MICHAEL LINDLEY

A FOLLOWING SEA

Book #2 in the Amazon #1 bestselling "Hanna and Alex" Low Country mystery and suspense series.

First published by Sage River Press 2019

This novel is entirely a work of fiction. The names, characters and incidents portrayed in it are the work of the author's imagination. Any resemblance to actual persons, living or dead, events or localities is entirely coincidental.

First edition

This book was professionally typeset on Reedsy.
Find out more at reedsy.com

As always, special thanks to the many book retailers, distribution partners, fellow authors and marketing partners, and of course, my family for their continuing support in the pursuit of these stories. ML

"Though lovers be lost, love shall not."

Dylan Thomas

Also by Michael Lindley

The *"Troubled Waters"* novels of historical mystery and suspense.

THE EMMALEE AFFAIRS
THE SUMMER TOWN
BEND TO THE TEMPEST

The *"Hanna and Alex"* Low Country Mystery and Suspense Series.

LIES WE NEVER SEE
A FOLLOWING SEA
DEATH ON THE NEW MOON
THE SISTER TAKEN
THE HARBOR STORMS
THE FIRE TOWER
THE MARQUESAS DRIFT
LISTEN TO THE MARSH

The sequel to Amazon #1 LIES WE NEVER SEE, a riveting and twisting tale of crime and suspense in the Low Country of South Carolina and the always precarious love affair of Hanna Walsh and Alex Frank.

Amazon and Goodreads Five Star Reviews for _A FOLLOWING SEA_

If you love mystery and suspense with twisting plots, compelling characters and settings that will sweep you away, find out why readers are raving about _A FOLLOWING SEA._

Chapter One

Hanna Walsh stood on the beach in front of her old family home on Pawleys Island along the coast of South Carolina. She felt the low swells of the calm Atlantic Ocean wash over her feet. The moon was out full overhead and a canopy of stars shone bright in the night sky. The scent of nearby beach fires drifted by.

She found herself imagining similar nights, generations ago, when her distant great-grandmother, Amanda Paltierre Atwell, had stood on this very shore, looking up at this same incredible array of stars and moon. Amanda's family had owned a nearby rice plantation during the years before and after the Civil War. This beach house had been their refuge from the intense heat and humidity of the Low Country summers. Hanna had retained ownership of the house following a long progression of family hand-offs over the years.

She heard a splash in the water out in front of her as Alex Frank dove out into the cool summer ocean and disappeared from view. She took a sip from the glass of wine in her hand and cringed as she thought of the big sharks she knew came in close to shore after dark to feed. The reflection of the moon on the water was a long trail extending out to the far horizon. It faltered and sparkled, and Hanna felt a chill at the beauty and calm of the night. Alex surfaced and turned back to her.

"Come on," he said, motioning for her to join him.

"I'm fine right here!" she called back.

Hanna watched him turn and start swimming in a slow crawl out into deeper water. She looked up as clouds from the east started to blow in from behind, across the marshes and the mainland that led to Georgetown and down to her old home in Charleston. She sensed the smell of rain and an electricity in the air. Miles away, she heard the first low rumble of thunder behind the dunes and beach houses and the distant sky lit up with tendrils of lightning arcing across the dark and menacing clouds approaching. She turned to see Alex stop again and tread water.

"Not too far now!" Hanna yelled out across the calm surface of the dark Atlantic. She waded further out into the ocean and felt the coolness caress her bare legs. The line of her khaki shorts dipped beneath a low swell that swept in and caused her to shiver. A freshening breeze from the east came up with the coming storm and blew her brown hair from behind her ears and into her eyes. She swept it back and as she watched Alex swim, she thought back to moments from the past year and their time together since the dark days of her husband's murder and the events that led to her run-in with Ben's dangerous partners. It all led to the kidnapping of her son as her husband's so-called "associates" tried to recover money they thought Ben had stolen from them in the dreadful land deal that had cost him his life. Alex, a lieutenant and detective with the Charleston Police Department, had been there for her throughout that terrible ordeal.

When she thought about it now, Hanna knew she was attracted to Alex Frank in the early days when she first met him, and he was assigned to investigate her husband's murder. It wasn't so much a physical attraction, but more in the man's considerate manner and obvious concern for her dire situation at the time. During those first encounters, she was certainly in no state-of-mind for romantic pursuits, and it wasn't until much later that she began to notice more in her feelings for him.

While her marriage to Ben Walsh had been strained at times, she had loved the man. They had been together over twenty years and had a beautiful son together. There did always seem a thin veil of distance or aloofness about him, like you couldn't quite tell what he was really feeling or thinking. There were only a handful of times Hanna could recall they had really connected at the most basic level and truly been a loving couple.

When Ben's affairs came to light after his death and with his terrible judgment as the Osprey Pointe land development spiraled out of control and threatened all they had financially, it had taken months for the sorrow and embarrassment and grieving to even begin to fade. She came to realize how much the presence of Ben had permeated her life, how she reacted to events around her, how she planned her days and nights. After his death, the emptiness was like a surge of water that held her down and kept her from her next breath. Her son's abduction and ultimate return had taken a further toll.

Hanna had to admit her husband's affairs had really come as no surprise. She knew something had changed between them in the past few years, and she likely overlooked some of the warning signs in a naive effort to keep their marriage together for her son. What *was* a surprise was one of the other women in Ben's life was her best friend, Grace Holloway. She and Grace had become the closest of friends over the years as their husbands worked together at the same law firm in Charleston. She couldn't have felt closer to Grace if she was her sister. The night of her son's return, over a year ago now when she learned of Grace's complicity in her husband's murder, as well as their affair, continued to haunt Hanna's sleep. She still found it hard to believe her closest friend could have kept her betrayal and liaisons with her husband, Ben, from her as long as she had.

Grace was now in prison and her partner-in-crime, Thomas Dillon was dead. The family friend and real estate agent had also been in on the illicit land scheme and ultimately had killed Ben when the deal was headed south, and Ben had threatened to bring in the authorities. It was still unclear who had killed Thomas. He had run away to the island of St. Croix as the deal continued to fall apart. The FBI agents who had helped in her efforts to get her son back had convinced her the organized crime elements from Miami who were Ben's silent partner in the Osprey Pointe deal were certainly the prime suspects.

The betrayal of her husband and two of her closest friends continued to gnaw at her. She felt not just a victim, but a foolish innocent who should have seen it all coming long before it spiraled out of control. Alex Frank had been there as she fought to come out of the deep depression of loss and betrayal. He was just a close friend at first and his steady presence was a comfort and a safe harbor as she struggled to put her life back together again. And then, it became much more than that.

She took another sip from the wine and smiled as she thought about how they had become a "couple".

Hanna knew they both had strong feelings for each other, but Alex had always kept a distance, even when he became her closest ally in her recovery. Nearly six months after all had been resolved in Charleston and her son was back safely at school in Chapel Hill, Hanna had invited Alex out to the beach house on Pawleys Island for a weekend to thank him for all his support through the "dark times" as she often referred to them. In her mind, she had convinced herself it was a friend inviting another friend out for a weekend together at the beach. She had made up one of the guest bedrooms for his stay and honestly had no intentions of letting things go further than the close friendship and bond they had formed.

Alex came out on a Saturday morning and they got horses from a nearby stable outside Georgetown and rode together through quiet trails in the Low Country. She cooked a big dinner of local seafood and they drank too much good wine. They walked on the beach that night and he took her hand for the first time. When they got back to the house and were standing together on the big deck, looking out over the water, she thought he was going to kiss her, and she actually hoped that he would. Maybe it was the wine or the need to feel close to someone again, but she really felt she might be ready to get closer with this man. In the end, he stammered and stalled and an awkward kiss on the cheek was all he offered before thanking her for a beautiful night and going up alone to his own room.

It was three more weeks before she saw him again. He had sent her a "thank you" note for her hospitality at the beach house, but he didn't call. Hanna was tempted on several occasions to put her foolish female pride aside and just call the man, but she couldn't bring herself to do it.

Alex finally called and apologized about how busy he had been on several new cases. Hanna had been skeptical but cordial. He invited her to join him at his father's fish camp for dinner and a night on the marshes far upriver from Dugganville, his hometown just north of Charleston where his family had been in the shrimp boat business for many years. That was the night the ice was broken. She smiled again at the memory and then looked out when Alex called to her.

"Are you going to come in or do I have to come and carry you?" he yelled out across the water.

She started walking back to shore, the lights from her house glowing above in the low dunes. She yelled back, "I'll be waiting for you inside with a warm towel and your favorite robe. Don't dally!" She could hear him swimming now toward shore and she smiled as she made her way up the beach to the house.

Chapter Two

The sailboat drifted silently on the incoming tide, illuminated on the dark water of the bay by the full moon overhead. The summer air was thick with the musty smells of the Low Country backwater. An alligator grunted in the marshes along the shallows of the bay, lying in wait for its next unsuspecting meal to pass near.

Connor Richards had lowered the sails on his boat when they returned earlier from an afternoon out on the Atlantic Ocean, just offshore from Dugganville. His girlfriend, Lily, pressed closer as they sat together on the soft cushions lining the cockpit of the sailboat Connor had named *Allowance* when he had purchased it the previous year.

Lily reached for the bottle of red wine and refilled both their glasses. She raised hers in a toast and then kissed Connor on the cheek as she felt his arm come around her, pulling her in. The acrid-sweet smell of marijuana filled the air as Connor took another pull on the joint before passing it to her. She looked up when a large bank of clouds started to push across the moon and the darkness engulfed them. The air was getting cooler and she stood to go below for a sweatshirt.

"Do you need a jacket?" she asked.

"No, I'm fine, just fine," Connor said, smiling back and taking another hit from the joint.

Lily came back up a few moments later, pulling a gray University of South Carolina sweatshirt over her head before she sat back down next to him.

"Damn glad these clouds finally blew in," Connor said.

"When's the storm supposed to blow-up?"

"We have plenty of time," Connor said, reaching for his wine glass in the teak cup holder next to him.

He looked behind them and noticed they had drifted out of the channel that led into the little town of Dugganville. His house was further upriver, a sprawling ranch house built on the water with a long pier for his sailboat and *Donzi* "go fast" boat. He reached down and turned the key to the ship's engine. The low rumble broke the stillness of the night. Connor stood to steer the boat back into the channel and deeper water to keep his six-foot keel from running aground. To the west, he could see the horizon line of the Atlantic Ocean out beyond the entrance to the bay. He saw the light signal before he could see the boat... three long, two short. A few moments later he saw the signal again. He reached for a spotlight on the cockpit seat and returned the same signal, twice as he had just seen.

"OK, here we go," he said.

Lily stood and looked out toward the ocean. "They're here already?"

"Drop the bumpers over the port side," Connor said and Lily climbed a bit unsteadily out of the cockpit. She made her way forward, holding on to the mast shrouds and railing wires along the sides of the big sailboat. She dropped two large rubber bumpers over the side that were tied to cleats both fore and aft.

They could hear the approaching boat now and the shadow of another large sailboat began to emerge in the low haze coming in across the water from the marshes. Neither boat had any running lights on. Connor heard his radio squawk and then a quick, *"All clear."* He had a man in town monitoring the police and Coast Guard radio channels.

He looked around the small bay and took a deep breath when he saw no other boats out on the water. Only a few faint lights shimmered through the haze back in town. He pushed the throttle forward and steered slowly out toward the mouth of the bay and the approaching boat.

The two vessels slowed as they came alongside, and Connor maneuvered the *Allowance* carefully up next to the hull of the other boat. Three men were onboard, one at the helm and two standing at the rail to help tie up.

"Hey, amigo," Connor and Lily heard from the other skipper with traces of a Spanish accent.

"Let's do this, boys," Connor said. He went below and came back up with a large black duffel bag. He struggled with the size and weight of it as he came up the stairs from the cabin.

The other skipper said, "How you been, man?"

"Never better." Connor carried the bag over to the rail and handed it to one of the other men. "You need to count it?" he said and then laughed.

"You're good for it," the other skipper said. "Never a problem from you, man."

The two crewmen from the other boat took the money below and both came back up with large bails of pot, wrapped in heavy plastic. They began handing them over to Connor who placed them along the deck of the *Allowance*.

The skipper said, "Thought the Coast Guard was gonna bring us over this afternoon, south of Charleston."

"What the hell happened?" Connor said, his heart leaping in his chest.

"Some drunk kids overloaded on a wake board boat came screaming by and the Coast Guard took off after them."

"Any other problems?"

"Smooth crossing from Nassau," the other man said. "Damn glad the storm's coming in to block that moonlight."

In twenty minutes the cargo had been transferred and secured.

"Nice doing business with you," the skipper said as the lines were pulled in and the two boats began to drift apart. He fired up the "kicker" on the sailboat and slowly headed out toward open ocean.

Lily came up and put her arm around Connor's waist. "Shall we take her home, baby?"

Chapter Three

Alex Frank walked into the downtown precinct of the Charleston Police Department and across the long room of desks and other police officers scurrying on with the affairs of the day; phones ringing, suspects being led in, the normal chaos of a Monday morning. He sat at his desk and started to sort through the dozen pink phone message slips he pulled from his mail slot on the way in. He sorted them into piles based on *urgent, not so urgent* and the trash can.

He stood to get a cup of coffee from the kitchen along the back of the office. A few colleagues engaged in the usual banter as he made his way. His mind was faraway though, thinking of the past night with Hanna at the beach house. When he finished his swim, he found her upstairs in the bedroom under the covers of the warm comforter of her big king bed with nothing but her silk robe on.

He felt a sense of comfort and satisfaction he was growing more accustomed to as his personal life came to include Hanna Walsh. She was an incredible woman; caring and confident, and maddening at times as well, as her Scots temper could flare at a moment's notice. They had been together now as a couple for several months.

After her husband's murder case had been solved and they had been able to safely bring her son back, Alex had kept close to Hanna to help her through those tough days of recovery and return to a somewhat normal life. Their relationship had grown from police officer and crime victim, to friends and now lovers. He hadn't been this close to a woman in years since his divorce from Adrienne. The memory of his ex-wife put a quick damper on his good mood as he poured a cup of coffee and returned to his desk.

On the top of the *not so urgent* pile was a call from his father, Skipper Frank. He was about to put it aside until later when he thought better of the notion and reached for the phone. His father rarely called. *I'd better check on what the surly old bastard has to say.*

He heard the phone ring in the kitchen of their house in the village of Dugganville, a small fishing and shrimping hamlet just north of Charleston. The house was set in along a row old houses along the river behind big docks with shrimp boats tied up. Alex still couldn't get the boyhood smells of the river and the shrimp and the diesel oil from his mind. His father and grandfather had run the *Maggie Mae* as shrimpers out of Dugganville for many years. Alex had grown up on the boat and for a time, always thought he and his brother would take over the business. Then, the war in Iraq changed everything.

The ringing stopped. "Yeah, what?" he heard his father grumble.

"Hey, Pop, it's Alex. You called."

"Yeah, right. Haven't heard from you in weeks."

"Likewise."

"What the hell you been up to?" his father asked, clearly not really caring about an answer.

"Just work, Pop."

"Heard you got a new squeeze."

Alex cringed. "Where'd you hear that?"

"Have to hear it from my first mate on the boat. My own son won't tell me when there's a new woman in his life."

Charles "Chaz" Merton had worked for the family on the *Maggie Mae* for years and was a close friend of Alex. "I ran into Chaz a couple of weeks ago here in Charleston," Alex said. "He was down visiting some friends and was in a place I go for breakfast. Must have mentioned Hanna."

"So, Hanna's her name?"

"Hanna Walsh. She's a good lady."

"Well, good for you," the old man said.

Alex was surprised. His father rarely had much nice to say. His sour demeanor had begun when his wife and Alex's mother, Katherine, had died years ago after a car accident. Alex had seen little improvement in his attitude since. His father's drinking didn't help and a string of bad choices in women had continued to deepen the man's gloom and dark outlook on the world. His only comfort seemed to be his time out on the water on the *Maggie Mae* harvesting shrimp. It still grated on the man that his own son hadn't joined him in the business.

"So, why'd you call, Pop?"

Alex heard his father cough on the other end of the line and then churn up a big gob to spit into the kitchen sink.

"Late night, Pop?"

"Had a few down at *Gilly's* with the boys."

"A few, right." Alex said, seeing his father sitting at the bar with his shrimper buddies, telling tall tales and bad jokes, the beers and shots of whiskey going down far too long.

"When are you gonna come out and have a beer with us, son?"

Alex hesitated. "Soon."

"Right. Look, I need to tell you something," his father said. "I ran into Adrienne last night."

Alex felt his heart sink in his chest. His ex, Adrienne, had also grown-up in Dugganville and her mother still lived there, another drunk that spent too much time at *Gilly's*. His father had a brief fling with the woman that ended as badly or worse than Alex's marriage to the daughter.

"Adrienne?" Alex heard himself say, the bile rising in his throat. He and Adrienne had met in high school and had fallen in love, or so he thought in those days. He still wondered at times about the intensity of his feelings for the girl. They had been together two years as graduation from Dugganville High School approach and were trying to sort out college or shrimping, or whatever was to come next. Adrienne clearly wanted to get married. Alex was leaning toward going away to school in Columbia.

Then, his older brother, Johnny, was killed in action in Iraq. His Marine unit was attacked outside Mosul. He was shot and killed in a fierce battle that took three other Marines. One month later, Alex was enlisted in the Marines and on his way to nearby Parris Island for Basic Training. In his mind, it wasn't revenge that drove him to want to follow his brother to the war, but more a sense of duty to help finish what his brother had lost his life in trying to do. He had also decided to marry Adrienne before he left.

"She was down at *Gilly's* with her old lady." Alex could hear the displeasure in his father's voice in even mentioning Ella Moore.

"So, she's back in town. Thanks for letting me know."

"She needs to see you, kid."

Alex could feel a cold sweat all over. He didn't answer.

"Alex, I don't know what it is, but she seems real set on talkin' to ya."

"That's been over for a long time, Pop."

The old man said, "She looks pretty good."

"Come on, Pop!"

"Why don't you come out for dinner tonight. She is my damned daughter-in-law for God's sake."

Alex said, "Have a good time. Give her my best." He hung up the phone.

Chapter Four

Hanna parked in the drive next to an old Victorian house back in Charleston the next morning. She had run the free legal clinic for many years and restored the old house near downtown for her offices. She had an assistant and usually two or three volunteer lawyers who helped to serve those in the city who had no money for attorneys.

Since she had lost her family home in town on the Battery in the financial scandal her husband brought down on them, Hanna had converted the upstairs of the clinic into a small apartment she used when she was in the city. She found she was staying at Alex's townhouse far more often in the past months. Shortly after Ben had died and the troubles had all been resolved, she had also accepted a paid position with a small law firm on Pawleys Island to help pay the bills, and she split her time between the two locations.

Her assistant, Molly, was already in the office when Hanna came through the door. Molly was on the phone but nodded and gestured to a woman and small boy sitting against the far wall. Hanna immediately saw the frantic look on the woman's face and dark bruise beneath her right eye. She walked over and held out her hand. "Good morning, I'm Hanna Walsh." The woman shook Hanna's hand and then reached for her son.

Her voice cracked when she spoke. "I'm Jenna Hall. This is William," she said looking down at her son. The boy appeared to be around five years old. His blond hair had recently been combed back wet.

"Hello, Jenna. And William, good morning to you." The little boy kept looking down at the floor.

"Do you have some time to see us?" Jenna asked, almost pleading.

"Of course. Come back with me." Hanna led them down the hall and into a small kitchen. She poured them both coffee and got a bottle of juice from the refrigerator for William. "Let's go back to my office."

They sat around the small conference table in Hanna's office. "What's happened to your face, dear?" Hanna asked.

The woman hesitated and looked over at her son. Hanna went to her desk and called Molly out in the lobby. "Can you come and get William? I think he'd enjoy seeing your laptop and how the printer works."

When they were alone, Hanna asked again, "What's going on, Jenna?"

The woman was mid-twenties at best, Hanna thought. She was gaunt and pale, and beyond the bruise on her cheek, she could see a pretty face that obviously had seen some very bad times. Her sandy brown hair was pulled back tight from her face in a long pony-tail. She wore jeans that needed a good wash and a t-shirt with some rock band name that Hanna had never heard of. One arm was full of colorful tattoos all the way down to her wrist and another peeked out from her shirt on the right side of her neck. Each ear had multiple piercings and earrings and she had a gold ring through the right corner of her lower lip.

Jenna Hall finally gathered herself, took a sip from the coffee cup and said, "We've been staying down at the women's shelter for a couple of weeks. We lost our apartment when Moe lost his job."

Hanna saw a thin silver band on the woman's left ring finger. "And Moe is your husband?"

Jenna nodded.

"And where is Moe?"

Tears welled-up in the woman's eyes. "I don't know."

"Did he hit you there, on your face?" Hanna asked.

Jenna nodded again. "The clinic helped me get a restraining order against him," she said slowly, almost trance-like. "But, he knows where we are, and he tried to take William."

"Have you talked to the police?"

"I don't want him arrested," she said defiantly.

Hanna reached out and placed her hand on Jenna's. "How can I help you, dear?"

"The clinic sent me here. They said you've helped other women."

Hanna said, "Yes, that's true, but you already have a restraining order to keep this man away from you. The police can help you enforce that."

Jenna stood and walked to the window that looked out across the backyard of the house. She spoke, still looking away outside. "I thought maybe you could speak with Moe... speak with both of us. Help us get back together and sort this all out. I just need someone who can get him to listen."

Hanna took a deep breath and closed her eyes, trying to control her anger at another man and the unimaginable behavior she saw too often in this office. "I thought you didn't know where he is."

Jenna turned. She stared at Hanna for a few moments. "It's just a matter of time before he tries to take his son again. I could call you."

"This isn't the first time he's hit you, is it?"

Jenna shook her head and quietly said, "No."

"I don't want to frighten you anymore, but this can be a very dangerous situation for both you and William."

"You think I don't know that?"

Hanna said, "Look, I certainly don't know much about the two of you and what's happened, and I'm not a counselor, but my experience has been to have a woman in your situation get as far away from men like this as possible."

"I don't have anywhere to go!"

Hanna nodded. "I know the clinic is locked and you're safe there."

"We can't stay there forever, and William needs to get out to go to school."

Hanna stood and walked back behind her desk. "You can stay here for today. We'll get you some food and Molly can go out and get some toys for your son. I'm going over to the clinic. I know the director and I want to hear what she has to say.".

"Don't get me in trouble there!"

"Of course not," Hanna reassured her. "I just want to know what they've done to help with all this and then we can figure out how best to proceed."

"Thank you."

"I've got an empty office down the hall that you and William can stay in today. You're obviously not taking him to school?"

"No, I don't want Moe near him again until we can all talk."

Hanna had come back from the women's clinic and was returning phone calls and catching up on other client's files when Molly stuck her head through the door. "Your father is on the line."

She felt the same old sense of dread every time she heard from her father. They had a long history of always having to apologize for their last encounter. The most recent blow-up had been months after Ben's death when her father had called to admonish again her for staying in South Carolina after so much chaos. It was a consistent theme with the man, even before Ben's troubles.

Her father, Allen Moss, was managing partner with the prominent Atlanta law firm of Moss Kramer. At 72, he was still among the city's most sought-after attorneys by the elite and upper crust of Atlanta society who needed help with their frequent divorces or the many other unfortunate legal entanglements the rich seemed to find themselves in. Hanna had followed her father into the legal profession, not because she wanted to work with his affluent clients, but rather those who needed the most help but couldn't afford it. Under duress, she had returned to Atlanta after getting her law degree at Duke. She reluctantly agreed to join her father's firm when he had the first of his three heart attacks. Two years was all she could take.

She had met Ben Walsh in law school in North Carolina. They had dated and near graduation it had escalated to a fairly serious relationship. Ben wanted to return to his home in Charleston to practice and Hanna felt compelled to return to Atlanta to help her father. They continued to see each other on occasional weekends. Just when things were continuing to deteriorate for her with her father and her law career at Moss Kramer, Ben asked her to marry him. Charleston and a new start away from her father and the firm seemed the best new path.

Somehow, nearly twenty years had passed, and her father never gave up on his attempts to get her back. His efforts only escalated after Ben died.

Hanna looked down and saw the light blinking on her phone. "I'll take it, thanks." Molly closed the door.

She picked up the receiver. "Hello, Allen." He didn't like it when she called him *father* or *dad*. It wasn't professional in his mind.

"How's my best daughter?"

"I'm your only daughter." She heard his laugh on the other end of the line. His most recent cardiac event had been just two years ago, and his voice sounded frail and tentative. It was the first time she remembered ever hearing him sound anything but forceful and totally in control.

"And how is my grandson?"

"You should call him."

He didn't respond.

"So, Allen, to what do I owe the pleasure of your call today?"

She heard her father clear his voice and what sounded like taking a drink of water.

"I wanted you to know I have to go in for another procedure."

"For your heart?" she asked, a cold chill running through her. She really did love her father and his health had been so worrisome as he had repeated episodes over the years. He always insisted on going back to work much too early and here he was at 72, still working seven days nearly every week.

"Do you think you can come home on Thursday?" he asked. "Martha would appreciate your company. I'm afraid it's going to be a long day at the clinic. A couple of bypasses, I'm afraid."

"Oh, Daddy. I'm so sorry," she said, truly worried now and dropping all previous formalities. *Martha* was Martha Wellman Moss, her father's second wife. At 48, she was hardly much older than Hanna and she seriously doubted the woman would *appreciate her company*. Martha had married her father ten years after the plane crash that took Hanna's mother and brother. Their father was piloting the family plane to the Bahamas with the whole family onboard. He had insisted on leaving Atlanta even though the weather report was sketchy. It was typical of the man's arrogance, Hanna had always thought, and she had never forgiven him for his foolishness that day. The storms blew up on the crossing and he crashed the plane in the water short of the runway coming into Nassau. Her mother and younger brother were killed on impact with the water. She and her father were pulled out of the wreckage before it sank by two fishermen who saw them go in. Hanna had a long and painful recovery and still had trouble with her back. A small scar along her jawline was a constant reminder of the tragedy. She had never been in a small plane since.

"The doctor says it's preventative, whatever the hell that means," she heard her father say. "Seems they should just pull the damned thing out and give me a new ticker."

"You're talking about this Thursday?" she asked.

"Yes, dear. It would mean so much to us if you could come up."

"Of course. What time is the surgery?

"You should come in the night before. Stay with us at the house."

Hanna thought about her childhood home, the vast estate on West Paces Ferry Road in one of Atlanta's most prominent neighborhoods. The thought of an evening with Martha in the big old house was not appealing.

'I'll be there," she finally said. "I'll let you know when I can get away to drive up."

Chapter Five

Hanna and Alex sat across from each other at one of their favorite restaurants in Charleston, *Magnolias* on East Bay. Hanna liked the wine list. Alex liked the *"down south dinners"*, particularly the *Shellfish over Grits* that now sat before him. He scooped another scallop up in the creamy white grits and closed his eyes as he savored the flavors.

Hanna scrunched her face. "Never could see the fascination with grits," she said. "Tastes like sand."

"It's the lobster sauce."

"There's not enough sauce to make grits edible," she said, reaching for the bottle of Cabernet between them and refilling her glass. Alex hadn't touched his first, yet.

Alex finished his mouthful and said, "You uppity Atlanta types just don't understand good Southern food."

Hanna just shook her head and then took another sip from her wine.

"Tough day?" Alex asked.

Hanna forced a smile. "I've had better. My father called. He's having another heart procedure in three days."

"I'm sorry. Is it serious?"

"Another bypass," Hanna said. "This will be the third one for the old coot. He wants me to come up to Atlanta to hold Martha's hand." She did little to disguise her frustration. She had told Alex about her stepmother and he was aware of Hanna's disregard for the woman. "I hate to say this, but I feel like she's just waiting for him to pass so she can have all the money and start chasing her next catch. Is that harsh?"

"Just a bit.'

"You haven't met her."

The waiter came and checked in on them. Hanna hadn't even started yet on her entree of planked salmon.

"Not hungry tonight?" Alex asked.

"Sort of lost my appetite after working with one of my clients today."

"Who's that?"

Hanna sighed. "It's just the typical mess we see down there at the clinic. This beautiful young girl with a five-year-old son is homeless and living in the women's shelter for protection from her abusive husband."

"Is there enough evidence on this father to bring him in and scare the crap out of him?" he asked.

"She has a restraining order and Greta down at the clinic tells me he is a seriously messed-up kid."

"Will she file another complaint?"

Hanna hesitated. "I don't know. She thinks they can get back together, and she doesn't want to get him in any more trouble."

Alex shook his head in disgust, looking off across the room. "We see this so often and the woman only gets hurt worse by these guys."

"I know. I tried to tell her that."

"Let me know if we can help," Alex said. "I'd be happy to bring him in and try to talk some sense into him."

"Thank you. I'm going to see her again tomorrow over at the clinic.

Alex finally took a sip from his wine and said, "I had a little excitement today."

"What's that?"

"My old man called to let me know my ex is back in town up in Dugganville."

Hanna bristled and put her fork down. Alex had told her some of the details of his failed marriage, particularly the part about her affairs while he was away in Iraq and after he returned. "Where did he see her?"

"Down at his favorite bar, *Gilly's.* I've told you about it.

"You still have the stink of shrimp and stale beer on you," she said and laughed.

"It's not that bad. Adrienne was in there with her mother who is another "regular" at *Gilly's*. My dad had a fling with her a few years ago. Surprised they didn't kill each other."

"So, what brings her back to town? I thought she was remarried or living with someone down in Florida."

"So did I," Alex said. "I don't know what's going on, but she apparently wants to see me."

Now he really had Hanna's attention. All her trust issues with men came rushing back. Not just Ben, but even back in college with a young man she had fallen hopelessly in love with, who abruptly left her their junior year to take on a photography assignment in Europe. Sam Collins had never returned and still traveled the world as a photo journalist. She got word a couple of years ago he had married a French woman. There were still times she struggled to push her feelings for the man aside.

Hanna had no reason not to trust Alex, but she had to admit she barely knew the man after just a few months together.

"Don't be upset," Alex said.

"I'm not upset," Hanna said too quickly, reaching again for her wine.

"I'm not going to see her," Alex said. "I even hung up on my old man. He wanted me to come out to dinner at his place...invite Adrienne over. He's always been blind to her nonsense."

"And you're not going?"

"I told you I hung up on him."

Hanna put her napkin on her plate. Only a few bites of the salmon were gone. "I'm sorry, Alex. I shouldn't doubt you. From what you've told me about this woman, though, I have every reason to be concerned about her."

Alex didn't respond.

Hanna said, "I really need to get home and get some sleep tonight."

"I thought you were coming over?"

"I just need to get some sleep. I have an early day tomorrow. Let me get dinner tonight." She looked around for the waiter.

"It's my turn," he said. "You sure you're okay?"

She stood and walked around the small table and then leaned in and kissed him lightly on the cheek. She said, "I'll call you tomorrow," and then turned and walked away.

Alex watched her go out the front door and tried not to let his frustration boil over. Adrienne had done enough to ruin his life. He wasn't going to let her get another shot at it.

Chapter Six

It was 7:30 the next morning. Alex was on his way into work. His cell phone on the passenger seat started to buzz. He reached over and looked at the call screen. It was his father again. He was about to decline the call when he decided he needed to put an end to this *Adrienne* issue. He pressed the screen. "What is it, Pop?"

Alex could immediately tell something was terribly wrong. His father's voice was slurred and tentative, almost weak. "We got a problem, kid."

"What's that?"

"The sheriff picked me up this morning out at the house."

"What the hell for?"

"They think I killed a man."

An hour later, Alex walked into a small room with no windows in the back of the Sheriff's Department office on the outskirts of Dugganville. His father was slumped over an old metal table, his hands cuffed to a ring on the top of it. Jordan "Skipper" Frank had just turned 63, a few months earlier, but he looked ten years older. The years on the water and hard living had taken their toll. He was dressed in orange jail scrubs and his hair was all askew and as usual, he had a good week's worth of gray unshaven beard.

On his way in, Alex had spoken with the Sheriff, Pepper Stokes, an old friend of the family. There had indeed been a murder the past night. A rival shrimp boat captain that Alex's father had issues with for years had been found dead on the deck of his boat last night. There had clearly been a vicious fight and Horton Bayes came out on the wrong end of the scuffle. The left side of his face was caved in and there were multiple stab wounds. Unfortunately, Alex's father had several recent run-ins with Bayes out on the water and at the docks. Last night, they had a very public and drunken fight in front of everyone down at *Gilly's Bar*. Skipper had loudly threatened to kill the man before a few of his friends broke up the scuffle and got Bayes out of the bar. This morning he was found dead when his crew showed up for work.

Alex's father had no alibi. He claimed to have gone home and passed out until he was arrested this morning. He still had blood and bruises on his hands, likely from the fight at the bar, but it could have also come from another run-in on the deck of Horton Bayes' shrimp boat.

Alex pulled out a chair and sat across from his father. The man finally looked up. His face was ashen and swollen, a dark welt under his left eye.

"I didn't kill no one," he said weakly. "At least I don't think so."

"What do you mean, you don't think so?" Alex pressed.

Skipper Frank sighed and rubbed at his temples. "I've tried to remember, but the last thing I recall is Gilly pushing me out the door at closing. Had a few too many shots I suppose."

"You have no recollection of getting home or anything after that?"

His father shook his head.

Alex asked, "What the hell's been going on between the two of you? I know there's been bad blood for a long time."

"Bayes has been a thorn in my side for twenty years, dammit," the old man growled. "He's always jumpin' my best runs. That bastard couldn't find shrimp on his own if they jumped in his damn boat. And just last week I come out to the *Maggie Mae* and see my riggings have all been tampered with. I know that sonofabitch did it!"

"How do you know?"

"Who the hell else would do something like that?"

Alex said, "Pepper tells me you haven't given a statement yet or asked for a lawyer."

"I didn't do it, dammit!"

Alex tried to remain calm. "We need to get you a lawyer, Pop. This looks real bad."

The man looked up at his son through rheumy eyes, "I don't know what the hell happened, kid. I mighta killed the bastard."

"Don't ever say that again, you hear me?"

The old man nodded and put his head down in his arms on the table.

Alex said, "I'm going to call Hanna."

"I've never tried a murder case, Alex," Hanna protested. "I want to help your father, but we need to get the best murder trial lawyer we can find. I know of a couple here in Charleston we can talk to."

"I understand that, but I need someone up here today who can talk some sense into the man and not let him dig a deeper hole."

Hanna was sitting in her office, looking at the pile of open files on her desk. She also had an appointment to go over to the clinic to see Jenna and her son again before lunch. "Let me push some things back," she finally said. "I'll try to get up there before eleven," she said, looking at the old clock on the wall.

Hanna called Alex when she was ten minutes out of Dugganville and they agreed to meet in the parking lot at the sheriff's office. She pulled her Honda Accord into the lot and saw Alex leaning against his car in the shade of a big live oak at the back. The temperature was already past 90, and she felt the full force of the heat and humidity when she opened her door and stepped out. She and Alex hugged.

"I'm sorry about last night," she said.

"It's alright."

"I can get a little touchy on this former girlfriend and wife stuff. Just bear with me."

"I get it," Alex said. He had filled her in on the details of the situation during their earlier call.

"Has your father ever been arrested before?" she asked.

"Not for murder!" he said and then paused. "He gets tossed in jail a couple times a year, at least, on drunk and disorderly. The local cops do it more out of courtesy, so he doesn't hurt himself. He can walk home, so he wouldn't hurt anybody else, but if he fell off the docks on one of his bad nights, they'd find him floating face down the next morning, chewed up by the gators."

"He still hasn't given a statement?" she asked.

"No. I told him to keep his mouth shut until you got here."

They started toward the back door.

Alex saw her first and then Hanna looked up and saw a tall and pretty woman coming around the corner of the building. She was dressed in tight jeans and a two-sizes-too-small white tank top that showed more cleavage than a *Sports Illustrated* swimsuit cover. The woman's long red hair was piled on top of her head in bouncing swirls.

"Oh crap!" she heard Alex say.

Hanna said, "Let me guess, the ex-wife?"

Alex just grunted.

Adrienne saw them and waved. She made a beeline towards them. Hanna stopped and stood behind Alex. She watched as the woman came up and threw her arms around Alex. He let his arms hang straight as she cooed in a big Southern drawl, "Hello, honey. It's been too long."

Hanna noticed the woman was looking directly at her during the greeting.

Alex pushed her gently away. "Hello, Adrienne. Look, I don't have time right now."

"Heard about your papa," she said. "I can't believe old Skipper would do something like this. I know he and Horton have had this comin' on for a long time, but..."

Alex interrupted. "Really, we need to get inside."

Adrienne looked at Hanna again. "Aren't you gonna introduce us, honey?"

Alex looked over at Hanna who was trying her best to smile.

Hanna reached out her hand, "Hanna Walsh."

Adrienne returned the offered handshake and said, "Adrienne *Frank*," with particular emphasis on the last name.

Hanna said, "Yes, Alex has told me about you."

"Oh, I bet he has!" she replied. "Skipper told me you had a new girl, Alex."

Alex took Hanna's arm and started them off toward the back door of the sheriff's office. He said, "Whatever this is about, Adrienne, it can wait."

"I'm not going anywhere, honey," she said. "Let's have a drink later."
Alex hesitated and looked back as they continued away from the woman.
"Nice to meet you, Hanna!" they heard as they walked through the door.

Chapter Seven

Sheriff Pepper Stokes had been wearing his badge for nearly thirty years. Born and raised in Dugganville, he joined the department after two tours with the U.S. Army where he served with the Military Police at bases all around the world. He returned to South Carolina, married a girl from Georgetown he met one night in *Gilly's* in 1986, and went off to college in Gainesville, Florida on the GI Bill. With his Criminal Justice diploma in-hand, he was hired by the County Sheriff's Department in Charleston. He was eventually assigned to his current post in his hometown of Dugganville, and he watched over the one thousand, or so, residents with a firm hand for justice and adherence to the law and local regulations. He was well-liked by the local citizenship for his fairness and at the same time, tough position on indiscretions of the many tourists coming through town who got out of hand in local bars or out on the water.

At 58 years, he had slowed some from his more athletic days on the Dugganville football and baseball teams. His six-foot, two-inch frame was now amply filled-out with more than 250 pounds, much of which lopped over the front of his big gun belt. He'd shaved his head the past ten years when baldness took most of his hair anyway but kept a bushy mustache that was now mostly gray.

Sheriff Stokes and Skipper Frank had been friends since childhood and Alex could tell the man was deeply concerned about his father when he and Hanna sat down across from him in his office. Introductions had been made. Alex asked, "What else do you know about last night you can share with us?"

"I'll tell ya all I know, son," the sheriff said. "Afraid it don't paint a pretty picture." He repeated what they had already learned about the Frank and Bayes feud over the years and particularly the fight last night in *Gilly's* that led to blows between the two men.

Hanna asked, "Has anyone else come forward with information?"

"Afraid not, ma'am."

"Are there any other suspects who had issues with Horton?" Alex asked.

"Horton Bayes was the orneriest bastard in town," Stokes said. "Forgive my language, ma'am. Weren't too many people around here who would go out of their way to help the old SOB. Alex, I remember your father telling me once he wouldn't take the time for a piss on the man if he was on fire. Sorry, ma'am."

"So, who else would want him dead?" Alex asked.

The sheriff smoothed his mustache as he thought for a moment. "Don't know anybody with reason to take it that far."

"That's what I was afraid off," Alex said. "What did you learn at the crime scene?"

Stokes sat up in his chair and rubbed at his smooth head. "It was a damn mess, Alex. Never seen so much blood. Half the man's face was bashed in. Numerous other wounds consistent with a serious knife fight."

"A knife fight?" Alex thought about this for a moment. "I know my old man has a few bruises, but it doesn't sound like he's been through a war like that."

"I don't know, son. Could argue he was the one dealing out most of the damage," Stokes said. "Hopefully, your old man will sober up enough here soon to remember what in hell happened after he left *Gilly's* last night."

"We'll want copies of the crime scene photos," Hanna said. "Anything you suspect as a murder weapon?"

Stokes said, "We've got a large piece of rigging off the boat, a spare block that holds the lines to the net booms that was laying on the deck near the body. Lot of blood on it. They're checking for prints. No sign of the knife. Could've got tossed overboard or taken with the killer."

"So, you still haven't taken an official statement?" Hanna asked.

"Waitin' for his lawyer to show up."

"Who's the prosecutor and judge?" Hanna asked. "We'll want to talk about bail."

"Don't get too optimistic about bail in a capital murder case, ma'am," the sheriff said. I know damn well the county prosecutor won't go for it.

Alex said, "I want to sit in with Hanna when you take Pop's statement."

"Sure, don't see why not."

They all stood, and the sheriff led them down the hall to the small interrogation room. He called across the office to have one of the deputies bring Skipper Frank down from the lock-up.

Hanna and Alex were a few steps behind the sheriff. Hanna whispered, "Forgive me a moment for thinking about anything other than your father, but were you really married to that woman?"

"Don't even start," he hissed back and then tried to push thoughts aside at how he had really felt when he'd first seen Adrienne earlier that morning. She still had a hold on him and it infuriated him to admit it.

Nothing more was learned from the sheriff's interview with Skipper Frank. He claimed he was still in complete blackout from anything that may have happened after he got thrown out of *Gilly's Bar* at closing. Alex's father seemed more interested in getting to know his son's new girlfriend than he did in putting together a defense for himself.

When Skipper Frank had first come into the room, he saw Hanna first. "My, Alex was right when he said you was a "looker."

"I didn't say that, Pop!" Alex protested. "I want you to meet Hanna Walsh. She's a very good attorney and she can help you through the first stages of this process. She may want to bring in a specialist in a case like this."

"I don't have money for fancy lawyers, son," the elder Frank said as he sat down at the table.

"Don't worry about the money," Hanna said. "Nice to meet you, Mr. Frank," she said as she extended her hand.

"Thanks for comin' up," he grumbled. "Seems I got myself in a bit of a scrape here."

The sheriff said, "This is more than a damn scrape, Skipper. You're lookin' at the needle here if you don't come up with some kind of defense or alibi."

"Take a pretty big damn needle to take me out, Pepper."

Hanna broke in. "The sheriff needs to take your official statement. Tell him everything you can remember about last night. Answer all of his questions as honestly and completely as you can."

An hour later they were finished, and Skipper Frank was returned to his cell. The sheriff agreed to try to get the prosecutor on the phone later that afternoon for a preliminary discussion. He would call as soon as he could confirm a time. He also mentioned the coroner would be releasing a report on the death of Horton Bayes within the next day or so.

Alex and Hanna walked out into the bright midday sun and sweltering heat.

Hanna said, "I'm sorry, Alex, but this looks really bad."

"I know."

"One of the best trial lawyers for murder cases in Charleston is a man you already know," she said.

"Who is that?"

"Phillip Holloway."

"Grace's husband?" he said in surprise. "Could you work with him after all you've told me about the man?"

"I'll do what's best for your father. Look, I need to get back to Charleston. If the prosecutor is available this afternoon, you can link me in by phone. I really have to get back."

Alex said, "I understand. Thank you for coming up so soon." He took her in his arms and gave her a long embrace and then a kiss on the cheek. "I really appreciate your help with this."

"Just stay away from that crazy redhead!" she said as she closed the door of her car and drove away. Hanna was trying to sound funny, but she was not feeling good about the intentions of Adrienne *Frank*.

Chapter Eight

Driving back down Highway 17 to Charleston, Hanna tried to keep her mind on the murder charges pending against Alex's father. She was not very optimistic based on what she had learned so far. Forensic evidence would be critical. If there were any of Skipper Frank's fingerprints or DNA on that rigging on the victim's boat, it could well be over for the man. She cringed at the thought of him facing the death penalty.

She had been serious when she mentioned bringing Phillip Holloway in on the defense. He was truly one of the best trial lawyers in the state with a lot of experience with tough murder cases. On the other hand, the thought of working beside the slime ball was not something she was looking forward to. His repeated attempts to romance her, despite being her best friend's husband, had been disgusting and he knew exactly how she felt about him. *Maybe there's someone else?*

She was also deeply concerned about Jenna Hall and her son. She had asked Alex to get a police report on the husband, Moe, to see if there was anything else they needed to be concerned about or leverage they might have with the man. The report should be on her desk when she got back to Charleston.

There was a message in voicemail from Jenna while they were in the session with Skipper Frank. She had spoken to her husband and he agreed to meet with Jenna and Hanna later this afternoon to discuss the situation. Hanna was not excited about confronting the man, but knew she needed to do something.

Nagging thoughts about Alex's ex-wife, Adrienne, kept interrupting her concentration on these other situations. *What a piece of work!* Hanna thought. She was really struggling to see the Alex Frank she had come to know being with this woman. She realized they were much younger when they met in high school and later married. Certainly, she was an attractive woman, but the latest look was way over the top. She also had her doubts about the woman's common sense after their brief encounter this morning.

She wanted to trust Alex with all her heart. She was coming to believe the two of them had the potential for something very special. They enjoyed being together and had many of the same interests. *Who knew a cop would like flea markets!* She often found her mind slipping away to their times in bed together. There seemed to be a natural chemistry and harmony between them when they made love... nothing awkward or forced.

Again, she had no reason to doubt Alex's faithfulness or commitment. Neither had used the *"love"* word yet, but it was just a matter of time, or at least she believed that. The not so distant betrayal by her husband of over twenty years and memories of her first real love, Sam Collins, back in college when he left her to take a job overseas and never came back, still left doubt and fear in letting another man get too close. Hadn't she vowed to herself after Ben, *no more men!*

Hanna would occasionally see Sam Collins' photographs in *National Geographic* and other magazines. He was incredibly talented and one of the most sought-after photo journalists in the world from all she'd read. She had shamelessly followed his website and more recently, his *Facebook* and *Instagram* pages over the years to keep track of his travels and work. Several posts on his newsfeeds documented his marriage to a beautiful French woman. She couldn't deny there was still a spark there for the man, though she hadn't seen him in what, almost 25 years? *Definitely need to close that chapter.*

She was startled when her cell phone rang. The number on the screen looked like a local Charleston call. She pressed the *"accept"* button. "This is Hanna."

"Hanna, this is Jenna. Jenna Hall."

"Yes, are we still meeting this afternoon?"

"Moe definitely wants to meet with us at your office. He'll be there at four. He promised," Jenna said breathlessly. "He's sorry for all that's happened. I think he wants to get back together."

"Jenna, don't get too excited about this. Let's take things slowly here."

"He may have a new bartender job, and we might be able to get our own place again."

"Jenna, please, one step at a time, okay?"

The police report on Moe Hall *was* on her desk when she got back to her office. One of Alex's colleagues had pulled the report and emailed it over.

It only took a moment for Hanna to groan, "Oh, no!" The man had a long list of arrests for drugs, assault and other lesser crimes. *How was he not in jail?* There was also an open arrest warrant for him on a parole issue. He was only twenty-five years old and his sheet looked like John Dillinger. *How in the world did a seemingly nice girl like Jenna get involved with this jerk, let alone have a kid?*

Hanna shook her head in disgust and put the report aside. She looked at the clock and saw it was 3:30. They would be here in half an hour. She would have felt better with Alex joining her for this discussion but there was Molly and one of her volunteers in the office this afternoon. She wouldn't be alone with the idiot. She considered calling Alex about the open warrant. She could have the man arrested, but a parole violation probably wouldn't put him away for any significant time and they had to get this resolved for Jenna for the long-term. She would have to alert the police about her knowledge of the whereabouts of the man, but she wanted some time with him first.

Chapter Nine

Sheriff Stokes agreed to accompany Alex down to the crime scene, the deck of Horton Bayes' shrimp trawler, the *LuLu Belle*. The boat was tied up at a commercial dock one block up the river from where Alex's father moored the *Maggie Mae*. Bayes' boat was another of the typical double-rigged trawlers seen throughout the region with two tall booms to lower shrimp nets out to the sides. There was a time when these boats were seen in great numbers up and down the Low Country waters of South Carolina. The shrimp business was tough but lucrative for those who were strong and persistent enough to endure the long days and nights out on the water. More recently, the industry faced an alarming decline, not in the abundance of shrimp, but in the stiff competition from imported shrimp from around the world at far lower prices, as well as the continued pressures of increasing fuel costs and shortage of experienced labor.

Skipper Frank and Horton Bayes were two of the holdouts who continued to ply the waters up and down the South Carolina coast and its backwaters for the prize of highly regarded Low Country shrimp. Many of the shrimpers in the area had friendly rivalries with each other. Alex's father and Bayes had taken that to a far more escalated level. Over the years there had been numerous run-ins out on the water when one man felt the other had violated some sacred custom of navigation or shrimper etiquette. Occasionally, these disputes would lead to blows back onshore when the two hot-tempered men would reach a boiling point with the other. Their feud and fights were legendary at *Gilly's Bar* and up and down the waterfront of Dugganville.

Alex knew there was more to it than one man jumping a run on another or cutting the other off in narrow channels. He remembered his father sharing a story years ago during one of his drunken rants about both men's interest in Alex's mother before she married Skipper Frank. From what Alex could gather in his father's angry tirade, Bayes made repeated attempts to "steal his woman," even after they were married. Alex's mother, Katherine or "Kat" as she was always called, had denied any interest in Horton Bayes when Alex asked her about it one night when his father was out. She had laughed and said it was just her jealous husband imagining things. Whatever had happened, she took it to her grave when she died in a car accident on a rainy night trip to Georgetown at the far too young age of 53.

Alex and the sheriff walked down the dock and he saw Bayes' trawler tied up in its usual berth. The *LuLu Belle* was showing her age. The paint on her hulls was dirty and peeling and the windows were fogged with years of grime and sea salt. There was rust everywhere in the riggings and generally a feel of neglect and disrepair. There was also yellow crime scene tape strung the full length of the old boat. Both men stopped near the aft deck. Sheriff Stokes had been right about the blood, Alex thought. Though it had dried and turned brown in the hours since the struggle, there were pools and splatters all across the deck and on the walls of the cabin.

"Looks like a damn war," Alex said.

"Told you, son. Horton took a hell of a beating."

Alex thought again about his father's condition he had seen this morning. He had a bruise on his face and bloody knuckles that could well have come from the two men's fight at the bar earlier in the night. He certainly didn't look like he'd been in a battle that would lead to this kind of carnage. The sheriff had told him there was some blood on his father's clothes that were off to the medical examiner, but again, it could well have come from their scuffle at Gilly's.

Alex looked around at the riggings on the boat strung across the two long booms. "They took the block you were talking about you think was used to crush his face in?"

"Yessir," the sheriff said. "Forensics team will get blood and fiber samples, fingerprints. We'll see."

Alex could also see footprint smudges leading from one of the pools of blood. "What about the footprints?"

"They're looking at your dad's clothes and shoes."

Alex said, "No one's come forward that would have been out here on the docks last night?" He looked down the row of six other commercial and sport boats tied up.

"We've spoken to the owners of all these other boats and no one was out here past midnight. Horton and your dad had their fight at the bar around 1am."

"And when do you expect the medical examiner's report?"

"Should be just a day or so they tell me. DNA takes some time to get back from the State Police in Columbia."

Alex looked down the waterfront. He could see his family's own boat, the *Maggie Mae*, tied up at their dock. It was no more than a few hundred yards away, an easy walk down the piers, even for a drunk man. He shook his head. "Pop said he woke up on the deck of our boat, right?"

"Yeah, he was there when we came looking for him this morning," Stokes said.

"Any sign of blood tracked over there?"

"Not that we've found, yet. Just the splatters on your dad's shirt and pants."

"And the shoes?" Alex asked.

"Not that I could see, but let's wait until we get the report back."

"And they got pictures of the walk down to the boat and the dock for blood prints and splatter?"

"I watched 'em do it, son," the sheriff said.

Alex turned to leave. "I'm gonna take a look down at the *Maggie Mae*."

"Got that taped off, too, so we'll have to stay on the pier."

Sheriff Stokes followed Alex down to the family's dock in front of their house up the hill from the water. Images of his childhood running out of the house down to his father's boat came back to him. He had always loved going out with his father and he loved the hunt for big schools of shrimp, the joy of pulling in a big catch, sorting through the wriggling shrimp, selling them back at the docks. He and his brother had often talked about getting their own boats, figuring their old man would live forever. Saddam Hussein and George Bush had changed all of that.

Skipper Frank's shrimp boat was in far better repair and condition than the *LuLu Belle* they'd just left. Despite his father's crusty personal appearance, there seemed a fresh coat of paint on all the boat's surfaces. The windows were clean and clear. All the riggings were smartly stored. The only thing out of place was an empty bottle of Budweiser lying on its side near the back deck of the boat. "Looks like Pop had one more before he passed out last night."

"The techs got pictures and prints from that, too, I'm sure," the sheriff said.

As Alex walked back to his car, he thanked the sheriff for his help and told him he needed to get back to Charleston. Stokes promised to keep him informed of all the information coming back with the investigation.

"I'll be back up tomorrow," he said. "Tell Pop when you see him."

"Will do, son."

He drove back on the road that ran through the little village of Dugganville. Whenever he saw these familiar streets and storefronts, it seemed as if time stood still in this sleepy fishing and shrimp town. He saw *Andrews Diner* ahead on the right, an old family restaurant and coffee shop that had been there since Alex was a kid. He pulled in to an open parking space and got out to go inside. He heard a call from behind.

"Hey, handsome."

He turned to see Adrienne walking across the street. She had to wait for a pick-up truck to pass. The driver nearly ran into a parked car as he craned his neck to get a look at the striking woman crossing the street. She came up to Alex next to his car.

"Buy a girl a cup of coffee?"

Alex hesitated. "I really need to get back to Charleston."

"Why'd you pull over here?"

He looked at the familiar face of his ex-wife, still as beautiful as when he had first fallen for her in high school. The overall look had changed... too much make-up, big hair, tight clothes, even more severe than the last time he'd seen her five years ago in another chance encounter here in Dugganville. There were a few lines now at the corner of her eyes as the years had passed.

He hadn't been home two days from his first tour in Iraq when he learned of his new wife's first infidelity. She had taken up with one of their high school friends, a boy who Alex had played football with. Somehow, they patched it up before he left again for his second deployment. Her next affair was known all over town when he came home again. He also found her in his bed with his old teammate when he came back a day earlier than planned from a visit to the school he was considering in Columbia. There had been no shouting or fighting. The boy left, and Adrienne packed and left town. For years, he didn't even know where she went. His feelings for her had slowly died long ago during lonely nights in the deserts and dusty towns of Iraq. And yet, the sight of her now brought back flashes of earlier times together when he had loved her deeply.

"What do you want, Adrienne?" he finally said.

She took his arm, "Come on, let's get a cup of coffee."

He let himself get pulled across the sidewalk and into *Andrews*. A few heads turned as she led him to the last booth in the back. Lucy Andrews came up and Alex said, "How're you doing, Lucy?"

"Good, good Alex. Nice to see you," she said, a plump and graying woman who had worked this place with her husband most of her adult life. "How you been, Adrienne?"

"Never better, Lucy."

Alex noticed the old woman didn't smile or reply, just turned and went back to the counter to get their coffee. He saw his ex-wife staring at him across the table.

She reached for his hand and he pulled it away. "Missed you, honey," she said.

"Adrienne, don't start."

"It's been too long. Sorry I've been away and haven't kept in touch."

"No need."

"Been down in Ft. Lauderdale," she said, pausing while Lucy put two coffees down. "You heard I married again?"

Alex nodded.

"And I have a son." Alex remembered he had heard this from his father some time ago as word got around town from Adrienne's mother.

Adrienne reached below the table for a small purse on the bench. She placed it on the table between them and searched inside. She finally pulled out a photograph and slid it across the table. Alex noticed her hand was shaking. It was a picture of a young boy standing on the deck of a fishing boat, blue water stretching out to the horizon beyond."

"What's his name?" Alex asked.

"It's Scotty. He's ten." She looked intently at Alex.

He looked back down at the picture and a sinking feeling surged into his gut as he did the math quickly in his head... *ten years.* The resemblance was striking. He could be looking at one of his old childhood pictures his mother kept. He didn't know what to say but just kept staring at the picture.

Finally, he looked up at her. "Why'd you never tell me?" Surprise was now overcome with anger. He pushed the photo back to her. He saw tears starting to water in her eyes. "Why the hell didn't you tell me about this?" he said.

"I knew you'd never take me back. I met another man. He took Scotty as his own." She stopped and wiped at her eyes, tears now leaking down her cheeks.

Alex was furious and had to hold the table to control himself. "And you don't think he needed to know who his real father was?"

"I'm so sorry, Alex."

He slammed his right hand down on the table and everyone at the counter looked over at the two of them in the booth. "God, Adrienne! I can't believe this!"

She tried to sniff away the tears. "We're alone now. My husband left us. I don't even know where he is. We're back staying with my mother."

"For how long?"

"We don't have anywhere else to go," she said.

The emotions and anger and implications swirled through Alex's head." I need some time, Adrienne. I need some time to sort this through."

"He needs to know his father, Alex."

He held up his hand and took a deep breath. "Just give me some time with this."

"Of course," she said. "We're not going anywhere."

Chapter Ten

Jenna Hall was waiting in the lobby of Hanna's legal clinic with her husband, Moe. When Hanna came out to greet them, she was surprised by the man's appearance. She wasn't sure exactly what she had expected but based on his arrest record and treatment of his wife, she wasn't prepared to see a well-groomed young man dressed in jeans and a clean white shirt. His long blond hair was pulled back and held with a rubber band at the back of his neck. His face seemed hard-edged, though, almost chiseled with dark reddish tan from too much time outdoors. The couple sat on two of the lobby chairs, holding hands.

Jenna was scrubbed clean, as well, looking far more put-together than she had the past day. The son, William, must have been left at the shelter, Hanna thought. Both rose to meet Hanna and Moe Hall stepped forward to shake her hand.

"Hello, Miss Walsh," he said. "Thank you for seeing us."

His grip was warm and firm and he held on a bit longer than was comfortable for Hanna.

"Hanna," she said. "Please come back to my office."

When they were assembled around the conference table, Hanna reached for a file folder on her desk and placed it in front of her. She hadn't offered coffee or water. This wasn't a social call.

Moe Hall was looking around her office at the family and professional photos framed on the wall and her diplomas. "Duke University," he said, looking at the diploma for her law degree. "Very impressive."

Hanna didn't respond.

Jenna Hall cleared her throat, clearly uncomfortable and nervous.

Hanna said, "Jenna, I thought you had a restraining order preventing your husband from seeing you?"

Moe jumped in before she could answer. "We're patching things up."

"I'm going to ask for the order to be lifted," Jenna said.

"I've been a jerk, Hanna."

"Yes, you have," Hanna said, the condemnation in her voice was clear. "Your treatment and abuse of your wife is unacceptable." She watched as Moe bristled. Before he could speak, Hanna continued, opening the file in front of her. "I also see you've had some other issues with the law."

Jenna jumped in, "That's all in the past, Hanna."

Moe's face was turning even more red. His fists clenched in front of him on the table. "What the hell is this?" he said slowly, clearly trying to maintain his composure.

"Jenna, do you know there is an open arrest order for your husband?"

The young mother looked over at her husband with a confused look.

"That's all bullshit!" Moe said, standing and pushing his chair back against the wall.

Jenna was on the verge of tears now and pleaded, "Hanna, I thought you would help us."

Hanna looked up at the man leering down at her. "Jenna, my only interest is the safety of you and your son. This man is a serial abuser and I have no reason to believe he'll behave any differently if you two get back together. He also has an arrest record a mile long and the police are looking for him as we speak on a parole violation."

Jenna looked back, speechless, the tears now flowing freely.

Moe Hall grabbed the file in front of Hanna and ripped the contents in half. "I told you this is all bullshit!" He threw the torn documents back in Hanna's face.

Hanna stood to confront the man. "You need to stay away from Jenna and her son as the court has mandated. You also need to turn yourself in to the police to resolve this parole issue."

The man's jaw tightened, and he stepped toward Hanna, reaching out and taking the top of her blouse in his right hand. Before Hanna could react, he pulled her face close to his. "You bitch! You're just like all the others."

Hanna wasn't surprised by the man's outburst. With a calm and steady voice, she said, "Take your hands off me, now. Get out of my office. Stay away from Jenna and William and turn yourself in. If you don't, I will call the police and it won't go well."

The fury in Moe Hall's face was more than threatening, but Hanna didn't back down. The man still held her face close and she could smell soap and sour sweat at the same time.

Suddenly, he pushed her away, and she fell back over the top of her desk. Hanna felt a stab of pain in her back from the fall, the old injury from the long-ago plane crash flaring. The man came around the table after her as Hanna tried to stand again. She watched as Jenna got up quickly and threw her arms around her husband to stop him. He threw her to the ground and Hanna heard the woman's head hit the wall.

"Stop it!" Hanna screamed, now getting to her feet beside the desk, but Moe Hall kept coming at her and before she could defend herself, he slapped her backhanded hard across the left side of her face. The blow staggered her, and she stumbled back against the credenza behind her desk. He was coming after her again when the door to the office flew open and Hanna's assistant and one of the volunteer lawyers, Adam Preston, came running into the room. Molly had her phone to her ear, "Is this 911!" she yelled.

Adam yelled out, "Hey! Step back!"

Hanna watched Hall hesitate and then start to back away. He looked down at his wife on the floor holding the back of her head and sobbing. He started shaking his head and then he looked back at Hanna, pointing a finger at her. "This is not over!" he snarled. "This is *not* over!" He turned abruptly and ran out of the room.

Hanna could hear Molly talking to the police and watched as Adam leaned down to check on Jenna. The blow to her face was still stinging and she could feel a swelling sensation beneath her eye. She sat down in her desk chair, completely stunned by the attack.

Molly came over. "Are you okay?"

Hanna looked up and managed to nod.

"Let me get some ice," Molly said and left the office.

Jenna Hall got back to her feet and walked toward Hanna. "What have you done? I thought you would help us!"

Hanna took a deep breath and managed to finally speak, "You need to stay away from that man and keep your son away."

Jenna just kept shaking her head and then she turned and hurried out of the room.

Chapter Eleven

The familiar stale smells of *Gilly's Bar* swept over him as Alex walked into the old place along the waterfront. It was dinner time and the bar and tables were nearly full of workers off-duty and having a few drinks, as well as other "locals" in for a meal. A few heads turned as he walked toward the bar. News of his father's arrest had spread quickly through town. One man who Alex knew was a good friend of his father, patted him on the back as he walked by. "Sorry, Alex. Let us know what we can do."

Alex nodded back. "Thanks, Sully." He saw two open seats down at the end of the bar and took the furthest. Gilly was behind the bar and came over. He was a big man with arms that looked like they lifted beer kegs all day. His hair was long to the collar of a faded denim shirt and as gray as the beard that clearly needed a trim.

"Long time," the old man said.

"How you doing, Gilly?"

"Never better. Sorry about your old man. Got pretty ugly in here last night."

"So, I hear." Alex looked down the bar at the beer tap handles. "I'll have a *Bud Light*." The old bartender nodded and walked away. Alex turned when a man sat down next to him. It was a familiar face, his father's deck hand, Chaz Merton. Alex had known him since they were in school together. Chaz had obviously never made it out of Dugganville and over the years had worked on most of the shrimp crews in town, the past five years for Skipper Frank. The man looked ten years older than Alex, though they were in the same grade in school. A dirty and crumpled orange ball cap said "Clemson" on the front and covered gray hair that hung in greasy strands around his ears and down his neck. He smelled of beer and sweat and old fish. His t-shirt looked like he'd worn it all week.

"Hey Alex."

Alex held out his hand and the two men shook. "How ya been, Chaz?"

"Sorry about the Skipper, man," Chaz said. "Saw him near take Horton's head off last night here at the bar, but never thought it'd go any further."

Gilly came up with Alex's beer. Chaz held his empty up and the bartender took it and walked away for the refill.

"What in hell happened, Chaz?"

"Skipper and Bayes were both drunk and started jawin' about a run-in they had two days ago out on the Banks run. Skipper thought Horton jumped his run again. Before we knew it, they were tossin' each other around the place and throwin' haymakers. Gilly and me broke 'em up. Horton left first, then your old man had another beer before he left. It's been brewin' for a long time."

"I know," Alex said. Gilly placed Chaz's beer down on the bar.

"Alex, know there's not much I can do," the bartender said, "but you let me know."

"Thanks, Gilly."

Alex heard Chaz say, "Oh, shit..." He turned and saw an older woman coming through the crowd. He recognized her right away. Horton Bayes' wife, Meryl, had been one of his schoolteachers in grade school. He hadn't seen her in twenty years, but the aged and sagging face was still familiar. She made eye contact with Alex and came straight for him. He stood as she came up. "Miss Bayes," he started before she slapped him. He sat back on his stool, totally stunned.

"Your papa is a damn murderin' bastard!" she screamed out. The noise in the bar quieted and all eyes turned to Alex and Meryl Bayes. "What am I gonna do now with Horton gone?" Her face was flushed red with tears and swollen eyes.

"I'm sorry, Miss Bayes," he said. "I'm really sorry."

"Sorry! You're not sorry. You're a damn cop and you're here to get your old man off the hook!"

Gilly came around the bar and got between Alex and the woman. He said, "Meryl, you need to get home. I'll have Therese walk with you." Gilly's wife came up beside them and reached for Meryl Bayes' arm.

"Come on, honey. Let's get you home."

The woman kept staring at Alex as she was led away. He heard Gilly say, "Sorry, son. No reason for that."

Alex took a deep breath and then turned to the bar and took a long drink from his beer.

Chaz said, "Woman's a damn mess. Can't blame her. A blessing in my mind, the old coot's gone. Never treated anyone well, not even his wife."

Alex turned to his old friend, still smarting from the slap across his face. "What are you hearing down at the docks?

"Nobody saw nothin'," Chaz said. "It was real late, and no one was staying onboard any of the other boats."

"Right." Alex took another drink from his beer and looked off across the faces in the bar, many staring back at him. He saw a well-dressed man stand from a group at a far table and come toward them. He recognized Beau Richards, a local real estate developer and owner of half the businesses in the area. Alex had known the Richards family all his life. The son, Connor was two years behind Alex in school, but they had been on sports teams together. That's when he first met Beau Richards. The man always thought his kid should be the starting quarterback, but he rarely played. Connor also had a brief fling with Adrienne in high school, even after Alex started dating her. Richards came up and slapped Alex on the shoulder. "Good to see you, Alex," he said in a deep growling voice. "Sorry about Meryl. Guess you can't blame her." He was the only one in the bar with a sport coat on. His plaid shirt and khakis were crisply pressed. He had a white handkerchief showing from the breast pocket of his coat. His loafers must have cost more than most of the other men in the bar made in a week.

"You slumming, Beau?" Alex said. "Nothing good on the menu down at the country club tonight?"

Richards didn't seem to react to the sarcasm. "Can't beat *Gilly's* for their fried catfish."

Alex could tell the man was well into his cups.

"Just wanted to say how sorry I am about the mess your old man's in," Richards said. "Always liked Skipper."

"Thanks."

"You got a good lawyer?" Richards asked. "Know some good ones down in Charleston. Happy to hook you up."

Alex said, "No, got it covered, thanks."

"Well, you let me know." He shook Alex's hand again and walked away.

It was eight o'clock when Alex finished his third beer and left the bar. It was too late to drive back to Charleston and he'd been drinking. He knew his old room at the family house was always available. As he walked to his car, he pulled his phone out and checked the messages. He felt it buzz in his pocket a few times in the bar but hadn't looked at it. There were two calls from Hanna. He pressed the voicemail button on the second call. The stress in Hanna's voice was clear.

"Alex, please call."

He hit the "return" button and heard Hanna come on the line after two rings.

"Where are you?" she asked.

"I'm staying up in Dugganville tonight. I had a look at the crime scene earlier with Stokes and then my dad's boat. It's a real mess over there."

"Alex, I need your help."

"What's going on?"

"I need you to come back."

"I can't drive. I just left the bar. Met with a few people I thought might know something about last night."

He waited for Hanna's reply, but there was just silence for a moment.

"Hanna?"

"Don't tell me you were with her?"

Alex said, "What? What are you...?"

Hanna jumped in, "The redhead. Your wife!"

"She's not my wife and no, she wasn't there." He immediately felt guilty

49

for not going on to tell her of his earlier meeting with Adrienne.

"Hanna, what's going on?"

Again, a pause. "I'm sorry. I'm really upset. I was attacked by the husband of one of my clients this afternoon."

"What!"

"I told you about the woman and the restraining order on the husband."

"Right."

"I had them both in the office this afternoon. She wants to reconcile. His rap sheet is a mess and there's a warrant out for him."

"Oh, great," Alex said. "What happened? Are you okay?"

"A little welt under the eye."

"Hanna!"

"I'm alright, but I need you to get the Department on this guy and bring him in before he hurts Jenna again."

"I'll make a call."

"You really can't come back tonight?"

"I shouldn't drive and there's a few more people I want to talk to in the morning."

Hanna sighed and then said, "I'm sorry about the "redhead" thing."

Again, Alex felt the guilt rush through him. He wanted to tell Hanna about the whole situation but not on the phone like this. "I'll call you when I'm on my way in the morning," he said.

Hanna said, "I called Phillip Holloway about taking your dad's case. He wants to meet with us tomorrow."

"I'll call you," Alex said. "You get some rest." He listened for her response but there was just silence.

Finally, Hanna asked, "What aren't you telling me?"

Alex hesitated and then said, "There's a lot going on up here. I'll tell you in the morning."

As he ended the call, it suddenly occurred to him he wouldn't be going back in the morning. There was too much to deal with here. He had weeks of back vacation and he'd call his Captain in the morning.

He made one other call before he got in his car to drive to his father's house for the night. He reached his partner, Lonnie, and filled him in. He also asked him to get someone on the Moe Hall warrant. When he ended the call, he thought again about Hanna. He didn't want to tell her on the phone about a son he never knew existed. The picture of his son he'd seen that morning in the diner came back into his mind. Then he remembered Adrienne's words, *we have nowhere else to go.*

Chapter Twelve

Alex left his car in the parking lot at *Gilly's* and decided to walk home. He would stay in the old family house he had been born and raised in. He walked down the quiet main street of Dugganville. It was just past midnight. He took notice of familiar names of family businesses and other storefronts on both sides of the street as he passed. The old post office, *Gordon's Rexall Drug Store*, *Rouse's Beer & Wine*, the diner he'd spoken with Adrienne in earlier. Up ahead to his left, the wall of buildings ended as the docks along the river pressed out into the waters of the Santee River. There were sailboats with halyards clanging in the light breeze, larger cruisers, and a few of the outrageous wakeboard boats with towers and racks and speakers. There was a small fleet of charter fishing boats with their signs promising abundant catches of fish. Only two shrimp boats were tied up at the end. One was Horton Bayes' *Lulu Belle*.

Alex remembered as a kid, there would have been a dozen shrimp trawlers at the docks, back before the business began its slow but steady decline. His father's boat, the *Maggie Mae*, was further up the river, tied up at the dock in front of their house.

Several gulls were still flying over the docks, even at this late hour, illuminated in the dim lights along pier. They screeched at each other and swirled in manic circles over the boats. The pelicans were less energetic, and a dozen rested out on the calm water of the river, waiting for morning and the first light of day to start out on their search for baitfish and mullet.

The city park stretched up to his right from the docks, a small white gazebo just visible in the dim light. Alex remembered nights with his family there when local bands would play, and the Rotary Club would serve up shrimp and crabs to raise money. Then he remembered the first time he kissed Adrienne Moore. It had been late one night after a football game and he should have had her home. They stopped in the park and leaned against the railing of the gazebo, talking about the game and school. Then Adrienne pulled him close and kissed him, long and then again. They were juniors in high school and it was Alex's first kiss. He could still feel the shocking smooth wetness of it. They both lost their virginity a few weeks later... or at least Alex knew he had.

A car came around the corner in front of him and passed, headed back into town. He shielded his eyes from the bright light and then kept on down the street toward his old family home. His father had bought the house in 1965, from another shrimper's widow who was ailing and leaving town to live with her daughter in Atlanta. He could see the house now, sitting up on a small hill across the street from the dock that held the *Maggie Mae*. It was a small shotgun cottage with white clapboard siding and a green shingled roof and green shutters on the windows. There was a covered porch across the front with painted white wicker furniture with green and blue cushions his mother had made years ago. The walk up from the street was made of a pattern of flat stones, now edged in moss and green mildew from the shade of big live oak trees surrounding the house. He saw the birdhouse he and his brother had made, sitting atop a tall post with an aluminum plate halfway up to keep the squirrels out of the seeds.

Alex walked up on the porch and sat on one of the chairs, looking down the hill and across the river. There were a few lights on and he could make out the large buildings of the *Richards Seafood Company*, just one of Beau's many local businesses. They processed and distributed most of the fish and shrimp and crabs caught by the local crews. Alex remembered the days pulling up to the Richards docks with a full load of shrimp on ice in the hold of the *Maggie Mae*. The tall riggings of his father's old boat were just a shadow in the dim lights and he noticed a low haze was blowing in slowly from upriver.

He shivered when he thought he could hear his mother's voice inside the empty house, fussing at her husband and calling the boys in for supper. He pushed the sad memories of his mother's sudden death from his mind, only to be replaced by images of his brother, Bobby. Alex closed his eyes and could see the two of them wrestling on the front yard. He never got the best of his older and bigger brother in those furious struggles. One of the parents would always break it up, just when Alex thought he was surely going to reverse the tide of the battle. He hung his head low and listened to the real sounds of the night, crickets and tree frogs, an occasional splash from the river when a mullet flopped.

Alex stood and walked to the front door. It was never locked. No one locked their doors in Dugganville unless they were leaving for a long trip. He pushed open the front door and was greeted with the familiar smells of his youth. He found the switch to a lamp on a table next to the couch along the front window. The living room opened to a small dining room with the family's old oak table and four chairs. The kitchen was behind with the original white wood cabinets, old gas stove and a newer stainless refrigerator that looked out of place. The three bedrooms were at the back of the house. Alex and Bobby each had their own rooms. He knew they were still left the way the boys had them before they left home for the service. Alex had never been back in his brother's room.

He walked into the kitchen and opened the new refrigerator. It was nearly empty except for three beers, half a sandwich wrapped in cellophane and a quart of milk nearly gone. He reached for one of the beers and walked back to the dining table, sitting in his accustomed seat on the side facing the living room. He opened the beer and took a drink, the cool fizz chilling his throat. Taking a deep breath, he closed his eyes and tried to push the events of the day from his mind. There would be time for all that tomorrow. He thought of Hanna and cursed silently in not telling her more of what was happening.

Hanna Walsh. He could see her face now and he remembered their last night together out at the beach house. He could see the curves of her body in the dim light, the smell of her hair in his face. He had never been closer to telling her he loved her. Something kept him from it. He couldn't quite reason why. He had never felt more physically and emotionally attached to a woman, never had a woman make him feel the way he did with her, close and comfortable. They had their moments of anger and frustrations, but the outbursts were short. He sighed as he thought about what he would tell Hanna tomorrow about Adrienne and a young boy that was his son... a boy who needed a father.

Chapter Thirteen

Lonnie Smith had been Alex's partner in the Charleston Police Department for almost five years. Alex found a new brother in the long days and nights they spent together. Lonnie was born and raised in one of Charleston's toughest neighborhoods. Somehow, he'd survived and graduated high school on time, worked his way through college over six years and joined the Department. He was one of the first African Americans to make Lieutenant in the Detective Squad. He was two inches taller than Alex and a couple dozen pounds heavier. His head was shaved, and his chin framed with a well-trimmed goatee. He had a wife of ten years and three little girls, 2, 5 and 8. Alex teased him he needed one more for a full starting line-up on the basketball court. His wife, Ginny, was a physician's assistant for a dermatologist on the north side. His mother lived with them to help with the kids and their tough schedules.

Lonnie had called Hanna at 7am to ask if he could come by her clinic later in the morning to talk about the warrant for Moe Hall. They agreed to meet at 8:30 and Lonnie was standing on the front steps of her office when she came down the steps from her apartment. Hanna gave him a warm hug.

"Thanks for helping with this, Lonnie." She led him back and put some coffee on in the kitchen. In her office, he took a chair across her desk and reached for a file in the leather bag he carried. He pulled out the file on Hall.

"This guy's a real creep," he said, looking at the long list of infractions on his sheet. "How does a guy like this end up with a wife and kid he's never gonna take care of?"

Hanna sat at her desk, "I'm afraid he's going to hurt them again. We've got to get him off the street, Lonnie."

"The wife has no idea where he's staying now?"

"No, they lost their old apartment," Hanna said. "The only place Jenna could think of was a friend's place where they both stayed once when they were between permanent homes." She slid the address across to him on a piece of legal pad paper. "I had to press her to even get this. She wants to get back together with the idiot and doesn't want him thrown in jail."

"Love is blind."

Hanna said, "He came after me with the slightest provocation. Fortunately, Molly and one of my volunteers were here to get him to back down."

"This parole thing and assaulting you can take him down," Lonnie said. "It's not the first time he's skipped his mandatory Parole Officer meetings and he's been warned."

"How long can you put him away?"

"Not sure what a judge will do but probably not more than 90 days."

Hanna shook her head and walked to the window. "That's not good enough," she said, feeling the sad realization that women like Jenna Hall were victims of sociopaths who somehow entered their lives and often there was very little that could be done to free them of the dangerous burden.

"Lonnie said, "There was an arrest two years ago where Hall was a suspect in an apparent murder of another drug dealer. The case could never be made, and he was never charged."

Hanna turned. "I saw that."

"We're going to take another look."

Hanna tried to take a break a couple times a week to get out and run a few miles. It was her only way to get some time alone to think, unwind, reflect. It also helped balance a diet she never stuck to and she had to admit, too many glasses of red wine on too many nights. It was just past 10am and she was running now along the walk on the South Battery, the park to her left and the river off to her right. She saw her old house coming up through the trees but looked away and tried not to think about the terrible financial loss her husband's indiscretions had caused. She was not a fast runner and wasn't training for any marathons, she just liked the time alone, the race of her heartbeat, sweating out the day's stress.

Alex hadn't called her yet. She thought about their conversation the night before. He was going to call when he was headed back to Charleston. Phillip Holloway was standing by to meet with them to discuss Skipper Frank's murder case. She was still upset with herself for accusing Alex of having drinks with his ex-wife. She couldn't help herself when she thought about this woman back home and clearly intent on seeing Alex. Old jealousies and doubts of who she could really trust continued to haunt her.

Hanna picked up her pace a little to get her mind off Alex and his ex-wife. She ran hard for a hundred yards until she had to walk to get her breathing back under control. Her cell phone was in a waist pack she always used when she ran because she didn't want to be totally out of touch. She thought about calling Alex but didn't want to seem desperate.

And then her phone rang. She stopped and spun the pack around her middle so she could unzip the pouch and get her phone. She looked at the screen and smiled. It was her son, Jonathan.

"Hello, honey," she said, putting the phone to her ear and trying to catch her breath."

"Hey Mom! Got a minute?"

"Of course." The sound of his voice always brightened her day, the few times he did call. She didn't blame him. His life was hectic at school and he had a part-time job to help with the expenses. He was living off-campus now at the University of North Carolina in Chapel Hill in his second year. He shared an old three-bedroom house with two other friends. His abduction the past year during the horrifying ordeal with the men trying to recoup money from Ben's land deal still kept her awake at night. She tried not to imagine how wrong things could have gone. The men involved were truly ruthless and it could have ended much worse.

Jonathan said, "Mom, I want to come home this weekend."

"Great!"

"Will you be out at Pawleys Island?"

Hanna thought for a moment. She hadn't spoken with Alex about weekend plans, but they often stayed out at the beach. "Not sure yet but, I imagine we'll be out there if the weather looks good." Jonathan knew about her growing relationship with Alex Frank and Hanna was relieved to see the two of them were getting along well. "Why don't we plan on it," she said.

"I'm bringing a friend."

"Sure, one of your roommates?"

Hanna waited a moment for his response. She could tell he was nervous about something. Finally, he said, "No, I want you to meet someone."

Hanna grinned and looked out over the water. "A girl?"

"Yeah, I want you to meet Elizabeth."

"Elizabeth?"

"She's a friend," Jonathan said. "She's great, Mom. I really want you to meet her."

Hanna felt a little pang of remorse as she thought about how quickly her "little boy" was growing up. Jonathan had always had girlfriends in high school and she knew he was meeting plenty of girls up in Chapel Hill, but this was the first time *he was bringing a girl home to meet mom.* She pushed her motherly concerns aside. "That would be great, honey. We'd love to meet her." She realized she'd said "we", but Jonathan didn't seem to notice or care. He liked Alex, and Hanna had been relieved when Jonathan had accepted their new relationship, even with his father's death so recent.

Jonathan said, "We can come down Friday night."

"Let's plan on it."

"Great. We don't have any classes on Friday afternoon, so we'll probably get down there before you."

Hanna said, "I'll pick up some fish and shrimp and we'll have a big dinner and maybe a beach fire later."

"That would be great, Mom. You're really gonna like Elizabeth."

"Can't wait to meet her."

They said their goodbyes and Hanna checked her messages before putting her phone back in the pack. Still nothing from Alex.

Chapter Fourteen

Alex woke with a headache from the beers. He'd finally fallen asleep on the porch, well after 2, sitting on one of his mother's wicker chairs. He was startled awake an hour later by gulls or some other noises down at the dock and had gone inside and fallen into his old bed with his clothes on. He looked around now at the room he had grown up in. Light was coming through the window above him. He looked at his watch and it was already 8:30. He sat up and rubbed at his temples. There was a half-empty beer on the nightstand and the sight of it made him cringe.

The walls of his room were still adorned with the same music and sports posters. His desk had the five books that had been there for years, held between jumping fish bookends that had been a gift from his parents. The titles were all detective stories he had loved as a kid. He thought about how he rarely found time to read any more. When he looked down, he saw he'd slept with his shoes on and he realized he didn't have a change of clothes for the coming day. He doubted anything in the drawers here would still fit him. There wasn't a lot more weight on his frame since he left home for the service, but he knew his waistline had grown a couple of inches and he wasn't keen on wearing a Rolling Stones t-shirt. He'd either have to do a little shopping at *Troy's* downtown, the only clothing store in town, struggling to keep their doors open with the new *Walmart* just five miles away, or run home to Charleston later in the day.

Alex pulled his phone out of his pants pockets. There were two calls from his partner, Lonnie, but no messages; nothing from Hanna. He knew he was supposed to call her this morning. He felt a tinge of nausea rise in his throat as the night's excesses continued to punish him and he thought of the discussion ahead with Hanna about Adrienne... and his son, Scotty.

Walking into the kitchen to try to find some aspirin in his father's cupboards, he pressed "call back" on one of Lonnie's messages.

He heard his friend and partner say in the familiar deep voice, "Where you at, man?"

"Up in Dugganville, still." Alex had talked to Lonnie yesterday several times about his father's arrest and the attack on Hanna at her clinic.

"You finding anything?"

"No, not yet," Alex said.

Lonnie said, "Met with Hanna this morning on this deadbeat of a husband."

"Thanks, man."

"We're gonna take another look at that murder beef he got brought in on."

"Good, good," Alex said. "Really appreciate you taking the time on this."

"No problem."

Alex was tempted to tell his partner about Adrienne and the new developments in his life. There wasn't much they didn't share. He knew he needed to talk to Hanna first. "You sure you're okay with me takin' a little time off?"

"You need to take care of this thing with your old man," Lonnie said. "We'll cover the shop."

"Hopefully, we'll get this sorted out soon," Alex said, though he knew in his gut there was a lot stacking up against his father's guilt in the death of Horton Bayes.

Later, Alex was sitting in the same booth at *Andrews Diner* he'd been in with Adrienne the day before. He had showered and put his same clothes back on. His hair was still wet. Lucy put a cup of steaming coffee down in front of him and he ordered three scrambled eggs, whole wheat toast and bacon.

"Got an appetite this morning, hon?" Lucy asked.

"Trying to soak up the booze," he said and then regretted he'd mentioned it.

"Heard you had a late night down at *Gilly's*," she said.

Alex wasn't surprised people were talking about it. Dugganville was a small town. Lucy walked away, and Alex looked across the restaurant. He didn't recognize anybody at the other tables or the few people up at the counter. He was far enough away from everyone, he decided he could make a call without everyone hearing his business. He pressed Hanna's number.

The tone of her voice had an edge when she answered his call. "Good morning." To Alex, it sounded like an accusation, not a greeting. He knew it was his guilt creeping in.

He started to speak and then paused, struggling to sort out what he was going to say. "Good morning. Sorry I couldn't get back."

"What's the latest?" he heard Hanna ask.

What's the latest? he thought.

"Alex?"

"I have to stay for a few days, Hanna."

"Okay." Again, the edge in her voice.

"I let the Department know I'm going to take some time to help my dad."

There was a slight pause before Hanna said, "Of course."

"I do need to get back to Charleston to get some clothes and things, maybe this afternoon. You mentioned Phillip Holloway wants to meet. Could we do it then?"

"What time do you think you'll be back?"

"Can we plan on 4?" he asked.

"I'll check with Phillip and let you know."

There was silence between them for a moment. Alex knew he had to speak with Hanna in person about Adrienne... and Scotty. Finally, he said, "Thanks for your help with all of this, with my dad."

"Anything new?" she asked.

Anything new? He tried to put the picture of his son he had never met out of his mind. He couldn't help but sigh when he said, "It looks real bad."

Hanna said, "You can fill me and Phillip in this afternoon."

"I will."

They ended the call. Lucy came up with her coffee pot and held it up for him. He nodded for a refill. "You got a phone book, Lucy?"

He found Adrienne's mother's phone number in the directory and wrote it down before he left the restaurant. He walked down the street to the park across from the docks and sat on a bench along the sidewalk. He put the phone number in his cell and then heard the phone begin to ring on the other end. He still didn't know quite how to deal with this or what he should say. After the third ring, he heard, "Hello?" It was Adrienne's mother, Ella Moore.

"Hello Ella," Alex started and then paused to take a breath. "It's Alex. How are you?"

Her tone brightened noticeably. "Alex Frank! How nice to hear from you, boy. It's been too long."

"Is Adrienne there?"

"She sure is, let me get her. You come by and see me now, you hear?"

"Sure, Ella."

"Hold on, let me get her."

He heard the phone lay down on the counter. He could see the old kitchen in his mind. He'd been there enough back during their time together.

"Alex?"

She seemed surprised to hear from him. *Did she think he was going to just walk away from this?* "Adrienne, I'm still here in town. We need to talk."

"Of course."

"I'm down at the park. Can you come over?"

"Sure. I can be there in ten minutes."

"Does your son... does Scotty know about this? About me, I mean."

"No, I haven't talked to him yet."

Alex watched as one of the charter fishing boats pulled out of its slip for a day out on the Atlantic. "I'll see you in a few minutes."

She clicked off the call without answering.

Chapter Fifteen

The heat was building, and Alex walked towards the shade up the hill in the park. He thought the gazebo had too many old memories, so he kept walking until he found another bench under a big, sprawling live oak. It was a bright day with only a trace of wind. A few billowy white clouds drifted by slowly overhead. Shadows spread across the burned grass of the park. The smell of fish and diesel oil drifted up from the docks. He thought for a moment about what his life would have been like if he'd come back to Dugganville and joined his father on the *Maggie Mae* or eventually got his own boat. After last night at *Gilly's*, he felt relieved this place wasn't his daily life. The small town and the same people knowing everything about you seemed overwhelming.

He saw Adrienne coming down the sidewalk and turn up into the park. He stood and waved when she looked his way. She was dressed much differently from the previous day. Her jeans looked like they were loose enough she could actually breathe. She had on a white sleeveless blouse, buttoned up the front with none of yesterday's display of breasts showing. Her hair was down and pulled back behind with a blue ribbon. There was only a trace of make-up on her eyes and lips. For a moment, it was like they were back in high school.

Alex tried to force a smile as she came up. She didn't hesitate and came into his arms as if nothing had ever come between them. He returned her embrace with a tentative wrap of his arms around her back. She smelled of shampoo and coffee.

She spoke first. "Thank you for staying to see me."

"I'll be in town for a while to help with my dad's case."

She pulled back and looked up into his face. She was just a few inches shorter with flat leather sandals on her feet.

Alex said, "Let's sit."

She sat beside him and said, "Alex, I'm so sorry about this...about not telling you."

Alex couldn't think of anything to say.

"I found out I was pregnant when I moved down to Florida. For a while, I didn't know what I was going to do. I started seeing Derek a couple weeks after I got there. We were working at the same bar in Ft. Lauderdale. His name is Derek Crandall. Scotty's name is Crandall. I told you we got married."

"Yes, you did," Alex said. "And now he's left you."

"It's been bad for a few years. He couldn't keep a job and he drank like a fish. He was good to Scotty, though."

Alex said, "Thank God for that."

Adrienne looked back and nodded as if it was time for Alex to share his feelings on the situation.

Alex looked out across the docks and took a couple of deep breaths. "I want to do the right thing here, Adrienne."

"The right thing?"

"I assume he really is my son, unless this Derek guy looks like one of the Frank brothers."

"No, he has red hair and freckles," she said. "He's not the father."

Alex was trying to keep his emotions under control. He wanted to come out and challenge her on who else she had been sleeping with in Dugganville before she left town for Florida. He held his tongue.

"I want you to meet him, Alex... to meet your son."

Hearing her say it sent his emotions flaring again. He couldn't help himself and he blurted out, "Who else were you with?"

"What do you mean?"

"You know what I mean," he said quickly. "Who else were you with before you left town that year?"

He could see the hurt in her face, but he didn't care at this point. All the frustrations and betrayals with this woman were coming back to the surface.

She put her hand on his knee and it startled him. He thought of Hanna again and what she was going to think about all of this.

Adrienne said, "You have to believe me, there was no one else... then."

Then. There certainly were other men before that, he thought.

"We can get a test, Alex... a paternity test, if you don't believe me."

Alex pushed her hand away and stood up.

"I don't know, Adrienne. How do you expect me to deal with something like this? You go away for ten years and come back and tell me we've had a child together and you decided not to tell me!"

"I told you I was sorry!"

"Sorry! I'm afraid that's not good enough."

"What are you going to do?" she said, a look of panic on her face.

Alex walked around and held on to the back of the wrought iron bench, looking down at her. He suddenly remembered times when he had enjoyed looking into those beautiful brown eyes. He pushed the thoughts away. "How do you plan to explain this to the boy," he asked.

She shook her head, looking away.

"Adrienne?"

"I don't know!" she said, the panic rising now in her voice. "You're a friend I want him to meet."

Alex shook his head in disgust. "You're not thinking!"

"Sooner or later, I'll have to be honest with him. When he's a little older and can understand."

"And until then?"

"Alex, I told you I'm alone now. I need help. I can't raise him alone."

Chapter Sixteen

The women's shelter in downtown Charleston was just down the street from the Farmer's Market in an old warehouse building that had been renovated years earlier. The fading brown brick building looked well past its prime. There was a very small sign next to the glass door sitting a few steps up from the sidewalk that read, "Women's Home". It was four stories tall and stretched half the block. As Hanna walked up to the building, she thought about all the women taking refuge in this sad place and the devastating issues they were dealing with; homelessness, abuse, addictions. She knew the director of the shelter very well and was grateful they provided a tremendous resource for women and their children who had nowhere else to turn.

She climbed the steps and pressed the button on the box by the side of the door. She looked up at a security camera pointed down at her as a voice from the box said, "Can I help you?"

Hanna introduced herself and was buzzed in. She was escorted to the director's office. Greta Muskovicz was away in another part of the building for a moment and Hanna was offered a seat. She had met Greta years ago when one of her clients needed resources and sanctuary. Greta was a tough woman of German descent who ran this establishment with efficiency and a remarkable kind heart. At 52 years of age, she had never wed. Her job was her life and she even lived in an apartment on the top floor of the shelter. They had become close friends over the years. Hanna looked around the sparsely furnished and decorated office. Her desk was cluttered with too many files. *This woman is truly a saint for the work she does.*

Greta came in and touched Hanna on the shoulder. Hanna stood and they both hugged before Greta sat behind her desk. "Good morning, counselor," the woman said.

"Hello, dear."

"Let me guess. You want to talk about Jenna and her son?"

Hanna said, "I know they're safe here with you and thank God for that."

Greta just shook her head.

"I wanted to make sure you knew her husband has a long and dangerous rap sheet with the Charleston PD," Hanna said.

"I'm not surprised."

"There's also an open warrant for his arrest. I met with the police this morning and they're going to step up their efforts to bring him in. Hopefully, they'll be able to put him away for a while."

Greta asked, "What's that welt on your face?"

"Courtesy of Moe Hall."

Greta sighed. "You know Jenna's bent on getting back with this jerk?"

"I know. That's why I'm here. Can I see her for a few minutes?"

Jenna Hall and her son, William, walked into the living room area of the shelter where Hanna was waiting for them, looking out a window over the city beyond. Hanna turned when she heard them come in. Jenna nodded and took her son over to a box of toys. When she had him settled there, she joined Hanna on one of the couches.

Jenna started, "I'm just so sorry about Moe coming after you."

"Jenna, you need to listen to me carefully," Hanna said. "Your husband is obviously a very dangerous man. The police are looking for him as we speak..."

The woman started to protest, but Hanna continued. "I know you think you can save this, Jenna."

"I want my son to have a father. I want us to be together again. We can't live in this place forever. William needs a home and a father. Moe has a new job again."

Hanna listened patiently, then said, "You need to believe me when I tell you I've seen this same story play out too many times before. It always ends badly. You know your husband is not going to change. You and your son are in grave danger every time you're with him."

"I know he has a temper and sometimes it's my fault..."

Hanna interrupted, "No! It's not your fault!"

Jenna stood up. "You can't stop us from leaving here!"

"I'm here to plead with you not to. Just give the police a little more time to find your husband."

"I don't want him locked up!" Jenna pleaded.

"There may be no choice in the matter. He's wanted on a parole violation and there's some doubt about a past murder investigation your husband was a suspect in, even though he wasn't charged."

"Can't you please just leave us alone now?"

"You need to help us find him, Jenna. Can you give us any other possible places he may be staying?"

She shook her head. Hanna could see the clueless defiance in her eyes.

On the way back to her office, Hanna continued to think about how she could protect Jenna Hall and her little boy. It broke her heart to think about the two them abused by this wretched husband and father. Greta had promised to keep a close watch on them.

She remembered she had to leave for Atlanta tomorrow to be there for her father's heart procedure... and a day with her stepmother, *the lovely Martha Wellman Moss!* It grated on Hanna that the woman continued to use her previous husband's last name, surely because Terrance Wellman was from a prominent family in Georgia and he appeared to be a front-runner for the next governor's race.

One of her other not so favorite people was on her calendar in a couple of hours. She and Alex were meeting Phillip Holloway at his office at four to discuss Skipper Frank's murder case. The thought of having Holloway anywhere near her made her skin crawl, but she knew he was one of the best in the business in Charleston to handle a case like this. Then, there was the matter of his fee. She planned to ask him about dramatically lowering it. There was no way Alex, or his father, could afford Phillip's normal compensation. Based on the inappropriate way Phillip had behaved during the events surrounding her husband's death and the subsequent drama leading up to the discovery of his wife's crimes, Hanna felt she had some significant leverage. *The man should take the case for free*, she thought.

Chapter Seventeen

Sheriff Stokes read through the last page of the Medical Examiner's forensic report and closed the file. He reached for his fifth cup of coffee and shook his head. If the preliminary murder case against Alex's father, Jordan "Skipper" Frank, had already looked bleak, it was now damn near a death sentence for the man. He started typing on the keypad for his laptop to bring up his contact numbers. He got the cell number for Alex Frank and called. On the third ring he heard the man answer.

"This is Detective Frank."

"Alex, it's Pepper." He paused for a moment. "You need to get down here to my office, son."

"What have you got?"

"Forensics are back. It's not good."

"I'll be there in five minutes," Alex said.

The sheriff heard the call disconnect.

Alex was putting some groceries away he'd picked up at the *Winn Dixie* out on the west side of town when Sheriff Stokes' call had come in. When he ended the phone call, he quickly got everything stored away.

His mind had been swirling with questions and doubts since he'd left his ex-wife in the park. Adrienne's desperate appeal for help now that she had been abandoned by her second husband surely wasn't sitting well with him and yet, he did feel a nagging sense of responsibility for the woman and certainly the son they had together. He had left her in the park with a promise he would come by her mother's house later in the day to meet the boy and discuss the future. *And how am I going to explain this to Hanna?*

Alex was led back to Stokes office. The sheriff was on the phone and he motioned for Alex to sit in one of the chairs across from his desk.

Alex listened as Stokes said, "Right, we'll bring him down first thing." He hung up the phone. "That was the District Court office in Charleston. The preliminary hearing for your dad will be at ten tomorrow morning."

Alex said, "I'll let Hanna know. We're meeting with another attorney in Charleston this afternoon who may join the defense with her."

"I'll be taking him down in the morning," Stokes said. "Spoke with Jewel Clarke, the DA, about an hour ago. They have this same Medical Examiner forensics report." He pushed the file across to Alex. "I told you, it looks bad. The prosecutor's office is going to file for murder first degree."

Alex started looking through the report. "Tell me the worst."

"The blood evidence puts your old man on the deck of Bayes' shrimp boat. His shoe prints are in the blood on the deck. He's also got Bayes' blood on his clothes."

"That could be from the fight in *Gilly's*," Alex said quickly, looking up from the pages in front of him.

"Could be. We're still doing interviews with witnesses at the bar."

"What else?" Alex asked.

"Remember, we've got that rigging block with Bayes' blood all over it. Could be the murder weapon."

"Right?"

"Your old man's fingerprints are on it."

"You're kidding?" Alex said, closing the file and hanging his head. "Is there a copy of this file I can get to Hanna and this other attorney this afternoon?"

Stokes said, "That's the second copy for the defense."

"You see anything in his favor?" Alex asked.

The sheriff shook his head *no*. "Sorry, Alex."

When Alex parked in front of Adrienne's mother's house, he saw Adrienne hurry out the front door and down to his car. When he got out, she rushed into his arms.

"Oh Alex, thank you.".

He stood there with his arms at his sides, surprised and confused, not quite sure what to say.

"I told Scotty I had a special friend coming over for a visit. When I told him you were a policeman, he got all excited."

Alex gently pushed her back and looked up to the house to see Ella Moore coming out the front door holding the boy's hand.

Adrienne yelled out, "Scotty, come on down here. Want you to meet Detective Frank."

Alex felt a chill as he watched the boy come toward them. Scotty Crandall did indeed look like young versions of him and his brother at the same ages. The resemblance was incredible. The boy started running down the hill toward them. He was barefoot with cut-off jeans and a Miami Dolphins t-shirt. His brown hair was wet and brushed back. Alex could see the sunburn freckles across his nose as he came closer.

"You really a cop?" Scotty asked as he stopped by the car.

Alex bent down so they were almost eye-to-eye. "I sure am, Scotty."

"A detective?"

"That's right." Alex held out his hand to shake with the boy. "It's really nice to meet you, Scotty."

"Nice to meet you, sir. Where's your gun?"

Alex laughed. "It's in the car right now."

"Can I see it?"

"Scotty!" Adrienne scolded.

Alex said, "Maybe a little later."

Ella Moore had come up beside them all. "Nice of you to come by, Alex." She had a suspicious look on her face and from her tone it wasn't entirely clear if she was really that happy to see him. She did give him a hug and kiss on the cheek. "Nice to see you."

"Hello, Ella," he said and then turned back to Adrienne. "Thought we might walk into town for ice cream. What do you think, Scotty?"

"Yessir!"

"You want to come with us, Ella?" Alex asked.

"No, you all go on ahead. I got to get some dinner going. Not too much ice cream now. Don't want you spoilin' this boy's appetite."

"We'll be fine, Ma," Adrienne said and then reached for Alex's hand.

He pulled away and said, "Let's go."

Scotty ran up ahead as they walked down the street shaded with tall live oak. The early afternoon heat and humidity was building.

Adrienne spoke softly so the boy couldn't hear. "So, what do you think?"

Alex took a deep breath and look over at her. "I think he's a fine boy."

"I know this a lot to handle all at once," she said.

He just looked at her.

"What are you thinking?" she asked

Alex thought for a moment before saying, "I think there's a lot of history between you and me that needs to get talked about."

Adrienne watched her son running ahead. "I was hoping we could put that behind us."

"It's not that easy," Alex said.

"I know," she said, putting her hands in the back pockets of her jeans. "You said you're staying in town for a while to help your dad?"

"A few days," he said. "They're taking him down to Charleston in the morning for a preliminary hearing and charges to be filed. They may keep him down there unless we can get bail. Not very likely."

"But you'll be back?" she asked.

"I'll be back later tomorrow. Got a lot of people here I want to talk to about what happened that night."

"Can you come for dinner tomorrow night?" Adrienne asked. "Ella wants to cook dinner for all of us."

Alex hesitated, then said, "I'll have to let you know. Not sure yet when I'll be able to get back."

"Don't you want to get to know your son?"

Alex stopped, and she turned to look at him. "You need to give me some time on all this."

"Take as much time as you need," she replied.

Alex looked up ahead and watched as Scotty Crandall stopped to pick up a rock in the road and then throw it out into the river.

Chapter Eighteen

Hanna couldn't remember the last time she had been down to the law offices of Phillip Holloway and her deceased husband, Ben. It may have been shortly after his death when Grace Holloway had helped her clear out Ben's office. That had been one of the most difficult times of the entire ordeal. Ben had a wall of photos with him standing by family and friends, celebrities, sports figures. She wasn't sure at the time what she was going to do with them, but everything went into boxes and then home. She was still struggling hard at the time with the sudden loss of her husband. She would wake and find it impossible to believe he was really gone. That day in his office seemed to begin some closure on the realization she would be living without him now. He was really gone and here was all the stuff of his professional life that needed to be gathered and sorted, discarded or stored.

Her son, Jonathan, had helped her with all of it, wanting to keep a few things but agreeing with Hanna to throw away much of Ben Walsh's personal effects, donating most of his clothes. When they found they had to sell the Charleston house and move out, there was a steady purge of not only Ben's things but much of what Hanna had accumulated over the years.

As Hanna walked into the reception area of the law firm, she was greeted by the familiar face of the long-time receptionist, Helen Bray. The older woman with neat gray hair and well-tailored navy suit stood and said, "Hello Hanna. It's been too long."

Hanna walked up to her desk and shook hands. "Helen, good to see you." The woman had always been cordial and gracious with Hanna and a real help in dealing with the firm after Ben's death.

"How have you been, dear?"

"I'm good, Helen. Thank you."

"We still miss Ben so much.

"Yes... " she replied and hesitated. "I have an appointment with Phillip at four." She looked her watch and she was five minutes early. "Someone else is joining us. He should be here shortly.".

Helen Bray stood and said, "Yes, I know, dear. Let me take you back to the conference room. There's coffee and water there for you to help yourself."

Hanna followed her down the hall. They passed a few offices, some with familiar faces, some not. They walked into a large conference room with a wall of windows looking out at the skyline of Charleston.

"I'll bring your other party back when they arrive," Helen said.

"Alex Frank," Hanna said. "Detective Alex Frank."

As Helen walked out, she said, "Mr. Holloway should be with you in a minute. He's very prompt you know."

They smiled at each other and she left the room.

Hanna placed her bag on the table with the few files and papers she had brought along. Alex had called her on his drive in from Dugganville to review the findings of the Medical Examiner's report. It was not a happy conversation. His father's case looked very bleak. She also sensed Alex was terribly distracted and when she asked him about it, she got little in response. He said he was just tired and very upset about his father's arrest.

She looked up when Holloway walked in with his typical broad smile. He was dressed immaculately, as always. His hair seemed to have a bit more gray since she'd last seen him.

"Hello, Hanna." He came quickly around the table and gave her a warm and thankfully, professional embrace.

"Phillip, thank you for seeing us on this."

"Of course. Of course." He went over to the credenza and poured some coffee. He held up an empty cup for Hanna.

"No thanks." She sat down. "Alex should be here in a few minutes. I spoke to him just a while ago on his way into town."

"How is Mr. Frank?" Phillip asked as he sat across the table from her.

"I'm sure he's been better. This case against his father looks very bad."

"Yes, well, we'll take a look at that."

"Alex has a copy of the ME's report to share with us," Hanna said. "The prelim is tomorrow morning here in Charleston."

"What time?"

"Ten o'clock."

"I'll clear my calendar for the morning."

"Thank you, Phillip. So, you'll be able to join me on this?"

"Certainly.

"Well, again, thank you," Hanna said. "Before Alex gets here, I wanted to speak with you about your fee. He and his father won't be able to pay your typical rates."

Phillip didn't hesitate. "I understand. That won't be a problem. We'll work this out. I feel like you're family, Hanna, and I'm glad you've come to me for help on this case."

"Thank you, Phillip. That's very kind."

"So, you and Detective Frank are a couple now?"

Hanna took a deep breath before speaking. "Yes, we've been seeing each other for a while now."

Holloway smiled and nodded his head, then said, "Good, good. Always liked Alex. Glad to see you're moving on with things."

"Phillip...," she started, but he interrupted.

"Just visited Grace last week," he said.

Hanna noticed he didn't say the word "prison". She had mixed feelings as she thought of her once dear friend in the state's women's prison. Hanna finally managed to ask, "And how is she doing?"

He started nodding his head again, seeming to try to find the right words. "Well, as you can imagine, it's a tough place."

"Yes, I've visited clients there," Hanna said.

"She feels horrible about all that's happened."

Hanna didn't respond.

"She hopes one day you'll be able to forgive her."

Again, Hanna didn't say anything and then Helen Bray showed Alex into the room. Holloway stood and walked over to greet him.

"Hello, Detective."

Alex shook his hand. "Thank you for seeing us."

"Really sorry about your father."

Alex turned to Hanna who was sitting across the table and nodded.

"Welcome back," she said.

"Thank you for putting this meeting together," Alex said. He placed his bag on the table and pulled out the file from the Medical Examiner's office.

Holloway said, "Helen, can you make copies of this for us?" She took the file and left the room. Phillip motioned for Alex to take the chair beside him. "Hanna filled me in on some of the details earlier on the phone, Alex, but what's the latest?"

Alex looked across the table and wanted more than anything to reach for her hand, but instead he looked back to Holloway. "The evidence is real bad. There's little doubt my father was at the crime scene. Many people had witnessed their earlier fight and my dad's threat to kill the man."

Holloway nodded slowly and attentively as he listened, then said, "Things aren't always as they seem."

"Well, let's hope so," Hanna said. "Alex, has your father been able to recall anything else?"

He shook his head "no".

Holloway said, "We need to get a doctor in to see your father right away. I want his wounds examined. I also want a psychiatrist to spend some time with him, maybe help with his memory."

"Okay," Alex said. "They're bringing him down to Charleston in the morning for the arraignment."

"Right," Phillip said. "I'll talk to the DA about getting some time with our client in the morning before the hearing."

Helen Bray came back in with copies of the file and handed them around the table before leaving again.

Holloway started looking through the report. Alex turned to Hanna and forced a smile. This time, she reached across the table for his hand and Holloway noticed and looked up from his reading for a moment before continuing.

Hanna said, "How are you doing?"

Alex squeezed her hand and said, "Not one of my better days." They stared at each other for a moment before Holloway interrupted.

"So, tell me about the knife wounds. They haven't found a weapon yet?"

Alex said, "No. They do have a piece of boat rigging they think caused the massive head wound. You'll see they found my dad's fingerprints on it." He watched as Phillip Holloway continued to read and shake his head in concern.

"Did your father own a knife?" Holloway asked.

Alex thought for a moment. "Always carried a big knife in a belt scabbard when he was on the boat."

"Have they found it?" the lawyer asked.

Alex said, "No, and my dad doesn't know where it is. It wasn't on him when he was arrested."

"Yes, I see that here," Holloway said as he continued reading. He looked up. "We need to find that knife."

After the meeting with Phillip Holloway, Hanna invited Alex to her apartment for dinner. She had shopped earlier in the afternoon and had some things to pull a salad together. Alex told her he needed to go by his own place first to change and get some clothes to take back to Dugganville after the hearing in the morning.

Hanna heard a key turning in the lock at the door to her offices downstairs. She went down the back stairs and out to the lobby to meet Alex. She closed the door and turned to reach for him. He took her in his arms and held her, their cheeks together, then she kissed him. "Welcome back, Detective."

Alex forced a smile. "Not sure how I'll ever be able to thank you. Holloway talked to me about his fee on the way out when you went to the restroom."

Hanna nodded as they turned to go up to her apartment. She took him by the hand. "What did he say?"

"It's on him, gratis."

"Really!" Hanna was truly surprised. "I knew he felt guilty about Ben and how all that came down."

"He's damn good, Hanna."

"Yes, never a doubt he's a good attorney," she said. "Has a few personality issues as you know."

Hanna's apartment on the top floor of her office building had a small living area that led to an even smaller kitchen with a table only big enough for two people. A single bedroom and bathroom were at the back of the place. It was beautifully decorated with some of the few pieces of furniture and artwork Hanna had kept after the sale of her house down on South Battery.

She had a bottle of wine open on the counter and poured a glass for Alex. She noticed he didn't take a sip but placed it over on the table. The salads were already served and they both sat down across from each other, unfolding napkins and placing them on their laps. Hanna studied Alex's face for a moment as he started in on the food. He looked tired and gaunt, understandably after the ordeal with his father and all that lay ahead.

"Not much chance for bail in the morning?" he asked.

Hanna looked up. "No. We will certainly try, but it's very rare in a case like this to let a "murder one" defendant out on bail."

"How long will it take to come to trial?"

Hanna took a bite and swallowed. "Depends on the prosecutor, the assigned judge's schedule. Could be quite a while. The DA's office will want to build a solid case."

"My old man is not gonna do well in jail."

"No one does, as you know," Hanna said.

Alex finally reached for his wine and took a sip, then said, "I'm sure the prosecutor is looking at the evidence and thinking this is a "slam dunk" case. I sure as hell would if this was handed to me."

"What else have you learned?" Hanna asked.

He stood and walked to the sink. "Mind if I get some water?"

"Sure, I'd like a glass, too. You know where they are," she said, pointing to the cabinet to the right of the sink.

Alex poured the drinks and came back to the table.

"So?" Hanna asked.

Alex seemed distracted and paused a moment. "I'm sorry?"

"So what else have you found?" she asked.

He stared at her for a moment, gathering his thoughts. "There's no doubt about motive. The two have been at each other for years and the fight the night of the murder at the bar obviously looks bad. There's clear evidence he was on the boat the night of the murder. His shoe prints from the blood spill are irrefutable."

Hanna interrupted. "And his prints are on that piece of rigging that looks to be one of the murder weapons."

"Right." Alex took a bite of food and thought for a moment. "There are a few things that could create *reasonable doubt*."

"Such as?"

Alex put his fork down. "The bruising and contusions on Pop's hands could have been caused during the fight at the bar."

"And the blood spills on his clothes?"

"Yes," Alex said. "It's also possible he was on Bayes' boat after he was killed. That could explain the shoe prints in the blood."

"It could," Hanna said, "But why would he be there and why didn't he report the attack?"

"Maybe he heard the struggle. Our boat's not far down the docks. He might have gone down to see what was happening and either panicked when he saw the body or was too damned drunk and just can't remember."

Hanna said, "You'd have to be pretty drunk to forget something like that. They did get a blood alcohol level on him, didn't they?"

"Yes, it was off the charts. Gilly says he was staggering drunk when he left the bar, almost incoherent. He tried to give him a ride home, but he wouldn't get in the car. Gilly was afraid he'd fall in the river."

"We can get a medical opinion on the man's mental and physical capabilities with that level of intoxication," Hanna offered.

Alex nodded. "The other thing is the knife wounds."

"They haven't found the knife, right?"

"No, but my dad's knife he carries on the boat hasn't been found yet, either. The scabbard he carries it in on the boat was empty on his belt when they found him the next morning."

"I saw that in the sheriff's report," Hanna said. "If they don't find the knife, I'm sure the prosecutor will try to show the wounds are consistent with whatever type of knife your father carries."

Alex took a deep breath and a long drink of water. "Sheriff Stokes is going to get a diver down around the boat in the morning."

Hanna thought for a moment, then said, "Could be good or bad. If they find your father's knife..." She shook her head.

"How is it good?" Alex asked.

"What if they don't find it or they find a different weapon that could have caused the wounds?"

Alex said, "Well, we'll see. I'm going back up in the morning after the hearing. Hopefully, I'll get there when the diver goes down. I also have a long list of people I want to talk to."

"I can't go with you," Hanna said. "I'm leaving for Atlanta after lunch tomorrow. My dad's surgery is on Thursday."

"Right," Alex said.

Hanna watched him and could tell he was still thinking about something else. "Alex?"

He looked up at her, seemingly surprised. "What? I'm sorry."

"I should be back on Friday," Hanna said. "We can stay in touch by phone and I'm sure Phillip will have a game plan for after the hearing tomorrow." She reached for his hand and it felt cold and damp. "What else?" she asked.

She watched as Alex scrunched his mouth, seeming to consider her question. When he didn't answer, she said. "Let's get you to bed." She stood and went behind him to pull his chair back. "I brought that robe you like back from the beach."

He stood up and took her in his arms and then stared back at her for a moment. "Best news I've had all day."

Chapter Nineteen

Alex was startled by the sound of running water. He opened his eyes and squinted at the sun coming through the window blinds. He realized Hanna was up and in the shower. Her robe lay on the end of the bed and thoughts of their lovemaking the night before came back to him. What he remembered most was the guilt he felt the whole time in not telling Hanna about Adrienne and the picture of his son he carried in his bag back from Dugganville. He had been trying most of the previous day to decide how best to share this with her. Several times he was about to go into it and then he hesitated and pushed it off. He knew the longer he waited, the more difficult it would make the whole situation. He wasn't usually this indecisive, he thought to himself. *Should I tell her before she leaves for Atlanta?*

He heard the water in the shower turn off and looked at his watch on the nightstand. It was 7:30. The hearing was at 10. He'd have time to go down to the precinct to check-in before taking his planned leave. He reminded himself to call his partner, Lonnie, to get an update on the situation with Moe Hall. He could hear Hanna moving around in the bathroom. His bag with the photo of his son, Scotty, was in the kitchen. He was about to go get it when Hanna came out with a towel wrapped around her. She was brushing at her wet hair.

"Good morning," he said. He looked at the pile of his clothes on the floor beside the bed.

"You slept like a rock last night," she answered, coming around the bed and stopping as he sat up against the pillows and the headboard. She sat beside him and started to brush at his unruly morning hair.

He grabbed her arm and pulled her into a tight embrace and said, "You did your best to keep me up half the night."

He watched as she smiled back at him, then she reached for his watch. "We have a lot of time before we have to get down to the courthouse."

He smiled back. "Yes, we do."

She pulled the towel off and dropped it beside the bed. "Don't want you drifting off to sleep again!"

Alex saw Lonnie coming through the door to their offices. He had been gathering files and paperwork he thought he might need up in Dugganville while he was away, but he was thinking mostly about Hanna. Their early morning tryst had left him with almost no time to get to the office before his father's hearing at ten. He still hadn't told her about Scotty. He felt a sick feeling in his gut as he chastised himself again for delaying the inevitable.

Lonnie stopped at his desk and said, "Wrapping things up?"

Alex nodded. "Anything on the deadbeat dad?"

"Got a couple of plainclothes checking some of his past known locations this morning."

"Okay, good." Alex quickly filled him in on the latest on his father's case.

"Sorry, man," Lonnie said. "You need help up there, you know you can call."

He saw Hanna standing next to Phillip Holloway in the hallway outside the courtroom as he came off the elevator. He watched Hanna smile as he walked up, and the guilt flushed through him again. He shook hands with Holloway and kissed Hanna on the cheek.

Phillip said, "Met with the prosecutor and the judge a few minutes ago. They're going to delay the hearing for fifteen minutes to give us more time to meet with your dad. They're bringing him up right now."

"Good, thank you," Alex said. "You got my note the sheriff has a diver going down today around the *LuLu Belle*?"

"Let's hope they don't find your old man's knife down there," Phillip said.

"When I get up to Dugganville this afternoon," Alex said, "first thing on my list is a thorough search of our boat and house to see if I can find the damn thing."

Hanna said, "Phillip has a forensic expert lined up to examine the knife wound evidence from the body. We'll need to know the exact size and manufacturer of the knife."

Alex thought for a moment. "It was a fishing knife he always carried on the boat. He'd use it to fillet fish that came up in the nets. Don't recall who makes it, but the blade was probably six to eight inches."

Holloway continued, "Sure as hell the DA will have their own witness on this, so we need to get out ahead of it. If the knife shows up, we'll have different issues to deal with." He started toward the courtroom door. "There's a conference room. Should have your dad up by now.

Hanna and Alex followed Holloway into the small conference room off to the side of the courtroom. Skipper Frank was already seated at the table there. A uniformed deputy stood against the wall and then excused himself when they were all seated.

Alex said, "Morning, Pop."

His father stared back through tired eyes and a face that looked like it hadn't seen sleep in days. He was slumped over the table, his hands flat on the old wood table. He was dressed in a jail jumpsuit and didn't respond.

"Pop," Alex said, "this is Phillip Holloway. He's the attorney who will be working with Hanna on your case."

Skipper watched as Phillip sat across from him. Hanna and Alex took seats on each side of Holloway.

Phillip reached his hand across the table to shake, "Good morning, sir."

The old man returned the hand shake and nodded.

Hanna said, "Good morning, Mr. Frank. We don't have much time, so let's get started.

"Name's Skipper, ma'am."

Phillip pulled a file from his bag and opened it on the table between them. "Here's what's coming down this morning in this hearing. The District Attorney will read the charges they're filing against you. The judge will ask how you plead."

The old man interrupted. "How I plead? I don't know what the hell happened. How do I plead to that?"

Alex started, "Dad..." then Phillip interrupted.

"Sir, you will plead *not guilty* this morning," Holloway said. "I don't want you saying another word. Do you hear me?"

Skipper Frank grunted and said, "Seems they got a damned open and shut case here, counselor. Why not just get this whole thing the hell over?"

Alex jumped in, "Pop, this investigation is just beginning. The evidence against you is tough, but there are also a lot of loose ends we need to tie up."

"Your son is right," Phillip said. "There is a lot of damning evidence, some of it circumstantial, but so far, nobody saw you kill this man."

"Don't tell me they don't have enough to convict my ass."

Hanna said, "If we do our jobs, that won't happen."

Skipper Frank stared at Hanna and considered her words.

Phillip said, "The DA is a man named Jewel Clarke. He's a tough customer. I don't want to distress you any more than necessary, but Clarke is damn good and rarely loses a case. You need to do exactly as we tell you today and throughout the trial. Don't give him anything else he can use against you."

The old man nodded, rubbing his hands together nervously.

Phillip continued. "I don't want you talking to anybody but us. Not the jailer, not other inmates. Do you understand?"

"Yessir."

"Good. Now, we're going to ask for bail, but I seriously doubt the judge will even consider it. You need to be prepared to stay behind bars throughout the trial. I'm sorry, but in a capital murder case, there is very little hope to get you out of here until we prove your innocence at trial. Do you understand?"

"Yessir."

Phillip looked at his watch. "We need to get into the courtroom. They'll bring you in shortly. I want you to sit up straight, pay attention and do exactly what I tell you to do."

Skipper nodded.

Alex walked around the table. His father stood and faced him. Alex couldn't remember the last time they had hugged each other, but he reached out and held him close. "We're gonna take care of this, Pop." He felt his father tighten his arms around him.

Skipper Frank whispered in his son's ear, "I can't tell you I didn't do this."

Chapter Twenty

"All rise."

Hanna looked up as the bailiff announced the entrance of Judge Susan Wilcox. The woman looked to be in her 60'S, gray having taken over most of her shortly cropped hair. She was a small and squat woman, her face round and fleshy with cheeks flushed red and an expression that looked like she was already angry about something. She took her seat behind the bench and signaled for everyone to sit.

Hanna was sitting at the defense table with Skipper Frank between her and Phillip Holloway.

As the judge went through opening remarks summarizing the purpose of today's arraignment proceedings, Hanna looked over at the District Attorney, Jewel Clarke. He was flanked by two younger attorneys, one man and one woman, both immaculately dressed in dark suits. Hanna had met Clarke before but had never tried a case against him. He was an imposing figure, standing well over six feet with a large frame that filled a crisply pressed gray and chalk-stripe suit with a bright red paisley tie that seemed the only color in the courtroom other than the American flag behind the judge. His twenty years serving in the District Attorney's office had allowed him to build a reputation of a pit-bull prosecutor of the law who had a nearly perfect record of convictions. Of course, most lawyers secretly believed he only personally took on the cases he knew he could win. The tougher cases got handed down to Assistant DA's. Hanna thought, it's not a good sign when Clarke shows up to personally try a case. He must have sensed she was watching him, and he looked back at her, expressionless and seemingly bored with the whole process. Hanna didn't respond and looked to her left at Skipper Frank. He was following Phillip's directions explicitly, sitting straight and attentive to the judge's comments.

When Judge Wilcox concluded her opening remarks and instructions, she opened a file in front of her on the bench. She looked up and said, "Will the defendant please rise."

Phillip turned to his client and nodded for him to comply. Frank rose slowly, pushing his chair back away from the table.

The judge said, "Jordan Charles Frank, you are here today charged with murder in the first degree of Horton Bayes by the County of Charleston District Attorney's office. I see you have legal representation with you."

Skipper Frank said, "Yes, ma'am. I mean, yes, Your Honor."

"And are you satisfied with your legal representation?" the judge asked.

Hanna watched as Skipper looked down at Phillip Holloway and then over to her. He turned back to the judge. "Yes, Your Honor."

Judge Wilcox made a note in her file, then said, "Mr. Frank, how do you plead to the charges of murder in the first degree."

Hanna breathed a sigh of relief when she heard Alex's father quickly and confidently say, "I plead *not guilty*, Your Honor."

Phillip's request for bail was quickly objected to by District Attorney, Jewel Clarke, and declined by the judge. Jordan Frank was remanded to custody in the Charleston County Jail. A trial date was set for six weeks out.

As Skipper Frank was being escorted from the courtroom by the bailiff, Hanna looked over at Alex who was sitting in the first row along the rail behind the defense table. Only three other people were in the public seating area. One appeared to be a reporter taking notes as the proceedings wrapped up. She could see the sadness in Alex's eyes as he watched his father led away by two Sheriff's deputies. She made eye contact with Alex and forced a thin smile of encouragement. Her effort seemed little consolation.

Alex was waiting for her and Phillip when they came through the courtroom doors into the hallway. Phillip said, "Alex, let me know what you hear on the diver's search this afternoon. Give me a day or so to sort through all this."

He motioned to the leather bag hanging from a strap over his shoulder."

Alex said, "Yes, thank you."

Phillip turned to Hanna. "I'll call you later this afternoon to discuss next steps."

"I'll be driving to Atlanta to see my father, so call my cell," she said.

Phillip nodded and said, "I need to get back. We'll talk soon." He patted Alex on his upper arm as he passed and walked away down the hall to the elevators.

Hanna said, "Well, your father held up pretty well in there."

"He's a tough old bird, but you can tell this has got him real scared."

"Who wouldn't be?"

Hanna noticed that Alex seemed uncomfortable, distressed about something which she assumed was the charge of murder just brought down against his father.

Alex said, "Hanna, I need to talk to you about something."

"Okay."

"Not here. Can we take a walk?"

Hanna was alarmed. "What is it?"

"Please, let's go outside."

They left the courthouse and turned down the sidewalk. The heat was building on another sweltering summer day in the city. Hanna noticed dark gray and threatening clouds had blown in since they had arrived earlier in the morning. They walked for a block without talking, the sounds of traffic and car horns, a distant siren breaking their silence. There was a bench at a bus stop coming up and Alex motioned for them to sit.

"What's going on, Alex?"

He sat beside her and looked away for a moment, seeming to gather his thoughts.

Finally, he said, "I need to talk to you about Adrienne."

Hanna's senses immediately went on full alert. She didn't respond.

Alex hesitated, clearly not sure how to proceed.

"What about Adrienne?"

He reached for the leather bag he held in his lap and opened the flap. He pulled out a photograph and held it so Hanna couldn't see the picture. "You know that Adrienne wanted to talk to me about something."

"So, you saw her?"

"Yes."

"And what did she want?" Hanna asked, her sense of dread rising.

"Adrienne left South Carolina shortly after I found out about her last affair. She's been gone over ten years," Alex said. "We've had no contact. I filed for divorce about a year after she left. Occasionally, I'll get some update from my father or someone I run into from Dugganville."

Hanna looked down at the photo he was holding but still couldn't see what it was.

"I knew she had a child after she left," Alex said, swallowing hard, speaking very softly. He took a deep breath. "I agreed to meet her for a cup of coffee. She wanted to tell me about her marriage and her son. Her husband has left her. She doesn't even know where he's gone."

Hanna had to interrupt. "That's her problem now, Alex. I don't mean to sound cruel, but..."

He handed her the photo and Hanna looked down at the picture of a young boy. She listened as Alex continued. "His name is Scotty Crandall. Adrienne married this Crandall guy who's now left her."

As Hanna listened to him speak, she looked more closely at the boy in the photo. She felt a chill all over.

"Does he look familiar?" she heard Alex ask.

"You're not saying?"

Hanna looked back to Alex as he said, "Adrienne had the baby" almost nine months after she left for Florida. We had still been living together when I found her in bed with another man, but..."

"So, you're telling me this is your son?"

Alex breathed deeply. "Look at his face, Hanna."

Hanna handed the photo back, not wanting to look at it any longer. "What about this other guy she was sleeping with here in South Carolina?" she asked, a tinge of hope in her voice.

Alex hesitated, then said, "He was black, Hanna. It wasn't him. She insists there was no one else, even after she got down to Florida. Not until after she knew she was already pregnant. She was pregnant when she met this Crandall guy."

Hanna's surprise was replaced with a slow building anger. Her face flushed red. "Why didn't you tell me about this earlier?"

"Obviously, I've been trying to sort this all out for myself."

Hanna looked away, trying to calm her emotions but having little success. She felt Alex's hand on top of hers and she pulled away. "So, what does Adrienne want?" She looked back at Alex.

"She wanted me to meet my son."

"So, you've met him?"

He nodded. "I went by her mother's house yesterday."

Hanna was shaking her head. "And he knows you're his father?"

"No. Adrienne hasn't told him. He thinks I'm a friend of his mother."

Hanna rubbed her mouth, trying to think through what to say. "He certainly looks like you, Alex. No one could doubt that. But, can you really trust this woman? Don't you want to get a DNA test or something?"

"I'm thinking about it."

"What do you mean, you're thinking about it?"

"Hanna, please."

"I can't believe you were afraid to tell me about this."

"I wasn't afraid. I was concerned for how you'd react."

"How did you expect me to react!" Hanna stood and walked a couple of steps away before she turned back to him. "First, I meet your ex-wife who is back in town to track you down. She looks like a stripper and starts coming on to you right in front of me. Then, you tell me you had a child together you never knew about. My God, Alex!"

"Hanna, please sit down."

"And what does she want?" Hanna said, the defiance in her tone crystal clear.

Alex looked back at her, almost helplessly.

"She wants you back," Hanna said. "She wants you to take care of your son. She wants you to be a family."

Alex started to answer, but Hanna went on, "And what did you tell her?"

"I haven't told her anything, yet," he said, standing and coming over beside her.

"But you haven't told her no?"

Alex didn't answer at first.

"What are you telling me, Alex?"

He reached for her arms and she didn't pull away this time. "I needed to let you know what was happening. I'm sorry I didn't tell you last night. I just couldn't find the right way."

Hanna felt an incredible sadness deep inside. Just hours ago, she and Alex had been together in the most loving way. She had sensed something was obviously bothering him but assumed it was his father's murder charges. Not really wanting to hear the answer, she asked, "And what does Adrienne expect now?"

"I haven't told her anything except I need time to think this all through."

"She knows you and I are together?"

"Yes, she knows. Of course, she knows."

"And obviously doesn't care," Hanna said, now pulling away from him. "So how much time do you need, Alex?"

He shook his head and looked back, almost desperately. "Please, Hanna. Please understand this is going to take a little time to process."

Hanna couldn't control her anger any longer. "You'll have all the time you need! I have to get to Atlanta this afternoon." She was determined not to let him see her cry, though she could feel the tears building in her eyes. "I have to go." She turned quickly and started walking away to her car. She heard him yell after her.

"Hanna, please!" then a brief pause before, "I'll call you tonight."

Chapter Twenty-one

On the drive up Highway 17 to Dugganville, Alex continued to think about his discussion with Hanna in front of the courthouse. He knew she would be upset about his indecision and uncertainty regarding Adrienne and Scotty. She had every right to be confused and angry. He had hoped she would be a little sympathetic to the situation he now found himself in, but when he put himself in Hanna's place, he knew he would probably react the same way.

He still couldn't sort through all the implications of the crumpled photograph that lay on the seat beside him. Certainly, he would take financial responsibility for the boy, but how would he insert himself into his son's life and what about Adrienne? Right now, Scotty Crandall thought he was just a friend of his mother. When would they talk to him about who Alex really was? What should his relationship with Adrienne be? He had to put his son as the first priority in wherever this was headed.

His cell phone was sitting on the dash and it started to buzz. He looked at the screen and saw a local area code, but he didn't recognize the number.

"Hello, this is Frank." There was no response at first and then he heard a woman's voice.

"Alex?"

"Yes, this is Alex Frank."

"Alex, it's Ella Moore."

He cringed and looked out across a vast pattern of marsh grasses and backwater channels. He could picture Adrienne's mother sitting on the stool in their kitchen with the wall phone to her ear. "Ella, how are you?" he replied tentatively, his senses on high alert.

"Alex, are you in town?" she asked.

"I'll be there soon."

"I need to see you."

"What is it, Ella?"

"I really need to speak to you about Adrienne. Can I meet you somewhere?"

Alex looked at the clock on the dash. It was near noon. "I'll be at my dad's place in about fifteen minutes."

"Oh, thank you. I'll see you there."

The line went silent.

As he pulled into the drive of his father's house, he saw Ella Moore sitting on the front porch steps, her arms wrapped around her knees. When she saw Alex's car, she stood and began walking over. She was an attractive woman and had many of her daughter's features. The red hair was more a dark brown after years of coloring away the gray. She was wearing khaki shorts and a sleeveless blue t-shirt with a white *Hilton Head* logo on the front. Her arms and legs were deeply tanned. Alex knew she worked as a waitress at a waterfront restaurant up in Georgetown and she must have had a lot of shifts on the outdoor deck. Normally, she wore too much make-up, but today, Alex was surprised to see her face plain as she came up.

He watched as she came around the front of the car and without hesitation, threw her arms around him. "Thank you for seeing me," she said softly as she pushed back.

Alex said, "Let's go inside. It's cooler."

They sat across from each other at the kitchen table, two glasses of ice water in front of them.

"How's your dad doing?" she asked.

"Not great, as you can imagine."

"Always liked your old man," Ella said. "Too bad it didn't work out for the two of us."

Alex remembered the short and tempestuous relationship a couple of years after his mother died. He was surprised one of them didn't kill the other.

Stories of their fights were legend around town and down at *Gilly's.*

Alex wasn't in the mood for small talk. "What do you want, Ella?"

The woman squirmed in her chair and took a drink. "It still hurts me every day, the two of you not being able to make it work."

Alex started to protest, but she continued.

"I know my daughter didn't behave well... the other men and everything."

"Ella, please. We don't need to go through all that."

"I'm so glad she's home now where she belongs."

Alex looked back without responding. He watched as Ella Moore took a deep breath.

"She's been away so long. She's really changed, Alex. She's finally grown up. Maybe it's the boy. She's a mother now and has to think straight about things."

Alex had no patience to listen to the supposed new virtues of his ex-wife. "Ella, I'm sorry, but what do you want?"

"I want Adrienne to stay here in town, to raise her son here."

"That's up to her," he said. He reached for the glass in front of him, cool sweat streaking down the sides. He took a long drink.

"I'm afraid she'll head back to Florida," Ella said.

"Again, that's up to Adrienne."

"I don't want her getting back with that Crandall man. He was never good to them," she said. "I'm glad he left."

Alex placed the glass of water back down. "Ella, Adrienne and I need to work this out. It's going to take some time. She doesn't want to tell Scotty about his real father yet. I honestly don't know how we should deal with this, but we will."

"Alex, my grandson needs a real father," she said. "He needs you."

"Ella..."

"Adrienne needs you, Alex!"

Alex dropped Ella Moore back at her house before driving down and parking in front of *Andrews Diner* to get some lunch. As Lucy brought over the iced tea he'd ordered, he thought about his final words with Adrienne's mother in the car in front of their house. She had pleaded with him again to take her daughter back. *He's your son, Alex. She's was your wife. You loved each other. You should be a family again.*

The bell on the front door of the diner rattled and Alex looked up to see the familiar face of Chaz Merton walking in. He and Chaz had been boyhood friends growing up in Dugganville. When Alex left for the Marines and later to college, Chaz never got away. He'd spent his adult life working a variety of odd jobs, most on the shrimper fleet. He had worked for Alex's dad for many years on the *Maggie Mae.*

Merton saw him and came over.

"Join you?"

"Sure," Alex said, motioning to the seat across the booth from his. "How you been, Chaz?"

The man sat down, and Alex noticed the deeply lined creases on his face from the toll of hard work and harsh elements on the water. He suspected too many late nights at *Gilly's* had also taken their toll. He could smell alcohol on his friend's breath and it wasn't even one in the afternoon yet.

"Heard they took your old man down to Charleston."

Alex nodded. "His arraignment was this morning. They'll hold him down there now until the trial."

Lucy came up and Chaz ordered a cup of coffee and a grilled cheese sandwich.

"Seen this comin' for a long time, Alex," Chaz said as the waitress walked away.

"How's that?"

"Your old man and Bayes. They been at each other for years."

Alex said, "I know the history."

"Hope to hell he's got a good lawyer."

Alex nodded.

"It don't look good, Alex," Chaz said, shaking his head and looking up when Lucy put his coffee down.

"Who else was in *Gilly's* the night of the fight, Chaz?"

The man scratched at his unshaven chin, then said, "The usual crowd."

Alex said, "I want to talk to everyone who was there that night." He reached into the bag beside him on the seat and pulled out a notepad and pen. "Can you write down everyone you remember?"

Chaz took the pen. "Everybody saw the fight, Alex. Ain't no mystery there. Your old man was jawing with Horton about something happened out on the water and the next thing you know, they're throwing each other around the bar."

"I know that, Chaz. Just write down the names you can remember."

Alex watched his old friend start writing names on the pad. He looked at his worn and weathered face and remembered times when they were boys. Chaz had been a great pitcher on their high school baseball team. A few small colleges had shown interest in bringing him in on scholarship until they saw his grades. He barely made it out of high school and would have no chance in college. It wasn't that he didn't have the intellect, he just could never focus on anything but girls and parties. Alex was sad to see how little his life had become.

Chaz was still writing names when he said, "Saw Adrienne this morning down at the docks. She was walking with her boy."

Alex just nodded when Chaz looked up at him.

Chaz said, "Damn, she's a looker. Sorry 'bout you two, man."

"Just give me the names, Chaz."

Chapter Twenty-two

Hanna drove down the tree-lined West River Drive in Atlanta on the way to her father's house. The massive old brick and stucco homes were set well back from the road, many with ornate gates closing off long curving drives through the trees. She had grown up here and many of her friends had lived in some of these houses. She knew her childhood was not ordinary. The wealth and excess had always embarrassed her. Friends had often teased her about shrugging off the trappings of her family's abundance. When others were driving Mercedes and BMW's to school, Hanna had insisted on a used Honda Accord when her father offered to get her first car. She named the car "Harry" for some reason she couldn't remember now and had driven it all through college up in North Carolina. She was driving a new Honda now and prided herself on her frugality and the good mileage the car got her.

When she faced near complete financial ruin after her husband's death, Hanna never considered calling her father for help. She refused to take anything more from the man. He had been incredibly generous with her throughout her childhood and all the way through law school, but in Hanna's mind, that was enough. As an adult, she always felt she needed to face life on her own, good and bad, and take responsibility for her own future. She was never sure if it was just foolish pride or some deeper resentment of her father and continuing efforts to control her life and bring her back to the family law firm in Atlanta.

Hanna saw the drive to her parent's house coming up on the left and she slowed and turned in. Tall brick columns held a bronze gate that was closed and locked, weathered to a blue green patina over the years. She opened her window and reached for the keypad. The four numbers were her mother's birthday... 8643. She forced thoughts of the plane crash and her mother's death away every time she came back here and had to enter the code. She was surprised her father's new wife hadn't changed the number.

The two-story white brick house could be seen up ahead through the tall oaks and pine trees. A broad veranda ran the full length of the first floor of the enormous house that had the look of a classic southern plantation but was far bigger than any she had ever seen. Hanna thought of her ancestor's old plantation house, *Tanglewood*, near Georgetown, back in the Low Country and her great-grandmother, Amanda Paltierre Atwell. She still kept and often read the woman's journal that had proved such comfort to her during the difficult times after Ben's passing. The old photo of her family from the Civil War that was a gift from the new owners of *Tanglewood*, now hung in Hanna's house out on Pawleys Island.

Hanna pulled to a stop in the circle drive around the front of the house. She sat for a minute trying to push thoughts of her long drive up from Charleston and the relentless doubts that had been swirling through her mind about Alex Frank and the conversation they'd had that morning about his ex-wife and a new son in his life. At times, she was so frustrated with the whole situation, she was tempted to call Alex back and tell him to stay in Dugganville with his ex and his son and never call her again. She thought about how many times in her life she'd vowed to never let her guard down again. Her first love in college, the photographer Sam Collins, had left and never returned. Her marriage to Ben Walsh had been, for the most part, a happy union, but the last few years had turned into a nightmare beyond belief. His betrayal had pushed her to make the vow again... *no more men!* And then Alex Frank had come along and eventually that promise to herself slowly faded.

Hanna knew in her heart that Alex was caught in an untenable situation. She knew he didn't intend to hurt her. The fact he'd had so much trouble telling her the truth about what he was faced with, did trouble her. She would have hoped they'd become close enough he would be able to share anything with her. *Apparently not.*

Alex said he would call tonight, she thought. She sighed when she considered he may well tell her he was taking Adrienne back, that he wanted to raise his son in a real family. Would Alex Frank just be the latest man in her life to leave her alone and devastated? She cursed silently for letting herself fall vulnerable again.

She got out of the car and looked up at the big house and the double doors that led into a grand entry. Thoughts of her mother came back. She would always come hurrying out that front door when Hanna came home for a visit. Her mother had been gone now nearly twenty years, but the pain of her passing in the plane crash in the Bahamas still cut deep and Hanna thought of her most every day since. Her brother would have been forty-two now, she thought, closing her eyes and trying to push back the dark mood coming over her.

The front door did open, but it wasn't her mother. Martha *Wellman* Moss, her father's second wife, came through the door with a flourish of smiles and colorful scarves flowing in all directions. Hanna immediately noticed the hair was a new shade of blond and cut more severely than her previous long and curly styles. She was still trim and fit in her mid-fifties, near daily workouts with her personal trainer in the massive gym in the basement of the house having their effect. Hanna cringed at the woman's fake enthusiasm at her arrival.

"Oh, Hanna!" she said, rushing down the long row of brick steps. "Welcome home, dear!" She rushed up to Hanna and gave her an effusive hug. The perfume was overpowering.

Hanna pushed back. "Hello, Martha."

"Oh dear, I'm so glad you've come," her stepmother said. "I must tell you, your father is not doing well at all. You'll be quite surprised when you see him. He's lost so much weight and he's become quite weak the past month or so."

Hanna was suddenly alarmed. She knew her father was facing a serious follow-up surgery for his heart disease, but he hadn't let on how poorly he was feeling. She remembered how weak his voice had sounded on the phone earlier in the week.

"Where is he, Martha?"

"Up in our room, dear. He's so excited you've come."

Hanna went to the back of the car to get her bags, but Martha said, "Don't worry about your things. I'll have Anna bring them in for you."

Anna Parsons was the long-time housekeeper and cook who had been with the family since Hanna was in grade school. The old black woman was one of Hanna's dearest friends and confidants. She had helped to keep her and her brother grounded in their earlier years when the wealth and privilege could have easily been taken for granted and expected.

Hanna saw Anna in the kitchen and had a quick reunion with her before heading upstairs. She gasped when she came into her father's bedroom and saw him sitting up against the headboard reading the *Atlanta Constitution*. He looked even worse than Martha had described. His face was not only gaunt, but a sickly pale. She rushed over to the bed and sat beside him, taking his hand.

"Hello, Daddy." His grip was weak and the skin on his hand was mottled with dark spots. She felt it quiver in her grasp.

"Hey, Kiddo," he said slowly, smiling now with surprising white and even teeth.

"How long has this been going on?" she asked.

"Oh, I'm just a bit rundown," he said. "I've been a little worried about them carving open my chest again tomorrow."

Hanna felt Martha sit beside her on the bed. "Dr. Mason is the best," the woman said. "He's taken very good care of your father."

It certainly doesn't look that way, Hanna thought. She couldn't believe the difference in appearance from the strong, dynamic litigator and community leader she was accustomed to seeing on her visits home.

Her father said, "Thank you for coming. It means a lot."

"Of course," Hanna said. "What time is the surgery tomorrow?"

Martha jumped in. "We're taking him to the hospital at seven and Dr. Mason has the procedure scheduled for late morning."

Hanna looked back at her ailing father. "Daddy, you should have called me earlier."

"I don't like to bother you. I know you're busy with your clinic and this new man in your life. What's his name?"

She was sure her father knew Alex's name, but she didn't protest. "Alex Frank."

"Right, Alex..."

Martha said, "We do hope to meet him soon, dear."

Hanna felt a surge of doubt and uneasiness. *Would they meet Alex someday soon or was that chapter closed now?*

Martha stood and reached for the newspaper he was holding. "I've been trying to get your father to rest all afternoon."

He replied, "I want to talk to Hanna for a moment, dear."

A cell phone started to buzz, and Hanna watched as Martha pulled her iPhone out of the white silk pants she was wearing. She walked toward the door, waving to them as she answered the call and then she was gone.

Hanna turned back to her father. "I'm sorry, Daddy, but you look like hell."

He laughed weakly. "Never felt better."

"How long have you been doing this poorly?"

He scrunched up his face in thought. "A couple months, maybe."

Hanna felt a flush of anger that no one had alerted her to this. Again, she had the nagging suspicion that Martha, the new wife, would prefer her father be on his way to the Pearly Gates. God only knows what she's managed to get put in his will, she thought.

He squeezed her hand and said, "Hanna, I know how you feel about the firm here in Atlanta, but..."

"Daddy, can we not do this now?"

"Moss Cooper has been led by our family for decades now."

"I know that. We've had this discussion a dozen times."

She watched his face sag even more and his eyes began to mist. "Hanna, dear, I may or may not even survive this procedure tomorrow." Hanna began to interrupt but he continued. "But, that's not what scares me today. What really scares me is the thought of someone else taking over our family's law office."

"The firm will be fine, Allen," she said, returning to his preferred name use. "Cooper has two sons who've joined the office, right?"

"They're total idiots," her father hissed.

Hanna looked back at her father and his almost pleading expression. "Let's just worry about your health and getting you back on your feet."

Chapter Twenty-three

Chaz Merton had never owned a car. He occasionally managed to keep enough money together from odd jobs that he considered buying an old pick-up truck for a few hundred bucks, but he always decided against it at the last minute. His old Schwinn 3-speed bike got him around town and to work down at the docks just fine. He lived in a one room apartment on top of a garage just two blocks from Main Street. He'd rented the place for over ten years from old Mrs. Grange who lived in the main house.

Chaz had left Alex Frank at the diner just a few minutes earlier and was riding his bike back down to the Richards Fisheries plant across the river from the Frank's docks and house up on the hill. He got some part-time work there, filleting fish for the market the Richards had there in a storefront on the docks. He figured with the Skipper's boat no longer available for work and Horton Bayes about to be put six-foot under, his shrimping days would be limited for a while. Most of the seafood the Richards took in was sold wholesale to restaurants and grocery stores, but they kept some of each day's catch for the locals to get fresh fish.

He had been surprised to see his old friend, Alex Frank, back in town and in the diner for lunch. He was also surprised he was taking a leave from the Charleston PD to help with his father's trial. He wasn't exactly sure what Alex planned to do with the long list of bar patrons he'd just given him, but he *was* sure that some of the people he had written down would not be happy about getting drawn into the case. He'd asked Alex not to tell anyone he had provided the names.

He pulled his bike into the drive at Richards and laid it against the wall of the building that held the market store. He saw Connor Richards come around the corner and get an angry look on his face.

"Merton, where the hell you been?" Connor yelled. "You're twenty minutes late from lunch and we got fish stackin' up in there. I give you a damn job and this is how you start?"

"Sorry, boss," Chaz said. "Won't happen again. Ran into an old friend down at *Andrews* and the time got away from me."

"Get your ass on the line in there," Connor hissed. "And there won't be any second chances, you hear me?"

"Yessir, boss!"

Alex was finishing his iced tea at *Andrews* and considering the list of names Chaz Merton had just left him. Most of the names were familiar to him as long-time residents of Dugganville. Several he knew were "regulars" at Gilly's and friends of his father. A few names didn't ring a bell. He noticed both Beau and Connor Richards had been in the bar that night, *slumming again*, Alex thought.

He reached for the phone directory Lucy Andrews had brought over for him. He found the number he was looking for and dialed.

"Richards Industries," may I help you?" he heard a young woman's voice say.

"Yes, is Beau Richards in this afternoon? This is Detective Alex Frank."

"Let me check for you, sir."

He had been waiting for over a minute before he heard the line click back on. "Alex? That you?"

"Hey Beau, sorry to bother you on a work day like this," Alex said.

"Never a problem, Alex," the man said with his low confident voice. "How's your old man holdin' up?"

"Had his arraignment down in Charleston this morning," Alex said. "They'll be keeping him down there 'til the trial."

"Damn! You sure there's nothing we can do to help?"

Alex paused for a moment as Lucy refilled his glass of tea. "You got a few minutes for me to stop by this afternoon, Beau?"

"Just on my way out," Richards said. "Say, why don't you come out to the house tonight for dinner. Connor and his girl are comin' over. Got some big Porterhouse cuts from our beef over on the ranch in Bluffton. Don't think you've met my new wife, Amelia?"

"I just need a few minutes, Beau."

"We'll have plenty of time over dinner. Come by around five and we'll have a cocktail first." Before Alex could respond, he heard, "Okay, great. See you at five," and then the line went dead.

Alex spent the rest of the afternoon back at his father's house, reaching out to other names on Chaz Merton's list by phone. He was looking for any small detail or observation someone might have remembered about the fight or what led up to it. When he looked at his watch it was 4:30. He had picked up very little he didn't already know from the sheriff, Gilly the bartender and owner or from his friend, Chaz.

He took a quick shower and changed into a clean pair of khaki trousers and a white golf shirt. As he drove out the back roads to the Richards' estate west of town, he was thinking about Hanna. She would be in Atlanta by now to be with her father. Alex knew she was furious with him and she had every right. He'd promised he would call her tonight, but he had little news to share. He'd tried to keep focused on gathering information that might help at his dad's trial, but his thoughts kept drifting back to Adrienne Moore and young Scotty... his son.

He knew in his heart he would do what was right to support the boy, but he couldn't imagine a way he would ever want to get back with his ex-wife. She had not only cheated on him repeatedly but had taunted him with the details during their last argument before she left town for Florida ten years ago.

And then the doubts would come back. How was he really sure this boy was his son? The timing of her pregnancy, the picture and remarkable likeness, and Adrienne's story left little other explanations. He thought again about a paternity test and then felt guilty for looking for a way out. He had only spent a short time with Scotty, but he felt an obvious connection.

He saw the long white three-rail fence that stretched for over a mile along the property that led up to Beau Richards' house. He had acquired several thousand acres years ago and built the sprawling Low Country house and stables for his first wife. She had left him for reasons unknown and he kept the house for the next wife, Amelia, who Alex had not met. Three beautiful Appaloosa horses grazed in the pasture just before the gate to the drive up to the house. Alex turned left and stopped at the closed gate. A brass sign beside the gate announced he had arrived at *Foxmoore.* Alex remembered Beau telling him once it was an old family name. There was a speaker on the keypad and he pushed the intercom button. A voice came on that he didn't recognize, probably one of the servants. "Yes?"

"It's Alex Frank. Beau invited me for dinner."

"Yes, Mr. Frank, Come right up to the house. Mr. Richards is expecting you."

The gate began to swing open, obviously well-oiled as it hardly made a sound. Alex noticed two security cameras placed on the brick columns built on each side of the drive. He felt like waving.

The drive up to the house wound through low hills with plantings of new shrubs and trees mixed in with many towering live oaks strung with Spanish Moss swaying in a light breeze. The fence continued up both sides of the drive and Alex saw several more horses grazing. *Business is good!*

The house came into view through the trees. Alex wasn't surprised by the size and grandeur of the place. He and his father had been out for a big barbecue the Richards had thrown several years ago. In the circle drive in front of the house was parked a long white Cadillac Escalade next to the biggest Mercedes convertible he had ever seen, white with tan leather interior. He parked his Ford behind the SUV and got out. The smells of the ranch were mixtures of hay and manure and sweet flower aromas drifting on the wind. Out beyond the house was a barn and stable that looked as big as a football field. The front door opened, and Beau Richards walked out. He was dressed in white linen pants and a *Tommy Bahama* light blue shirt untucked. His brown leather loafers shined in the late afternoon sun through the trees. His hair, as always, was brushed back with some product to keep it perpetually in order. His face was deeply tanned showing off the bright white of his teeth as he smiled at Alex's arrival.

"Welcome to Foxmoore," Beau said, coming down the broad row of steps from the veranda. He came up and gave Alex a firm handshake and pat of the shoulder.

"You didn't need to go to all this trouble, Beau," Alex said. "Just had a couple of questions about the night of my dad's fight down at *Gilly's*."

"Whatever you need, Alex. Let's go out back. Got some drinks ready and Hessy has made up some awesome steamed oysters. Hope you like steak."

Richards led Alex up the stairs and through the house. It was a wide-open flow of elegant, yet comfortable groupings of furniture and incredible white painted woodwork and beams across the vaulted ceilings. On every wall there were bright splashes of color from Beau's vast collection of contemporary paintings. Alex could see their cook, Hessy, off to the left, working in the massive white kitchen. She looked up at him for a moment, then returned to her work.

As they approached the back of the house, a wall of windows revealed an incredible view that spread across a large lake and forest-covered hillsides far beyond. Alex walked out onto the back veranda and saw Beau's son, Connor Richards, standing with two women by an outdoor kitchen and dining area next to a large pool. Both women were dressed in colorful flowing sundresses.

Beau Richards yelled out, "Amelia, I want you to meet an old friend, Alex Frank."

Alex watched as the woman turned. He was immediately struck by the stunning beauty of her face. It was dark and Mediterranean, perhaps Italian. Her long brown hair fell in loose curls around her tanned bare shoulders. She walked up confidently and shook Alex's hand. "Amelia Richards," she said, and he tried to place the faint accent.

Beau said, "I told you Alex is a detective with the Charleston PD, but he grew up here in Dugganville."

Amelia said, "I'm very sorry, Alex, to hear about your father. I hope there's been some mistake with his arrest."

"Thank you." Alex said, then noticed Connor and his girlfriend walking up. Connor had a big smile and also slapped Alex on the back like his father did when they shook hands.

"Don't think you've met Lily, Alex," he said, turning to introduce the woman. She was a cute and curvy twenty-something blond with a pronounced tan line from swimsuit straps across her bare shoulders.

"Alex, nice to meet you," she said, offering him her hand.

Beau said brightly, "Let's get you a beverage!"

They all walked over to a fully stocked bar in the kitchen area. "What can I make for you?"

"Cold beer would be fine," Alex said.

Beau opened a large refrigerator. "How about a *Stella*?"

"Fine." Alex said and then the man freshened drinks for the others. They walked over and stood by the long pool together.

Beau said, "So, you can't get your old man out on bail then?"

"No, not in a capital murder case."

"Right."

Connor said, "He's been charged then?"

"Yes, his arraignment was this morning."

"Who you got for the defense?" Beau asked.

Alex took a sip from his beer, then said, "Phillip Holloway works for one of the big firms in Charleston. He's got great experience on cases like this."

Beau nodded back. "Yeah, I've heard of him. Good, you're gonna need the best."

Connor said, "So I hear you're in town for a while to help with Skipper's case."

Alex nodded. "Not sure how much help I'll be, but I have to do something. I'm talking to people who were in the bar the night my dad had the fight with Bayes. You never know what details you might turn up that can lead to something."

"Me and Connor were there. I told you the other night," Beau said.

"Right, that's why I called earlier," Alex said.

Amelia said, "Alex, since you are a detective, you can work on the case then?"

"Not officially. I'm taking a leave."

"Well, I hope your efforts will be productive," she said. "We will say a prayer for your father."

Alex was a bit surprised. For some reason, he didn't take her for the praying type. "Well, thank you."

Beau broke in. "How you like your steak, Alex?"

The five of them sat at a long wood dining table near the pool for dinner. Beau had three bottles of different wines open and they had just finished fine salads Hessy had brought out.

Beau took a long sip from a Napa Valley cabernet he had just raved about, then said, "So what are you trying to find out about the fight that night, Alex?"

Alex still had his first beer in front of him. He looked over at Beau Richards. "Did you hear any of the back and forth between Bayes and my dad before it got ugly? I heard it was something about Bayes jumping in front on a shrimp run out in Bulls Bay off White Island a couple days earlier."

Beau thought for a moment and took another long drink from the wine glass. "You know, I spoke with Skipper earlier that night, maybe a half hour before he and Bayes really got into it. He was pissed at Horton. Excuse my French, ladies. He did say... I won't mention what he called him in front of the ladies. He said Bayes couldn't find shrimp if they jumped in his damn boat."

"Anybody else there that night have words with Bayes you remember?" Alex asked.

Beau looked over at his son. Both men shook their heads, *no.*

Connor's girlfriend, Lily, spoke up. "Always hear what a tough bunch those shrimpers are."

Connor turned to her, agitated. "Come on, Lily, not now."

Amelia said, "Alex, do you really have hope of finding evidence to free your father? I'm sorry, but the case sounds very strong against him."

"I have to try."

"And you damned well should, Alex," Beau said. "If we think of anything that could help..."

"Thanks, Beau," Alex said. "I wanted to ask you about Horton Bayes. I know he was not a very popular fellow around here. What do you hear about others who might have a beef with him?"

"Half the damn town," Connor said, the wine starting to have its effect.

"Not a real popular guy," Beau echoed. "Went out of his way to irritate just about everyone he came across."

"But who else would have reason to want him dead?" Alex said with purpose, all four around the table turning to look at him.

There was silence for a moment, then Beau said, "Nothin' worth killing for, I know of."

Chapter Twenty-four

The late evening sun in Atlanta was low in the trees behind the house, a bright orange with flares of yellow through the pines. Hanna sat on the broad porch in a grouping of couches, still stunned by the condition of her father. Though she had her issues with the man over the years and had never fully forgiven him for his foolish attempt to fly the family to Nassau in questionable weather, Hanna truly loved her father. She also respected him and what he had accomplished at his legal practice and his work in the City of Atlanta. The thought of his passing was hard for her to even consider now. All her family would be gone, except for her son, Jonathan. Just the two of them would be left to carry on the Moss/Walsh lineage.

She thought of her son to get her mind off her father's health and declining condition. Jonathan would be bringing a new girlfriend to Pawleys Island for the weekend. There would be the promise of new relationships, new futures. Hanna smiled as she pictured her beautiful son and images of him growing up out on the island. She secretly couldn't wait until Jonathan brought grandchildren with him to visit.

Her mood grew quickly dark again when her step-mother, Martha, came out the back door and sat across from her.

"Hello, dear," Martha said. "Can we bring you anything?"

Hanna already had a half empty glass of red wine in front of her on the low table. "I'm fine, Martha. Thank you."

"I'm sorry your father's condition was such a shock to you. He didn't want me to tell anyone, particularly you, how bad he was. He didn't want people worrying about him."

Hanna tried to check her anger, but said, "He's my father, Martha! You should have let me know."

"I'm sorry, dear. Your father insisted." Hanna had little patience with the woman and was about to let it all out when Martha continued, "Would you like to get something to eat down at the Club?"

Hanna knew she was referring to the old Piedmont Club, north of downtown at Piedmont Park. She wasn't the least bit hungry and an evening with this woman was more than she would be able to tolerate. "No, but thank you."

"Dear, you have to get something to eat. It's going to be a long day at the hospital tomorrow and God knows, the food there will be simply dreadful."

"Martha, you go ahead. I'll find something in the kitchen."

The woman looked out across the vast lawns down to the woods and a small creek that ran through the property. Still looking away, she said, "I need to discuss something with you, Hanna."

"And what is that?" Hanna reached for her wine.

Martha turned back and said, "I know this is not the time, but just in case."

"Just in case, what?" Hanna demanded.

"I don't want this to be a surprise," Martha said.

"What surprise?"

"Your father told me recently he will be leaving the house to me when he passes."

Hanna's anger flared to near boiling. She could care less about the house, but the fact this woman was talking about her father's death in such greedy fashion was unbelievable. She took a long drink from her wine before she said, "I don't care about the damn house, Martha or anything else in the man's will for that matter. The fact you're even bringing something like that up tonight is beyond..."

Martha held up a hand. "Please, Hanna! I didn't mean to upset you."

Hanna stood and walked back into the house.

She was sitting on a stool at a long granite island in the kitchen when her cell phone rang. She looked at the screen. It was her friend, Greta Muskovicz, from the women's clinic in Charleston. She felt her heart sink, dreading what news Greta must have to call at this hour.

"Greta?"

"Hanna, where are you?"

"I had to come up to Atlanta. My father's having surgery in the morning."

"I'm sorry," Greta said, a sadness and sense of defeat in her voice. "I had to let you know Jenna Hall and her son are gone."

Hanna was afraid this would happen. "How long?"

"Normally, Jenna brings William back from school late afternoon. They're still not back."

Hanna looked at her watch. It was 10:30.

Greta said, "I had one of the girls keeping an eye on Jenna, but we can't lock her in."

Hanna shook her head, trying to think what could be done at this point. "Let me call Alex's partner at Charleston PD. He can put out a bulletin to keep an eye out for them."

"Okay, good," Greta said. "I'm sorry Hanna. I don't feel good about this. The husband is *bad news*."

"I know. Please let me know if you hear anything."

"Of course."

Hanna ended the call and placed the phone down. She looked around the opulent kitchen and then placed her face down in her hands. Everything seemed to be pushing in on her and she was about to burst under the weight of it all. Alex was off in his old hometown with a terrible woman trying to take him back into her life with a son she claims is his. She had dropped her guard and let another man get close again. Her father looked as if he was on his death bed when she arrived this afternoon, with the dreadful Martha hovering nearby. And now, a young vulnerable woman and her son were back with a dangerous man who should be in jail. *Why couldn't I protect them?* Hanna thought as she tried to hold back tears.

She grabbed her phone again to call Alex. He would alert his partner, Lonnie. The phone rang six times before it went to voice mail, "Hello, this Alex Frank. Please..." She pushed the pound button to interrupt the message.

"Alex, it's Hanna. I need to speak with you tonight. Jenna Hall has run away with her husband. We need to alert Lonnie. I'll try to reach him, too, but please call."

And why couldn't he answer his phone?

Chapter Twenty-five

The noise in *Gilly's Bar* was typically loud and raucous. Even on a weeknight, the place was packed with the usual array of locals, enjoying too many drinks, most looking for some respite from what the coming day would bring. Alex sat at the bar with a beer in front of him. It was his third, though he wasn't counting. He thought about going back to his father's house after leaving dinner at the Richards' place, but in the end, didn't feel like being alone in the old place.

The dinner with Beau Richards and his family had been an extravagant affair, as expected. The steaks were huge and perfectly prepared. The wine was incredible. Alex was thinking about Beau as he looked down the bar at the other patrons. He was one of the few who pulled himself out of the normal "just getting by" existence of so many of Dugganville's residents. In fact, many of these people had jobs thanks to Beau Richards.

Alex thought about his discussion out at Beau's house. He had learned little of value in his father's case. It just reinforced what he already knew, that half the town had reason to hate Horton Bayes, but none enough to kill the man.

Ella Moore, Adrienne's mother, had come into the bar about a half hour earlier. She hadn't noticed or cared not to notice Alex. She was sitting with a man Alex didn't know, laughing and drinking heavily. Adrienne must be home with Scotty, he thought. He knew he couldn't keep putting off the inevitable with Adrienne. He would have to settle on a course of action and commit to it, commit to Adrienne that he would be there for her and their son. *Their son,* he thought again.

Alex turned when he noticed Ella Moore getting up and leaving with the man she'd been talking to. They were arm-in-arm as they went out the door. He shook his head in disgust. The woman's reputation was legendary here in town, including affairs over the years with both his own father and the now deceased, Horton Bayes. He always knew Adrienne didn't have the best influences in her life. Her father had run away years earlier and had never returned. Ella was a mess and never gave her daughter much attention or guidance. *Adrienne,* he thought. *I have to go see her in the morning.*

Alex didn't check his phone until he was back home at his father's, sitting on the front porch with another beer on the table next to him. He cursed when he saw that Hanna had called two hours earlier. He hadn't noticed the call in the noise and nonsense down at *Gilly's.* He listened to the message. Jenna Hall was gone, back with her deadbeat husband. *Just great*, he thought in anger.

It was now close to one in the morning. He didn't want to call Hanna this late. He decided to send a text message. *Got your call. I'll call Lonnie in the morning. Sorry. Alex.*

He wanted to say more, to give her some reassurance about how he felt about her and what was happening here in Dugganville, but he couldn't find the words. *Sorry. What was he sorry for? For not calling back? For Adrienne. For Jenna Hall running back to her abusive husband?* Yes, he was sorry for all of it. *But, what was he going to do about it?*

He looked up when he heard someone coming up the walk to the porch. In the dim light from inside the house behind him, he finally saw it was Adrienne. He felt an empty panic in his gut as she came up the steps and sat next to him.

"Thought you'd still be up," she said. "Mom came home a while ago. Said you were down at *Gilly's.*" She put her hand on his thigh. "How're you doing, soldier?" It was an old greeting she often used when they were married.

He looked back at her and consciously thought about pushing her hand away but didn't.

"It's late," he finally said.

"Mom's home with Scotty. He's been asleep for hours," she said. "I've been waiting to hear from you."

Alex didn't respond, not sure of what to do or what to say.

"Alex?"

This time he did push her hand away and he turned to face her. Before he could speak she leaned in and kissed him.

It caught him completely by surprise and he stood up. "Adrienne! I'm not ready for this."

She looked up at him with a smile in the dim light. She reached for the belt of his pants and said. "I remember what you like."

His cell phone lit up and buzzed on the table next to where they'd been sitting. He saw Hanna's name on the screen and his heart sank.

He reached for the phone. "Adrienne, you need to go." When she didn't move and started pulling at his zipper, he backed away and walked down the steps onto the front yard. He pressed the button to take the call.

"Hanna."

He heard her say, "I got your text. Thought you'd still be up, so I wanted to talk."

He started to reply when Adrienne called down from the porch, "Alex, who's that? The little woman from Charleston?"

He couldn't cover the phone in time and he knew Hanna had heard her. There was silence for a moment, then, "Good night, Alex." The line went dead.

Chapter Twenty-six

Hanna threw her phone into the pillow on the bed beside her. *No wonder he didn't call!*

She was seething at the thought of that woman mocking her on the phone, knowing full well she could hear. She tried to think about what they'd been doing in the middle of the night together. She felt sick deep in her stomach and thought she might throw-up. She started for the bathroom but the feeling subsided and she sat back on the bed.

Damn you, Alex!

If she was looking for a "last straw" in their free-falling relationship, this would surely be the one. She had to come to grips with the fact that her feelings for the man had been real, but it was not meant to be. Maybe it was better she'd found out now before things got too much further along. A deep sadness washed over her again. She wasn't going to make any more vows about men, she thought. *There just won't be any more men!*

She had her son and his adult life was just starting. There would be a future to share there. She had her work and her clients, her beautiful family ancestral home out on Pawleys Island which was always her sanctuary.

She didn't need the company or comfort of men in her life. Certainly, not anymore.

Hanna shook her head to clear her thoughts. She knew sleep would be slow in coming. She'd been able to reach Lonnie Smith on his cell when Alex hadn't returned her call. Lonnie was going to call in an alert to the Department right away. All the street cops would have the search for Jenna Hall and her son on their bulletins. She said a silent prayer for Jenna, hoping she was somewhere safe.

The alarm on Hanna's phone went off far too early. She had set it to allow time for a shower and something to eat before they left to take her father to the hospital. Her first waking thoughts were of Alex and the voice of his ex-wife in the background at 1am in the morning. *Is that the little woman...?*

She wished she could get her hands around Adrienne's neck now but pushed the thought aside.

Thirty minutes later, they were all getting into her father's big Cadillac SUV. Hanna would drive. She helped her father up into the passenger seat and Martha climbed in back. They drove in silence for a while. The drive to Piedmont Hospital would normally take just a few minutes, but the morning rush hour traffic had already slowed most roads to a crawl.

Allen Moss spoke in a hoarse voice, "Martha told me last night you got upset about the will and leaving the house to her."

Hanna's senses went on full alert. "I certainly did not!" she protested. "I really don't care what you do with your house and anything else, I was just upset we were even discussing it at a time like this."

Martha chimed in from the back. "I'm really sorry, honey."

"I'm not your honey!"

"Ladies, please," her father said. "Hanna, I know you never cared for the big house and all the trappings. I felt it would mean a lot to Martha to know she can stay in our house when I'm gone."

"I don't want to talk about this now!"

After they had her father checked-in and had a brief conversation with the surgeon, Hanna and Martha were directed to the Surgical Waiting Room for a long and tedious day waiting for updates from Dr. Mason's team. Hanna purposefully sat several seats away from her step-mother. It always galled her to think of the woman in that way. Martha was barely ten years older and Hanna certainly didn't consider her a mother-figure in her life.

Hanna pulled out her phone to check messages. Alex had called again and left his third message of the morning. She hadn't answered any of the calls and she wasn't about to listen to his messages. She deleted them all.

There was a voicemail from Lonnie Smith that word was out on the street to look for Jenna and her son, but nothing yet. She was about to put the phone down when it rang again. The screen said it was Phillip Holloway.

"Good morning, Phillip."

"Hanna, hello," he answered back. "Are you up in Atlanta?"

"Got in last night. Just dropped my father here at the hospital. He's in surgical prep right now."

"Well, my best to him," Phillip said. "I hope everything goes well today."

"Thank you, Phillip."

"Will you have some time today to discuss Mr. Frank's case?"

Hanna had to think for a moment. She honestly hadn't even considered how she would handle being on the legal defense team for Alex's father. She made a quick and conscious decision. "Phillip, I need to withdraw from the case."

"What in the world for?"

She hesitated to explain, then decided just to get it all out. "Alex and I have had a falling out. I don't think it would be fair to his father for me to be involved. There are just too many distractions."

"Hanna, I'm not very pleased about this. You bring me in on this case, ask me to cut my fee and then you bail on me."

"I'm sorry, Phillip," but I just can't be involved." She paused, then feeling even more guilty, she said, "If you need some help on the side, research, whatever, I'll try to help."

"Well, okay," Phillip said. "So, what's between you and Alex?"

"I don't want to talk about it, Phillip."

Her next call was to Greta at the clinic. She knew Greta would have called if there was any news about Jenna, but she wanted to check anyway.

"She's taken everything," Hanna heard her friend say. "Her room is cleaned out completely."

"How could that happen?" Hanna protested. "I thought you had people watching her?" Hanna immediately felt bad for chastising her friend. "Look,

I'm sorry. I'm just so worried about Jenna and her boy."

"The police are searching?" Greta asked.

"Yes, the alert has gone out across the city."

"Good. Good." Greta said.

Chapter Twenty-seven

The pain in his temples was the first thing Alex noticed as he began to come out of a deep sleep. The sun was just starting to lighten his room. He looked at his watch and it was almost 8am. As he rubbed his head and tried to swallow, he remembered the previous night. He'd had too much to drink. Back here on the porch, Adrienne had come on to him. He shouldn't have been surprised. It was her typical MO. When all else fails, seduce the guy. He winced when he thought about Hanna calling and hearing Adrienne in the background. After he finally got Adrienne to go home, he had tried Hanna's phone twice without success, leaving messages each time.

He had fallen asleep in his clothes and his phone was still in his pocket. He pressed the number for Hanna again. It went to voicemail after a few rings. *"Hanna, it's Alex. Please call me back. I have to explain. Adrienne came uninvited and I made her leave. Nothing happened. I'm sorry you had to hear that. Please call."*

He went into the bathroom and ran cold water, splashing his face over and over to clear his head. He took a long drink right from the faucet. His phone started buzzing back in his bedroom and he rushed back. It wasn't Hanna. He saw on the screen Pepper Stokes was calling.

"Good morning, Sheriff."

"Alex, wanted you to know we got two divers going down around the *LuLu Belle* starting at 10am."

"I'll be there, thanks."

The coffee at *Andrews* was hot and strong. Lucy had been keeping his cup full for twenty minutes while he worked on the eggs and bacon in front of him. He had started to call Hanna again but put his phone down. He figured her father was in surgery by now and she needed to focus on that. It was in her court to call back. *God, will she ever call me back?*

He was seated at a booth that gave him a view out the front window of the diner to the main street of Dugganville. There were a few cars parked on each side of the road and three storefronts in his limited view; the drug store, a lawyer's office and the hardware store. He hadn't been paying much attention to who was passing by, still thinking about last night and Adrienne... and Hanna.

He was still furious with his ex-wife for coming on to him like that. Did she really think that sex would bring him running back to her? If anything, he was more disgusted with her than ever. Hanna must surely think the worst, he thought. How would he feel if he called her in the middle of the night and heard another man mocking him in the background? *Why did I answer the damn phone!*

He looked up when he noticed two women walking with a young boy. It was Adrienne and her mother with Scotty. They were on the far sidewalk and slowed to go into the hardware store. Alex took a deep breath. He was not in the mood for another encounter. He signaled for Lucy to bring the check, left some money on the table and hurried out.

He was just getting into his car when he heard his name called out, "Alex, wait!" he turned and saw Adrienne coming across the street. He was tempted to get in the car and drive away, but he stood there. He watched her stop for a car to pass. Her face was not made up and she looked tired and drawn. He saw Ella and Scotty come out of the store and hurry away in the other direction.

She came up to him, breathless. "Alex, I have to apologize. I don't know what..."

"Adrienne, I don't want to hear it."

"Really, I don't know what I was thinking," she said. "My mother came home and told me she'd seen you down at *Gilly's*. I'd had a few glasses of wine after Scotty went to bed. I just wanted to see you and for some crazy reason, thought maybe we could be together again. It must have been the wine."

Alex looked away for a moment. He was tempted to tell this woman to go away and never come near him again. There had been enough pain between them in the past. But, then he thought of the boy. "Adrienne, listen. I'm in a relationship. You know that. Your little act last night may have killed it, but let's hope not."

"I said I was sorry..."

"That's not good enough!" he said, trying with all his will to control his anger. "Look, I have a full day." He stared at her for a moment, thinking about the boy. "I'd like to spend some time with Scotty later. Maybe we can get a burger or something for dinner."

Adrienne smiled and said, "That would be great. Thank you, Alex."

"You're still telling him I'm just a friend, right?"

"Just friends."

When Alex walked down the dock to the *LuLu Belle*, he saw a flurry of law officers assisting two divers who were preparing to go into the murky water around the boat crime scene. The sheriff was standing nearby, and Alex came up to him.

Stokes turned. "Hey, Alex. They'll be going down in a minute."

Alex said, "It will be tough to see down there, and the bottom is soft mud."

"They have metal detectors," the sheriff said.

They both heard someone else coming down the dock. The murder victim's wife, Meryl Bayes was walking fast, an angry and determined look on her face.

"Oh great," the old sheriff said.

Meryl yelled out, "Sheriff Stokes!"

"I'll let you handle this," Alex said and started to walk further out where the divers were assembling."

"You wait right there, Alex Frank!" the woman said.

She came up to both of them, her hair a wild mess like she'd just come through a wind storm. Her clothes looked like she'd had them on for a week."

As she came up, the sheriff said, "Meryl, you can't be out here."

"Why the hell not? It's our damn boat!"

Stokes said, "It's still a crime scene and I'd think you would want us to get to the bottom of your husband's attack."

"You mean his murder!"

"Yes, ma'am."

She turned to Alex. "Why is he here, Sheriff? You two are both working to get his father off, right?"

Alex didn't respond. The sheriff said, "We're doing no such thing, Meryl. We're just trying to get the facts. These divers will be going down to look for a murder weapon or any other evidence that may have gone overboard that night."

"Well, I need to get my boat back," she said. "Can't make any money with it sitting here tied up. Got a crew pulled together to get her back on the water."

"Who is that, Ms. Bayes?" Alex asked.

"Chaz Merton's gonna captain and he's got two men lined-up. My son, young Horton, is coming home from school to help."

Alex said, "Good, I'm sure Chaz can use the work with my father's boat out of commission."

"When can I have my boat back, Sheriff?"

Stokes thought for a moment, then said, "Don't see why we can't release her later today. I'll check with the prosecutor's office and let you know, Meryl."

She seemed satisfied. "Thank you." She turned to Alex. "You know, son, I hope your old man rots in that jail for what he's done."

Stokes said, "Meryl, that's not..."

She was getting fired up again and her face was turning a deep crimson. "Alex Frank, your dad has been out to get my husband for years. He finally got what he wanted."

Alex said, "Look, Ms. Bayes, we both know this was a terrible thing and whoever is responsible will have to pay for it for the rest of their lives."

"It was no damn *thing* and your old man will rot in hell for what he's done!"

She moved toward Alex like she was going to strike him, and the sheriff got between the two of them. He said, "Meryl, you need to go home now. Plan on having your boat back to make a run tonight if you want. I'll call to confirm after I talk to the prosecutor's office in Charleston."

She slowly backed away, not taking her eyes off Alex. "Sheriff, don't let him pull any nonsense with the evidence here."

"That's not gonna happen, Meryl. Now you go home."

Alex and the sheriff watched as the first diver resurfaced about ten feet out from the boat in the main channel of the river. He kicked his fins to move slowly back toward the dock, holding a mesh bag out of the water in front him. The bag appeared to have several muddy items inside including a couple old beer cans. The second diver came up a few dozen yards away and started back to the dock. He also had a bag he held out of the water. The two men placed their bags on the dock and began removing masks and fins to get out of the water.

Sheriff Stokes stood on the dock over the divers. "Anything interesting here?"

The first diver shook his head. "Nothing but a lot of old trash."

"Didn't find a knife or anything that could have caused those stab wounds?" the sheriff asked.

"No, sir."

Stokes turned to Alex. "Well, where in hell is your old man's knife?"

Two hours later, Alex stood with the sheriff on the dock next to Skipper Frank's boat, the *Maggie Mae*. Stokes took off his hat and wiped his sweaty forehead with a handkerchief. He looked at his watch. "Should be coming up in a few minutes, son," he said.

Alex watched bubbles coming up to the surface from the two divers making their way around the boat, looking for any evidence in the death of Horton Bayes. It had been a long sweltering day down on the docks. The divers had been making ever-widening circles around the boat in their search.

"Here we go," Alex heard the sheriff say as the first diver's head and face mask broke the calm surface of the river. The diver had come up about twenty yards out from the end of the dock and began slowly swimming back. He lifted a mesh bag from the water and held it up as he kicked his fins.

The diver spit the air regulator from his mouth and yelled out, "Sheriff, you need to see this."

Alex and Sheriff Stokes both walked out and knelt at the end of the dock. The diver handed the bag up to Stokes. He laid it carefully down on the dock. Alex felt a sick feeling in his gut when he saw the sun glint off the blade of a long fillet knife.

Chapter Twenty-eight

Hanna had done her best to ignore her stepmother for the past two hours in the waiting room. Her efforts were helped by the woman's constant chatter on her cell phone. Hanna overheard numerous conversations about charity galas, her golf league, getting a new workout trainer, someone's divorce. She seemed to have no shortage of friends to keep her occupied.

She looked at her phone. The three messages from Alex Frank were still on her call list. She finally decided to listen to the last one. She found little solace in his apology and explanation. Her senses continued to warn her, *close the chapter, Hanna!*

She looked up as her father's cardiologist, Dr. Mason, came into the waiting room in his blue surgical scrubs and mask hanging from his neck. He saw Hanna and Martha and came over and sat next to Martha. Hanna went to join them.

The doctor took a deep breath, clearly tired. "Ladies, we have good news and bad."

"Good news, please," Martha said.

"Your husband handled the procedure satisfactorily. He's in recovery and doing well."

"Well, thank goodness," Martha said.

"And what's the bad news, doctor?" Hanna asked.

"The bypass was successful, Hanna, but I'm afraid it's only a temporary solution. I had hoped this procedure would be sufficient, but it's clear he's going to need a transplant if we want to keep him going longer-term."

"A transplant." Hanna repeated, resignation clear in her tone.

"A complete heart transplant?" Martha asked.

"I'm afraid so," the doctor said.

"How soon?" Hanna asked.

"Well, the healing process for the procedure today will take time. I'd say we're looking at several months from now. Once he's fully recovered, we can get him on the donor list. Then, it's a matter of time until the right donor is available and he's on the top of the list. Sometimes it takes more than a few months.

Hanna was somewhat relieved her father's condition seemed to be stabilized. On the other hand, a heart transplant was a frightening prospect.

"When can we take him home, doctor?" Martha asked.

"A few days, if we can get him to sit still for that long."

"He'll want to get back to the office tomorrow," Hanna scoffed.

The doctor frowned. "I'm going to insist he take a significant leave of absence to get his strength back and avoid the stress of his work."

"Good luck with that." Martha said. "Allen will go crazy sitting around the house."

"When can we see him?" Hanna asked.

"Should be an hour or so. I'll have the nurse come and get you."

It was nearly two hours before a nurse came out to escort them back to her father's room. Hanna and Martha followed her down a long corridor and then into a room filled with monitoring equipment and nurses taking readings. He lay propped up with pillows, tubes running out from numerous locations on his body and an oxygen feed in his nose. She thought he looked ten years older than when they took him in earlier in the morning. She watched a thin smile come across his face as they entered. The two women sat on opposite sides of his bed, the nurses moving aside to make room.

"Hello, girls," he said, weakly.

"Sounds like you've had quite a day, Allen," Hanna said.

"Wouldn't recommend it on *Trip Adviser*," he replied.

"How are you feeling, dear?" Martha asked.

He licked his lips and reached for a cup with a straw to get a drink of water.

Hanna watched his hand shake as he tried to drink. She reached to help him hold it.

"Got some real good drugs running through these hoses," he said gesturing up to the fluid drips hanging beside the bed. "Never felt better."

"Dr. Mason told you about the transplant." It wasn't a question. Hanna knew the doctor had already shared his prognosis with the patient.

Her father just nodded.

"You're going to need to cut back on your schedule," Hanna said.

"Maybe we can take a trip," Martha said, trying to sound cheerful.

Hanna scowled. "You need to take it easy for a while. Get your strength back."

She watched him take another sip from the straw, then he looked back at her. "I have too many open cases pending. I'm going to need your help."

Hanna knew this was coming. "You've got plenty of talented attorneys down there who can pick up the slack."

"But they're not you, daughter."

"Let's not talk about this now," Hanna said, panicking at the thought of stepping into her father's role at Moss Kramer.

Martha made a flourish of looking at her watch. "Dear, get some rest. We'll be back soon. I have a hair appointment but will be right back to see you."

Hanna shook her head and reached for her father's hand. It felt damp and cold and it gave her chills to think of his failing health. "You get some rest. They can come and find us if you need anything."

Hanna was sitting alone in the Waiting Room. Martha was still away having her hair done. There was one other family on the far side of the room. Two small children were playing with the toys in the corner. The mother was reading a *People* magazine. Hanna had been on the phone several times with her office, trying to keep on top of the open cases on her desk. Her assistant and volunteers were trying to pick up the slack while she was away.

She noticed Alex's messages again on her call screen. She knew she had to get this over with sooner or later. She pressed the *Return Call* button. He picked up on the second ring.

"Hanna!"

She didn't respond.

"How is your father doing?"

"He's okay, but there's a long road ahead."

"I'm sorry." He paused and there was silence on the phone between them. Finally, he said, "You got my messages?"

Hanna sighed and closed her eyes. "Alex, I know you're in a tough situation up there with your father and now all this with your ex."

"Hanna..."

"No, let me get this out," she said. "You need time to see this all through."

"What are you saying?" he asked.

"I don't want to be a distraction."

"You're not a distraction," he insisted.

"I've told Phillip I can't work on your father's case."

"What?"

"Alex, I'm sorry. I let this go too far between us. I just can't be in another relationship this soon." She felt a cold chill as goosebumps flushed all over.

"Hanna, I want to see you."

She didn't respond.

"Hanna?"

"I've offered to help Phillip in the background if he needs any assistance with research or motions, but I can't be directly involved anymore... with your father's case... and with you."

"Hanna, please. Let me explain."

"There's no need. You have to work this all out, Alex." She hesitated for a moment, then said, "Goodbye, Alex," and ended the call.

Her phone started buzzing almost immediately and she saw it was Alex, but she didn't answer. She hung her head and took a deep breath to gather herself. *Close the chapter, Hanna.*

Chapter Twenty-nine

Alex heard his call go to voice mail.

"Hello, this is Hanna Walsh..."

He didn't leave a message. She was leaving him. He had lost her, and he sat stunned in his car as he replayed the conversation in his mind. She thinks she's a distraction, he thought. *She's the only sane thing in my life right now.*

Then, the more he thought it through, the more he came to realize she was right. He needed time to help his father. He needed time to sort everything out with Adrienne. He needed time to work through this situation with his son, who thought he was just a friend of his mother. Despite all that, he sat heartsick at losing Hanna. He knew he would never meet anyone like her again, anyone who was so right for him.

The thought of having to see Adrienne later tonight sent a surge of anger through him. He knew if it wasn't for the son they now shared, he would have nothing further to do with her. But that wasn't the case. They did have Scotty, and he needed to face that and deal with it.

It was late afternoon and Alex was sitting on a folding chair on the aft deck of his father's shrimp boat, the *Maggie Mae*. He had been sitting there for over an hour, silently looking out across the river and the boats, thinking about all he had to work through. He was trying to keep Hanna out of his thoughts and focus on the murder case against his father and how he was going to move forward with Adrienne and Scotty.

He pulled his phone from his pocket and called Phillip Holloway. He answered his cell right away.

"Hello, Alex."

"Phillip, I should have called earlier. The divers found a knife in the water near my father's boat. I'm not sure, but pretty likely it's his knife. The Medical Examiner has it now for prints and blood trace."

"Okay, I'll check with the DA to get everything they have," the attorney said. "Did you get a picture of it we can show to your father?"

"Yes, on my phone," Alex said. "I'll email a copy to you."

"Alex, this is the last thing we needed." Alex didn't respond. "Anything else?" Phillip asked.

"No. I've spoken to several people who were in the bar the night of the fight. I'm not coming up with anything new or any other suspects who may have reason to want Bayes dead."

"Okay, keep asking."

"Phillip, I talked with Hanna this afternoon. She told me she's off the case."

"Right. What's going on between you two?"

"Long story."

Alex walked up the steps to Ella Moore's house, a sense of dread looming over him that he couldn't put out of his mind. *One step at a time*, he thought, as he knocked on the wood screen door.

Scotty came running to let him in. "Hi, Alex. Mom said we're gonna get some cheeseburgers!"

The boy's excitement made him forget his dark mood. "You bet. Where's your mom?"

Adrienne came up behind her son and tentatively said, "Hello, Alex."

"You ready to go?" he asked.

"We're ready!" Scotty yelled out.

"Thought we'd walk down to the Dairy Queen. Burgers and a shake. Whaddya think?"

Scotty pulled his mother's arm. "Let's go."

The boy ran out ahead of them as they walked back into town, kicking a stone down the sidewalk.

Adrienne said, "Alex, can we get past last night?"

He didn't answer right away, watching Scotty up in front of them. He decided not to mention Hanna and their breakup. "I don't know. Let's take this a step at a time."

She said, "I need to get Scotty enrolled in school for the fall. He's gonna be in fifth grade. I want him to go to school here."

"Okay," Alex said, hesitantly.

"We're gonna stay with my mother, if the two of us don't kill each other." She didn't explain why.

Alex just kept walking.

"I'm looking for a job. I need to make some money. Mom's a little tight right now."

"What are you going to do?" he asked.

"I don't know, wait tables, probably."

Alex said, "When are we going to tell him?"

"About you?"

"Yeah, he needs to know."

Adrienne hesitated, then said, "Derek called this afternoon."

"Your husband?"

"Yeah, he wanted to talk with Scotty. He wants us to come back to Florida."

"And what did you say?"

"After he was done talking to Scotty, I told him to go to hell!"

"So," Alex said, "you're definitely through?"

"You know a cheap lawyer?" she asked.

"I used to," he said, and then tried to put Hanna out of his mind.

She gave him a puzzled look. "I'm going to file for divorce."

"Okay," he responded, glancing over at her with a suspicious look.

She walked on a bit, then said, "Will you be able to spend time with us? If we tell him, I mean. You're gonna be back in Charleston."

He sighed. "Right, but it's not that far away."

"He needs a father," Alex. He needs his real father."

He looked over at her again and the serious look on her face.

"We'll make it work," he finally said.

On the way home from dinner, Alex had them stop at the hardware store. He bought two baseball mitts and a ball. He and Scotty were playing catch on Ella Moore's front yard. The boy was a natural athlete and had a strong arm. Adrienne sat on the porch watching, a big smile on her face. Alex was wrestling with the conflicting thoughts racing through his brain... the joy of playing with his son, the heartbreak of losing Hanna Walsh, the confusion in how to build a life and relationship with Adrienne to support his son. It was all just too much to sort through and he tried to just enjoy the moment with the boy.

He saw Ella Moore come out on the porch and sit next to her daughter. *What a family!*

Chapter Thirty

Hanna had come back to her father's house in Buckhead an hour earlier after spending much of the afternoon with him down at the hospital. She planned to get some dinner here and then go back to Piedmont Hospital for another visit before he went to sleep for the night. He seemed to strengthen some through the afternoon as the sedation wore off and the doctor and nurses were able to stabilize his pain meds.

She was sitting on the bed in her own room on the second floor of the big house with two windows looking out across the vast estate grounds. The bedroom was much the way she had left it when she went away to college. The room was much larger than her entire apartment back in Charleston. She wasn't wild about the pink walls and decor that had been her preference as a younger girl. *Different times*, she thought.

The family's long-time housekeeper and cook, Anna Parsons, was down in the kitchen making a quick dinner of salad and steamed vegetables for her. Martha had left earlier to go out to dinner with friends, her *support group*, she had said.

She raised her feet up on the familiar old queen-size bed and propped two pillows behind her. Though she tried to push thoughts of Alex away, she was failing miserably. She couldn't help remembering the many close and happy times they had spent together these past months. *Different times*, she thought again, her despair spiraling downward.

Her phone on the bed beside her lit up and she saw Detective Lonnie Smith's name on the caller ID. *Hopefully, they've found Jenna Hall and her son*, she thought as she answered the call.

"Lonnie, hi." He didn't answer right away, and alarms went off in Hanna's brain. "Lonnie, what is it?"

His voice was low and subdued. "Hanna, I'm really sorry. We found Jenna...
"

"What's happened?" she cried out.

"We found her in an alley downtown. She'd been beaten... she's dead, Hanna."

"Oh my God!" Hanna felt a surge of nausea race through her gut. She took several deep breaths to try to calm herself. "What about the boy?" she managed to ask.

"We haven't found him, yet."

"It had to be Moe Hall, the father, right?" she asked.

"We're not sure, but he's obviously first on our list of suspects. We have an "all points" out on him.

Hanna didn't think her gloom could grow any deeper. Shouldn't it be easier to find him if he has the boy with him?" she asked hopefully.

"If they're together, yes," Lonnie said. "We don't know for sure."

"Oh Lonnie, I wanted to do more..."

"You did all you could, Hanna. Sometimes people just can't accept our help."

"Have you called Greta down at the shelter?" she asked.

"No, you're my first call."

Hanna said, "Let me call her."

"Okay," she heard the detective say. "Hanna, listen, I heard from Alex. He told me about the two of you. I'm sorry."

"I'm sorry, too, Lonnie," she said. "Not meant to be."

Hanna skipped dinner and said goodbye to her friend and confidant, Anna Parsons, in the kitchen of the big house. She drove back to the hospital for another visit with her father. He was in a lot of pain and they had his meds pumped up. He hadn't been very coherent. He did make another appeal for her to come "home" to Atlanta. She hadn't responded to his plea.

She was on the expressway now, an hour out of Atlanta on her way back to Charleston. She had called Greta Muskovicz earlier and the two women had cried together on the loss of the young woman, Jenna Hall. Greta had promised to call if there was any news of the son, William.

Hanna drove on, numb in her grief for Jenna Hall. Such a beautiful and young life taken needlessly.

Suddenly, the thought of being alone in her small apartment over the legal clinic was more than she could tolerate. She looked ahead at the approaching headlights on Highway 20, coming into Augusta. She decided to go to the beach for the night, to the house on Pawleys Island.

Hanna poured her third glass of wine, sitting in a white Adirondack chair in the grouping around the fire pit in front of her beach house. Her bare feet were buried in the sand. She hadn't started a fire and she pulled the sweater up around her neck as the evening continued to chill. The tears were still wet on her cheeks when she started to cry again... for Jenna Hall, for all that was falling apart in her life.

There was a strong wind from the east blowing in across the dark ocean. Large waves were crashing on the shore with a relentless thunder. She leaned her head back against the chair and squeezed her eyes shut, trying to put images of Jenna's beaten body out of her mind.

She must have dozed or passed out. She woke with a start, the waves still crashing out in front her. Her wine glass had spilled over in the sand beside the chair. She reached for it and was startled by the dim silhouette of a woman sitting in the chair beside her. As her consciousness cleared, she started to stand. "Who are you?"

There was no answer from the woman and Hanna got to her feet and backed away. There were no lights from the porch above and she stood in near darkness, only the faint shape of the woman could be seen against the white chair. She appeared to have a long dress on and her hair was long around her dark face.

"Who...?" Hanna started to say again.

Then, she heard the quietest voice, just barely loud enough against the sound of the waves, say, "Follow your heart, Hanna."

"What?" She tried to clear her head. The wine and the nap had dulled all her senses. She squinted through the darkness, still backing away. And then, she realized the woman was gone.

Or was she ever there?

Chapter Thirty-one

Alex sat alone in a booth at the back of *Gilly's Bar.* He hadn't really eaten when he'd taken Adrienne and Scotty to dinner. He was too preoccupied with the reality of sitting there on the picnic bench outside the *Dairy Queen* with his newfound son and the woman who had been his wife. He had enjoyed the time spent back at Ella Moore's house with the boy. It reminded him of earlier days playing catch with his own father and older brother, Bobby.

His time with them had ended when he got the call from his partner about the death of Hanna's client, Jenna Hall. He had made up an excuse to call it a night with Adrienne and Scotty and left them there with a promise to *see them soon,* whatever that meant. He had no idea at the moment.

The crowd and noise at *Gilly's* were building and Alex tried to block it out as he thought about Hanna and how devastated she must be about Jenna Hall. He wanted so badly to call her but knew she wouldn't want to hear from him or talk to him about it. He pushed the half-eaten sandwich on the plate in front of him aside and decided to get home early to think about his father's case and what he could get done the next day. He stood to go to the bar to pay his bill with Gilly when he saw a young man walking through the tables towards him. He recognized the younger Horton Bayes, son of the deceased. Alex hadn't seen him in town yet but realized he must be home from school for the funeral and to help on their family's shrimp boat.

His eyes were trained right on Alex and he was coming up quickly. Alex could tell right away he'd had too much to drink.

He got to Alex and before he could do or say anything, the boy pushed him hard back down into the booth.

"Your old man's a sonofabitch!" he screamed through blurry eyes. "The bastard killed my dad!"

Alex stood up again and faced the boy, their faces just inches apart. "Horton, you need to take it down a notch." Alex noticed everyone in the bar watching them.

The boy tried to push him back again and Alex grabbed both of his arms and held him as he struggled to get loose. "Let go of me!" he yelled out.

Alex saw Gilly rushing over and then the young Horton Bayes pulled his right arm free and took a long roundhouse swing at Alex's face. It happened so quickly that Alex only partially blocked the blow and it caught him high on the side of his forehead. He stumbled back into the booth again and this time the kid came crashing in on top of him, his arms flailing. The blows began to land. Alex reacted quickly and threw a short punch that caught the boy square on the nose and sent him falling backward, sprawling across a table and chairs behind him.

Alex had lost all sense of reason and patience after what he'd been through all day, and he'd had enough of this. He got up and went after the kid before Gilly grabbed him from behind, holding his arms tightly in his grasp.

Gilly said, "Easy, Alex. That's enough. The boy was drunk when he came in here a few minutes ago. Should have sent him home right away."

Alex watched as Bayes struggled to get to his feet, pushing chairs aside and holding a hand to his nose. Blood was dripping down over his mouth and onto his white t-shirt. "You broke my nose, you mother..."

Another man grabbed the boy and said, "That's enough," and started pulling him away towards the door. Alex didn't know who the man was but was glad he was getting the kid away from him. He was just mad enough, he wasn't sure what he would have done if he'd come at him again.

Gilly said, "You okay, Alex?"

"I'm fine. Sorry to mess up your place," Alex said, looking at the table and chairs knocked over.

"Not your fault," Gilly said. "Saw the whole thing. The kid's got his old man's nasty disposition."

Alex settled his tab and was leaving when Chaz Merton stopped him at the door. He had a half full bottle of Budweiser in his hand.

"Hey, Alex, nice right jab on the kid," Chaz said. "You got to stop beatin' up my crew, though."

Alex said, "Heard you got a new spot on the *LuLu Belle.* Had a little run-in with Ms. Bayes, too. Said you were gonna captain the boat."

"Yeah, with your pop out of commission, I need the work."

"Sure, I'm glad for you. If you're going out tonight, you better lay off the sauce, Chaz."

"Just headed home now to get my stuff. I'll be fine."

Merton took a drink from his beer. "Say, heard they found a knife out there today. The divers, I mean."

Alex nodded.

"It's your old man's?"

"We'll see. Probably."

"Long fillet knife? Black handle?" Chaz asked.

"Yeah."

Chaz thought for a moment, then said, "You know, he used it mostly when we brought up fish in the nets to fillet 'em before we got back to the docks, to sell over at Richards Seafood."

Alex said, "I know he had a folding table he set up to clean fish."

Chaz scratched at his forehead and took a drink from his beer. "Sorry, Alex. Give my best to your old man."

Chapter Thirty-two

Hanna woke in her bed at the beach house the next morning, still groggy from the wine. Her head was on fire and she struggled to push the covers back. She looked down and saw she had managed to get her slacks and shoes off but was still wearing the blouse from yesterday. She walked barefoot into her bathroom and looked at the face staring back at her, then looked away in disgust. She ran some cold water to splash on her face, found some aspirin on the shelf beside the sink and then went to the toilet. As she walked back to her bed, she looked around for her cell phone. She didn't see it on the bed or nightstand. Her pants were in a heap on the floor next to the bed and when she picked them up, she felt the weight of the phone in one of the pockets.

As she sat on the bed and leaned back against the headboard, she suddenly had an uneasy feeling about the previous night. She remembered getting out to the beach house well after dark, grabbing a bottle of wine from the frig and a glass and going down to the fire pit. The wine was going down much too easily as she stressed about Jenna Hall and her father... and Alex.

Then, she had some recollection of talking to someone. Hanna thought about it for a moment and then recalled the other woman sitting next to her in the dark. She must have been dozing when the woman came up. She remembered then how scared she had felt when she woke and saw her there beside her.

The woman had said something about *following her heart*. As she thought about it, Hanna wondered if the woman was talking about Alex or her father ...*or what?*

She shook her head, trying to clear her memory. She got a chill when she remembered the woman had suddenly been gone.

Hanna chastised herself for drinking so much of the wine. There had been too much of that lately, she had to admit.

You're losing your mind, Hanna Walsh.

Hanna had showered and changed into fresh clothes she kept out at the beach. She looked out the back windows from the kitchen while she sipped her coffee. The morning sun was up high now on a bright blue-sky day. The surf was still heavy and rolling, lit with colors of blue and green. There were a few people setting up umbrellas and laying out towels up and down the beach. She decided to take a walk to clear her head and she refilled her coffee cup.

Walking down the back steps from the deck, she decided the shorts and shirt she was wearing seemed comfortable enough. The breeze off the water was keeping the day cooler, at least for a while. As she walked down to the water, she felt the cool loose sand beneath her feet. She unconsciously headed north along the water with no real destination in mind. She knew she needed to get back to work in Charleston. She had so many open cases to deal with and felt guilty about leaving the work with her associates. *Just a short walk,* she thought.

Jenna Hall's death was weighing heavy on her mind. She was still having trouble accepting she was really gone. Jenna and her son had just been in her office the other day. The woman loved her son so much and just wanted him to have a real family. Unfortunately, his father was a very dangerous man. Hanna chastised herself again for not being more proactive in protecting Jenna and William. She needed to call Lonnie and Greta to see if there was any news about the boy but knew they would most likely have already called if there was anything to report.

The only bright spot on her horizon was her son coming to visit the beach house this weekend. She was really looking forward to spending time with him and meeting the new girlfriend. She thought through her schedule for the next couple days before getting back out to the island by Friday night. She realized she better get back.

As Hanna walked by the fire pit before going up to the house, she thought, *who in heck was that woman last night?* She stopped for a moment and looked at the chair the woman had been sitting in. There were so many tracks in the sand it was impossible to tell where she might have come from or where she walked away.

Before she went up the stairs, she threw the rest of her cold coffee out onto the sand. Thoughts of returning from walks on the beach with Alex Frank crept into her mind, but she quickly pushed them aside. Twenty minutes later, she was on the highway back to Charleston.

Chaos greeted her as she entered the house that was now her legal clinic. Phones were ringing, people were rushing about. Three people were waiting in chairs along the wall to see attorneys. It was almost a welcome distraction. She could dive back into the work and put thoughts of the last couple of days out of her head. Her assistant had a phone to her ear and nodded as Hanna passed, handing her a pile of pink phone messages.

Back in her office, Hanna closed the door and sat down to sort through the messages and go through her calendar. She knew she had clients waiting to see her out there, but she needed just a minute to decompress and plan the day. She sorted through the messages and pulled out a note from Lonnie Smith at the police station. *Why hadn't he called her cell?*

He took her call right away. "Hanna. I tried your cell early this morning."

"Sorry, I didn't hear or see the call."

"We have the boy."

"Oh, thank God! Is he okay?"

The detective said, "He seems fine. We got an anonymous call he was down at the bus station. Figure his dad left him there and called us before he headed out of town."

"Where is he?" Hanna asked.

"We took him back to the shelter. He's with Greta there."

"Thank you, Lonnie," she said. "That's the best news."

"We still have the search on for the father, but it's likely he's left town. We're checking the security cameras at the bus station. We've alerted the State Police, too."

Hanna almost hesitated to ask but couldn't help herself. "Did you learn anything from the boy about what happened to his mother?"

"He apparently didn't see anything, or at least we don't think so. His father told him his mother had to leave on a trip but would be home soon and then he just left him at the station."

Hanna's heart was still full of grief for the boy's mother. Now, he faced an uncertain future with no mother and a father on the run from a murder charge. *Not a great hand to be dealt,* she thought.

Chapter Thirty-three

Enough dining out, Alex said to himself as he worked on a pan of scrambled eggs. *This town is just too small*, he thought. He wasn't in the mood to keep running into people he didn't want to see.

He finished his meal and cleaned the kitchen. Lilly Johannsen, the girlfriend of Connor Richards, was on the list of names Chaz had given him of people who had been in Gilly's the night of his father's fight with Bayes. He didn't have a chance to get her aside at dinner out at Beau Richards' place. He did find she worked in one of Beau's real estate offices out at a new golf course and housing development west of town.

Alex drove up to the ornate gated entry to the golf club neighborhood, an elegant sign announcing *Chesterfield Manor*. A security guard came out of the gatehouse to greet him.

"Morning sir, how can I help you," the guard asked.

Alex pulled out his credentials wallet and showed the man his Charleston PD identification card. "I need to speak with Ms. Johannsen. Is she up at the real estate office?"

"Let me check sir."

The guard went back in the gatehouse and made a call. Alex saw him speaking with someone and then nodding before he hung up. He came back out.

"Yessir, she's up ahead at the office. Second left, you'll see the signs."

Alex said," Thank you," as the guard pressed a button for the gate arm to come up.

He heard, "Have a nice day, sir," as he drove away.

Lily Johannsen met him at the door when he walked up from the parking area. "Good morning, Alex," she said, somewhat alarmed. "What can I help you with?" She was dressed smartly in casual business slacks and a sleeveless blouse, a bit more professional than the sundress she was wearing when Alex last saw her.

"Do you have a few minutes?" he asked.

"Sure, come back to my office."

They passed two other agents in their offices as they walked by who gave them puzzled looks. There was a large dimensional display on a long table that showed the holes of the golf course, the layout of the streets and building lots and little colored push pins that showed what was sold and what was still for sale. The walls were adorned with large posters of happy people playing golf, swimming in the pool and dining at the club.

Lily closed the door to her office behind them and had him sit on one of the small chairs beside her desk.

"Nice place out here," Alex said, looking out the window at several large model homes lined-up down the block.

"Yes, one of Beau and Connor's nicer developments," she said.

Alex said, "Sorry we didn't get to talk more the other night at Beau's."

"Wasn't that a nice evening?" she said. "Beau and Amelia sure know how to entertain."

"Yes, they do," Alex affirmed. "I've already spoken to Beau and Connor about the night my father got in the fight with the man who died."

"You mean Horton Bayes?" she asked.

"Yes. Did you know him?"

"Most people around here did, Alex," she said. "Not a very big town and the man was always in a ruckus or argument with somebody."

Alex continued. "I was told you were there in *Gilly's* that night."

She answered quickly. "Yes, I was there with Connor and his father. Amelia had other plans."

"I've been asking people if they saw anything different or unusual that night at the bar, anything that may have sparked the fight, anybody else who was involved in things getting out of hand."

She sat back, and her eyes opened wide as she thought about his questions. She finally said, "You know, I already spoke to one of the deputies from the sheriff's office."

"Yes, I know."

"Nothing out of the ordinary comes to mind," she finally said.

Alex could tell she was getting nervous and fidgety about something. "You sure, Lily?"

"What do you mean?" she asked, real concern now clear on her face."

"Anybody else you know have a beef with Horton Bayes that night, or maybe you heard about recently?"

She shook her head, too quickly. "No, no, just your father when he started throwing Bayes around the bar. It was really scary."

"Right, I know that," Alex said. He stood and handed her one of his cards. "You think of anything else, you call me."

He watched her look down at the information on his card. He noticed her hand shaking a bit.

"Sorry to bother you, Lily. Have a good day."

Chapter Thirty-four

It was past five and things were starting to settle down at Hanna's clinic. The waiting room was finally empty. The other two legal volunteers had their doors open and were catching up on calls and paperwork before heading home for the night. Her assistant, Molly, was cleaning up the carnage in the lobby from the long day.

Hanna had just finished a conference call with an attorney at the firm she worked for part-time back on Pawleys Island. She had three active clients there, paying clients. Her nerves were wired from the busy day and all that had happened during the past few days. She was tempted to get a glass of wine from the refrigerator in the kitchen but chastised herself after drinking too much the previous night. She thought again about the strange woman at the beach fire pit. She still couldn't piece together what had happened. *Maybe I dreamed the whole thing in my wine-induced stupor.*

Molly stuck her head in the open door to Hanna's office. "Phillip Holloway is in the lobby. He needs a few minutes, he says."

Hanna gave her a troubled look. She was tempted to tell Phillip she was too busy now and to have him call her in the morning. But then she thought he might have something important on Skipper Frank's case.

"Send him back, thanks."

Phillip rushed into her office with his typical confident flourish, dressed in an elegant suit and bright tie, his shoes polished to a blinding glare. "Hanna, dear, thank you for seeing me. Sorry I didn't call."

Hanna stood and came around her desk, motioning for him to join her at the conference table. Before she realized what was happening, he hurried over and enveloped her in a big hug that lasted much too long. She heard him say, "How are you holding up, kid?"

She pushed back, her radar on high alert. This was the creepy, lecherous Phillip Holloway she knew all too well. "I've been better. Please, sit down. What did you need?"

They both sat across from each other. Phillip said, "I just wanted to make sure you were okay after your father's procedure and whatever is going on between you and the detective."

"My father is fine, and we don't need to talk about my private life."

"Hanna, you know I'm always available to help. I'm your biggest fan."

Hanna thought about what he was really after, probably dinner and *whatever* later tonight. *Sure enough...*

"Have you had dinner yet?" he asked.

She tried to remain calm. "I have a lot of work to catch up on after being out of town. I'll probably be here half the night."

"You need to eat," he insisted.

"I've got food in the frig here, but thanks," she said. "What have you heard on Mr. Frank's case?"

"Not good, I'm afraid," he said, loosening his perfectly knotted tie. "Divers found a knife in the water near Skipper Frank's boat. The Medical Examiner's office is checking for prints, blood evidence, you know. Doesn't look good at all."

Hanna was truly saddened the case against Alex's father was growing worse. "What else has Alex found? I know he took a leave of absence to help the investigation with the sheriff."

"Nothing else so far," Holloway said. He paused and smiled that smarmy smile that infuriated her. "Look, the club's only ten minutes from here. Won't take more than an hour to get some good food in you," he persisted.

Hanna had enough. "Phillip, I'm not going to dinner with you! I'm not ever going to dinner with you. I appreciate what you're doing for Alex and his father, but *you and me* is not going to happen. Understand?"

He seemed to take her rebuff in stride, his face impervious to her comments. "Just trying to be a friend, Hanna. Sorry to bother you when you're so busy."

He stood to leave.

"Good night, Phillip. Thank you for the update on Mr. Frank. Again, let me know if I can help with anything behind the scenes."

She watched him turn and smile as he walked out the door.

It was near ten that night and Hanna was still at the office working through the last files on her desk, making a long list of follow-ups for the morning. She had resisted that glass of wine she considered earlier and had an open bag of potato chips to her side, half gone. She had thought about taking a break earlier to go visit William Hall at Greta's clinic, but she knew her friend already had her hands full trying to help the boy through the trauma of his mother's murder. She also thought about going down to the morgue to see Jenna's body... to what, pay her respects? She'd wait for the funeral. The whole situation was just sucking the life out of her.

The text chime on her cell rang and she looked at the screen.

"*Hanna, call as soon as you can. Martha.*"

She pressed the number on the text and heard the phone ringing. Martha's voice came over the phone. "Hanna, oh my God!"

"What is it, Martha?"

"I'm down at the hospital..."

Hanna stood up in alarm. "What's happened?"

She could tell the woman had been crying and Martha paused, trying to gather herself. "They called me down a half hour ago. Your father had some sort of cardiac arrest."

"What!"

"They've stabilized him according to the doctor, dear, but it's pretty bad."

Hanna felt her spirits sink. She had hoped her father was out of danger until whenever a transplant could be scheduled. "How bad, Martha?"

"The doctor thought you should try to get back here as soon as possible."

Hanna looked at the clock on the wall. There would be no way to get a flight tonight. She'd have to drive even though it would take over five hours. She couldn't wait until morning. "I can be there by three or so. I'll leave right now. Please call if there's any news."

"I will, dear. Please hurry. I keep thinking the worst, Hanna."

"Is Dr. Mason there?" Hanna asked.

"No, he's with your father in surgery."

"Have him call my cell in the car as soon as he has an update," Hanna demanded.

"I will. Please hurry!"

Chapter Thirty-five

The crickets and tree frogs were in full symphonic mode as the day's light faded. Alex sat on the porch of his father's house. He was thinking about his mother, Katherine. Everyone called her *Kat*, he remembered. He was thinking about the night of the car accident when they got the call from the sheriff. He was a senior in high school. She'd been driving back from a friend's house in Beaufort late one night when a deer ran out. She swerved and hit a tree head-on. They told him she died instantly, but he could never imagine how you were suddenly just dead with no pain or suffering.

He'd tried to block out the grief over the years for the woman he loved more than anyone in his life. He still had tough moments thinking back on his best memories of his mother when he was a boy.

Tonight was one of those nights. He was thinking about the time he'd asked Adrienne to his first big high school dance. He was worried about wearing the old blue sport coat that was worn and shiny on the elbows. He didn't own a suit. At dinner one night with his mom and dad there, he'd asked about borrowing money to buy a new suit of clothes.

His father had immediately put him down. "You don't need to spend good money on fancy clothes for some damn dance. Hell, me or Bobby got somethin' in the closet you can wear."

His brother had smiled at him and shook his head.

The next day, his mother asked him to take a ride with her. She drove him down to Charleston and a men's store at the mall. She had them fit him for a new suit, a shirt and tie and a new pair of black dress shoes. She paid for it with her teacher's money. His father never said a word.

Alex looked up when a car stopped in front of the house and turned out the headlights. From the street lamp down the road he could see it was a big white SUV. He watched as Beau Richards came up the walk to the porch. He called out, "Alex, that you?"

"What's up, Beau?"

"Got a minute?

"Sure, come on up. Get you a beer or something?" Alex asked.

"Love a cold beer."

"Grab a seat, be right back." Alex went into the kitchen and opened two bottles of beer and went back to the porch. He sat down and handed him the beer. "What're you doing out so late, Beau?"

"Just wanted to stop by, see how you're doing," he said. "Worried about you after the other night out at the house. You seemed pretty down about all this with your dad."

"Well, thank you," Alex said, a bit skeptical.

"Anything new?" Richards asked.

Alex thought for a moment and didn't see any reason to share news of the latest evidence they'd found. "No, it just looks pretty bad."

"I know, son." Alex watched as Beau Richards lifted his beer bottle in a toast. "Here's to the Skipper."

Alex tapped his beer with his and lifted it in a toast. "Thank you."

Beau took a few sips from his beer and the two men sat for a while looking out over the river and listening to the sounds of the night. Alex heard him say, "Heard you stopped by to see Lily today, out at the project."

"Yes, I did," Alex replied, suddenly on alert.

"She was kind of upset, Alex."

"How's that?"

"You're asking a lot of questions around town and making people nervous, son. Just thought you should know."

Alex bristled and said, "I'm trying to keep my father off Death Row, Beau. You got a problem with that?"

"No, no, I understand. I'd be doing the same if it was my old man, God rest his soul."

"So why the late-night social call, Beau?"

"Look, we been friends a long time. Just thought you should know people are wondering about all you're digging in to."

"What people?" Alex asked.

Richards didn't respond.

Alex said, "Beau, I got every right to look into who in hell else had reason to want Horton Bayes dead."

"Of course, you do, and you let me know if I can help with anything."

Beau Richards had left after the beers were gone and again, offered all his help in the investigation. Alex had walked down to the *Maggie Mae* and was sitting in the captain's chair in the cabin of the shrimp boat, another beer in his hand. He remembered so many times out on the water with his dad yelling orders to the crew from this chair. Tonight, the only sounds were the bugs and the frogs. The two big booms holding the nets loomed above him on both sides of the boat. The smell of old fish and shrimp was heavy in the air. He took another sip from his beer, thinking about Beau Richards and the strange visit.

His thoughts turned to Hanna and where she might be tonight, probably back in Charleston after her father's surgery. If he knew her, she was probably still down at her office working for free on her client's cases. He'd given up on trying to sort out how he was going to deal with Adrienne and Hanna. He'd just have to let things develop day-by-day and see where it all leads. He wished Hanna was still working with Holloway on his father's case. He wished she was with him here tonight.

Chapter Thirty-six

Hanna was still two hours out from Atlanta and on her third cup of bad convenience store coffee when she knew she couldn't stay awake much longer. Twice, she had nodded off and hit the rumble strips on the freeway, preventing her from heading off into the trees. An exit sign ahead had symbols for gas, food and lodging. She just needed to rest for a while and then get back on the road.

Dr. Mason had called an hour earlier. There was an infection in her father's heart that caused some sort of cardiac event she couldn't remember the name of. His prognosis was guarded at best. He encouraged her to get there as soon as she could.

She pulled off at the exit for some small Georgia town she never remembered seeing. Turning off the ramp, she saw lights down the road for another convenience store, *Come Get It*, or some such nonsense. The signs at the ramp said the nearest hotel was two miles down the road in the town. She wasn't in the mood for driving any further, or the thought of some small-town motel. She just needed a few minutes rest and then get back on the road.

She pulled in to the convenience store and found a dark parking space to the side of the building. There was only one other car in the lot. She looked at the clock on her dash and it was 1:15am. She made sure the doors were locked and was asleep moments after she turned the car off, her head back against the seat.

There was pounding, then loud voices. She came back from a deep sleep and tried to regain some sense of where she was. She was suddenly jolted by the sight of two men pounding on her window. They were dressed in black leather vests over their bare chests. She saw tattoos everywhere. Both had long greasy hair and beards. They were leering at her and yelling, and she couldn't understand what they were saying. She sat up, fully awake and reached for the keys in the ignition. She put the car in reverse and the men stayed next to the car, still pounding, now on the top of the car.

She felt the fear surge through her veins like the worst adrenaline rush. Panicked now, she looked around the parking lot for anyone to help. No one was in sight. She got back far enough to put the car in drive and didn't care if she ran over the men when she spun the tires to get away. The two of them were behind her now as she passed two big motorcycles and sped away.

Looking in her rear-view mirror, Hanna was sure they would follow her. She was quickly back on the interstate and still watching her mirrors. The clock on her dash now read 1:50am. After a few miles there still were no lights behind her and she started to breathe a little easier. She didn't have to worry about drowsiness now, she was wide awake.

Hanna got to the hospital at nearly four in the morning. She pulled into a parking space and lay her head back, taking a deep breath. There had been no more calls from Dr. Mason, so she had no idea what to expect. She willed herself out of the car, stiff and sore from the long drive. She hurried to the red *Emergency* door sign.

Dr. Mason's partner met her in the Cardiac Unit waiting room. She was a younger doctor. Her name was Gilbert.

"Your father is in Intensive Care," the woman said. "The emergency procedure stabilized the situation, but more tests are underway to know what's next."

Hanna was in no mood for pleasantries. "Is my father going to die tonight?"

The doctor was taken aback and seemed upset. "We will know when all the tests are completed. You'll need to wait."

"Is my father's wife here, Martha Moss?" Hanna asked.

"No, we sent her home a couple of hours ago. There was nothing she could do here."

"She didn't stay?" Hanna was flabbergasted.

Hanna felt someone pushing her shoulder. She'd fallen asleep in a chair in the waiting room. She opened her eyes to see the young Dr. Gilbert sitting beside her and then squinted and covered her eyes at the morning light coming through the windows.

"Good morning, Hanna," the doctor said. "I wanted to let you sleep as long as possible. I know you've come a long way."

"How is he?" Hanna asked, sitting up and brushing hair away from her face.

"He's stable. That's all we can say at this point."

"What is *stable*?" Hanna asked.

The woman hesitated. "Your father's heart is very challenged at the moment. We believe we've controlled the situation but, the next few hours will be critical."

"Can I see him?" Hanna asked.

"I'll take you back to the ICU, but he isn't conscious."

"I want to see him."

Hanna was stunned when she saw her father. She couldn't imagine he would look worse than the previous day but, she thought she was looking at a corpse. His face had a faint yellow pallor and his mouth was open, like a death mask she had seen in others when they'd passed. She pulled a chair up next to his bed and reached for his hand. "I'm here Allen... Daddy."

She jolted awake when a nurse bumped her, checking on the readings on the many monitors around her father's bed. There seemed no change in his condition. Hanna looked to the nurse.

"He's a strong man. He's fighting," the nurse said.

Hanna turned and saw Martha coming into the room.

"Oh, Hanna, I'm so glad you made it safely," she said. "I've been worried about you all night."

"Yes, thanks for waiting," Hanna said, not trying to hide her irritation.

"I had to take a break, Hanna. I'd been here for hours. The doctors said I should go home and get some sleep."

Hanna's mood softened a bit. "Have you seen Dr. Mason?" she asked.

"No, not yet."

They both looked at the lifeless form of Allen Moss lying weak and possibly dying on the bed beside them.

Martha said, "I love your father, Hanna. I don't know what I'll do if we lose him."

Hanna looked up at her stepmother, surprised at her honest feelings. She reached for her hand. "I love him, too."

Chapter Thirty-seven

Alex felt himself coming from a deep sleep. What was the noise he was hearing? His head continued to clear, the fragments of a dream now lost forever. It was someone knocking at the front door. He touched the screen on his phone and it lit up the room... 2:35am. *What the hell?*

He got out of bed, dressed only in his boxer shorts, and went to the front of the house. He'd left just the screen closed and had turned off the porch light. Even in the dark, he could see it was his ex-wife. Through the screen, he said, "Adrienne, what's going on?"

He turned on the porch light and could see she'd been crying. Her eyes were red and swollen, the tears still tracing down her cheeks, her make-up smeared. She wore torn cut-off jeans and a white sleeveless t-shirt. Her feet were bare.

Adrienne said, "Alex, my mother and I got into another huge fight. She threw me out."

"And why are you here?"

"Alex, you know I have nowhere else to go."

"Where's the boy?"

Adrienne tried to wipe the tears from her eyes. "He's still sleeping."

He opened the door to let her in. He could smell the liquor on her breath as she passed. "You want some coffee? I'll put some on."

"Yes, please."

Pointing to the couch, he said, "Have a seat. I'll be back."

He sat across from her, a cup of steaming coffee in his hands. Hers was on the coffee table. She sat with her elbows on her knees, hands crossed, looking down. "I really am sorry, Alex."

"What happened?"

"It's always a ticking time bomb with the two of us," she said. "Ma came home late from *Gilly's* after a few too many and she just lit into me about getting my life straightened out. I must have fallen asleep and knocked a glass of wine over on her couch."

"She has a point," he said.

Adrienne looked up and bristled, then shook her head. "She literally threw me out of the house."

"She'll sober up by morning," Alex said.

"It's more than that."

Against his better judgment, he said. "You can take Bobby's room. I'll get you some bedding."

She reached for the coffee and took a sip. "I really hate to be..."

"Adrienne, just get some sleep. We can talk about it in the morning."

Alex was helping her make the bed, tucking in the top sheet. She came around with a pillow in her arms and leaned in quickly to kiss him on the cheek.

"Adrienne..." he said, backing away.

"I just wanted to say thank you."

"Good night," he said, walking out and closing the door behind him.

Adrienne was still asleep when he left the house the next morning at eight. He drove down to the sheriff's office and found Stokes in his office on the phone.

"They're damn sure?" he heard the sheriff ask. He listened for a few moments, nodding and signaling for Alex to grab a chair. "Send me the full report," he said and hung up. He looked up at Alex and said, "DA's office in Charleston. They got the Medical Examiner's report back this morning on the knife. The saltwater and mud compromised some of the prints and DNA trace, but they're pretty sure they can make a firm ID on your dad's prints."

"What about blood?" Alex asked.

"Like I said, they've got some trace DNA they're running right now, checking it against Bayes'."

"Pretty sure?"

The sheriff nodded back. "Look, Alex, if they match Bayes' blood on that knife we found under your old man's boat... that's gonna be game, set, match."

"I know that." Alex felt his stomach churn as he considered his father's fate. The fact he may have killed a man in a drunken rage, stabbing him repeatedly, seemed impossible to believe. For the first time, he considered whether his father had been lying about passing out and having no memory of the night after he got back home.

He heard the sheriff say, "I'm sorry, Alex."

Alex walked back into his father's house around nine as the sun began to filter through the tall trees shading the old place. He smelled coffee brewing and found Adrienne in the kitchen, sitting at the table and sipping at her coffee, dressed only in the white t-shirt she had on the previous night and a pair of peach-colored panties.

She put her hands in her lap, seemingly embarrassed. "I'm sorry. I didn't think you'd be back so soon."

He went to the counter and poured a cup of coffee. "Not like I haven't seen you in the morning before," he said, turning to face her.

"Thank you for taking me in."

"You need to go home and sort this out with Ella," he said.

Adrienne hesitated and stared back at him. Then, she said slowly, "What if I don't want to sort it out?"

"What do you mean?"

She stood and walked over to him. Standing near, she said, "Alex, we have a son. We should be together."

"Adrienne, please..."

"He needs a family, Alex. He needs both of us."

He took a deep breath and looked at her face, weary from a late night and too much to drink, her hair mussed in all directions. He tried to push thoughts of their earlier times together when he truly loved and cared for this woman. He knew there was still some of that feeling left deep inside him,

Adrienne moved closer and put her arms around his waist. He didn't push her away. She lay her head on his chest and her hair piled into his face. He brought his arms up and slowly wrapped them around her.

They stood together, not moving, not speaking.

Chapter Thirty-eight

Hanna had fallen asleep in the chair in the hospital waiting room. The nurses had finally insisted she leave the ICU to allow her father to rest as much as possible. Her stepmother, Martha, shook her shoulder to wake her. Hanna came slowly out of a deep, yet troubled sleep where she was dreaming about the plane crash that took her mother's and brother's lives. She woke abruptly and looked around, not certain where she was.

"Hanna, I'm sorry," Martha said.

Hanna looked over and saw the woman sitting beside her. She glanced around and remembered she was in Atlanta and at the hospital and her father was deathly ill. "What?" she managed to say.

Martha said, "Dr. Mason is coming down to give us an update."

Hanna was still gathering her senses and pushing thoughts of panic and screaming on a falling airplane from her mind. She saw the doctor coming across the room toward them.

"Good morning," Dr. Mason said. He sat beside the two women. "The bottom-line is, Allen has fought back and seems to have passed through the worst of this. The tests look better this morning. We're going to keep him in ICU for now to closely monitor his progress, but I think he's through the worst of it."

Martha reached for the doctor's hand and said, "Oh, thank God! He's going to be okay?"

Mason said, "He's better, for now."

"Are you really certain he's through the worst of this?" Hanna asked.

"We can never know for sure, but I'm much more optimistic this morning."

"Can we see him?" Martha asked.

"He's awake, but not fully alert," the doctor said. "Let's give him a little more time."

It was mid-morning when the nurse came out to tell them they could spend a few minutes with the patient. Hanna followed Martha down the hall and into her father's room. She watched as her stepmother hurried over to the bed and sat beside him. She threw her arms gently around him and let her face fall gently on his stomach.

Hanna could see that he was barely conscious and seemingly confused about what was happening. She heard Martha whisper, "Oh, Allen, we're so glad you're back."

Allen Moss looked over and saw his daughter. Their eyes met for a moment and then a spark of recognition seemed to light up his ashen face and he smiled. He reached out a hand for her.

Hanna stepped to the side of the bed and took her father's hand. It felt cold and when she squeezed, his grip was weak and tentative. Martha was crying and still lying on his chest. Hanna said, "The doctor tells us you're a tough old bird and you're not gonna check out yet."

Her father smiled back and nodded but couldn't speak.

Hanna went back to the house, showered and changed and then drove to the offices of *Moss Kramer*, her father's law firm. The elegant suite of offices that housed the collection of 156 attorneys was located in a newer 80-story glass and steel tower just off Peachtree Street a mile north from downtown Atlanta. *Moss Kramer* occupied the top five floors. Hanna's father's office was on the top floor in the executive suite where the twelve members of the Management Committee, chaired by Allen Moss, were located.

A wall of glass greeted Hanna as she exited the elevator. Locked double doors were inscribed with the firm name in gold script. Through the doors she could see the rich decor of the lobby area with two young women with phone head-sets in their ear seated behind a long wood reception desk. She heard the door buzz as she approached and pushed through. She recognized one of the women from previous visits.

"Good morning, Hanna," the receptionist said. Her nameplate read *Sara Hamilton.* Hanna noticed the other receptionist look up with an almost apologetic look on her face, but she didn't speak.

"Hello, Sara," Hanna replied.

"How is your father doing?" Sara asked.

"Better this morning, thanks."

"We've been so worried about Allen."

"Thank you," Hanna said, coming up to the counter and placing her leather bag down. "I'm sorry for dropping by without an appointment, but I really do need a few minutes with Mister Kramer."

Both women looked at her with concern, as if this was the most unacceptable request.

Sara cleared her throat, looking at her computer screen, then said, "He's got a terribly full schedule this morning, I'm afraid."

"Please just let him know I'm here and need to speak with him for a moment."

"Of course." Sara touched a button on her ear-piece and then dialed the single number for the office of Gregory Kramer, her father's partner. Within moments she was obviously connected to the man's executive assistant. She shared Hanna's request for a quick meeting and then listened for a few moments for the response. "I'll let her know, thank you." Sara ended the call and looked up. "Let me take you down to the board room. Mr. Kramer will break free in a few minutes to see you."

Hanna noticed a look of thinly veiled surprise on the other woman's face. She followed Sara Hamilton down a richly-decorated hallway, dimly lit with a lavish collection of oil paintings along the way. The woman pushed open two large wooden doors into a long narrow room with a wall of windows facing them and a spectacular view of the skyline of downtown Atlanta. Hanna had seen the view from her father's office on her infrequent visits and she always marveled at the grand expanse of a city that seemed to have no limits for growth and development.

Sara said, "Hanna, there is coffee or tea in the kitchen through that door, or whatever you'd like from the fridge."

"Thank you, Sara."

"Give your father my best. We all hope he's back soon."

"Thank you," Hanna said, thinking to herself about no one from the firm coming to visit her father at the hospital or calling to check on his status. She watched the woman leave and close the double doors behind her, then went to pour a cup of coffee before returning to sit at the long walnut table surrounded by deeply-cushioned green leather chairs.

She had barely sat down when a door at the other end of the room pushed open and Gregory Kramer came in. He was twenty years younger than her father in his mid-fifties, the son of the last Kramer who had founded the firm with Hanna's father, now deceased for the past five years. He was a small man but exuded a powerful presence in a finely-cut gray suit and lavender silk tie, his blond hair balding some and his face deeply tanned. He came quickly around the table and gave Hanna a hug and kiss on the cheek.

"Hanna, so nice to see you."

"Thank you, Gregory."

"We've been so worried about Allen. What's the latest?"

Hanna tried to control her anger at the man's obviously false concern. "He's better this morning, but we had quite a scare last night."

"He's going to be okay?" Kramer said, motioning for Hanna to take a seat and then pulling up the chair beside her.

"His doctor is calling his condition, *guarded*," she said. "If he pulls through this latest..."

"If he pulls through!" the man said in seeming surprise.

"His heart is very weak, Gregory. We almost lost him last night."

"My God!" the man said. "We were told late yesterday he was recovering well from the surgery."

"There have been complications."

"I'm so sorry, Hanna."

"If he can get through this latest set-back and regain his strength, he's going to need a transplant."

The man looked genuinely concerned now and said, "I had no idea, Hanna.

I'm really so sorry. I had planned to stop down later this afternoon to check in on him."

"I'm not sure he'll be ready for visitors yet. You'd better call first."

He nodded and then said, "We have all your father's work covered with our best people."

"I'm sure you do. Thank you."

There was an awkward silence between them, then Hanna said, "Gregory, I wanted to let you know of my father's request for me to take his position here at the firm until he's strong enough to return." She watched as the man tried to hide his surprise and displeasure with the news. She continued, "This is what he wants."

Kramer paused a few moments, then said, "Of course, Hanna, whatever Allen feels comfortable with. I will say, though, it would be very difficult for you to just step into his role here and assume your father's work with his many clients. It would be very..."

Hanna cut him off, trying to keep her anger in check. "Gregory, please, I understand." She took a sip from her coffee to gather herself. "I have no intention of joining the practice at this point. I'm sure you have things well in control." She could see the obvious relief in his expression. "However, I did want you to know that if my father is ultimately unable to return to work, I will want to assume his responsibilities, again, at his request."

Kramer stared back at her intently for a few moments, his practiced and professional look doing a good job of masking his obvious displeasure at the notion of her taking on the senior role at the firm. He finally said, "I understand your father's wishes and concern, Hanna, but it's not quite that simple. The Management Committee has a role in determining a situation like this."

"I'm sure they do, Gregory. Just know that I will honor my father's desire to keep our family involved in the business here."

He looked like he was having a hard time swallowing, then he managed to say in a low and surprisingly calm voice, "Hanna, let's hope there is no need to worry about any of this. We all want Allen back as soon as possible."

Hanna was certain this was the last thing the man wanted as he would surely assume the Managing Partner role in the firm if her father was unable to return. "Thank you, Gregory." She stood, and he pushed his chair back and got up with her, offering his hand.

"We will stay in close contact about all of this, Hanna. Please keep us apprised of your father's condition."

Hanna nodded.

"Thank you for coming down under such difficult circumstances," he said.

She turned to leave, thinking about how much she would dread having to come to work in this place every day and dealing with these arrogant bastards.

Chapter Thirty-nine

Beau Richards closed the door of his Cadillac SUV and walked around his son's house to the expansive lawn that led down to the river. The mid-morning sun was high over the trees behind him and the last mist was burning off the dark river below. A long dock pushed out from the shore with his son's sailboat moored on one side and the speedboat on the other. The far bank of the river was lined with dense woods in both directions as far as you could see. Connor had bought all the adjoining property to prevent other development from destroying his view and privacy.

Beau had called his son ten minutes ago to request a meeting. Connor asked if he could come down to his boat where he was preparing for a sail with his girlfriend, Lily. He saw his son wave from the deck of the sailboat. Lily stepped down into the cabin as he approached. As he came out on the dock, a small alligator pushed away slowly from the shore, only its dark head visible above the flow of the river. As Beau came alongside the sailboat, he heard his son call out, "Come aboard."

Beau stopped and said, "Let's take a walk."

Connor hesitated, then said, "Okay." He jumped on to the dock and came up to his father, giving him a hug. "Morning. What's up?"

Beau turned without answering and started walking back to the shore. Connor followed and said, "Dad, what's going on?"

Beau didn't speak until they reached the shore. He turned along a path by the river and said, "When is your next delivery?"

"What? You mean the weed?"

"Yes."

Connor walked alongside his father. "Tonight, why?"

Beau stopped and looked out across the river to the far bank. "I don't want you out there tonight. Get someone else and this will be the last, do you understand?" Connor started to protest, but Beau held up his hand and said, "We don't need this anymore."

"What are you talking about?"

"We don't need to take these risks anymore, particularly with all the cops stirred up about the Bayes murder."

Connor didn't try to hide the panic in his voice. "We can't just shut this down overnight! We have partners..."

"They'll find someone else," Beau interrupted. "We don't need the money and we sure as hell don't need the risk anymore. I'm doing the same thing with the sports book."

"You're shutting down the gambling, too?" Connor said in exasperation.

Beau turned to face his son. "We have more than enough legitimate business now. We're not going to screw around with this crap. Do you understand?"

"So, it's about Bayes?" Connor asked. "They'll never find out he was taking deliveries out on the bay for us."

"We don't know who he talked to before he died," Beau said. "And Chaz Merton's been his crew on most of his drug trips. I trust that old drunk about as far as I can spit."

Connor said, "We can take care of Merton."

"No! There won't be any of that."

Chapter Forty

Hanna had spent most of her time on the drive back to Atlanta on the phone to her office in Charleston, trying to keep current on the cases she was working on at the legal clinic. One of her calls had been to Lonnie Smith at the Charleston PD to check on the search for Jenna Hall's killer. Lonnie was frustrated by how little progress had been made in finding the man. He was quite certain Moe Hall was far from Charleston at this point and they would have to rely on the State Police and others brought in to help with the search. Jenna's son was still being kept at the shelter under the care of Greta Muscovicz.

She had also checked in with Phillip Holloway on progress on the Skipper Frank murder investigation. There was nothing new since she had learned of the discovery of the knife and blood evidence, further strengthening the case against Alex's father.

Hanna had left Atlanta in the late morning after another visit with her father at the hospital. She was encouraged by the progress he seemed to be making in recovery. The doctors also provided a more optimistic view of his improving tests and response to treatment.

Her father was coherent enough to understand the discussion she shared with his partner at the *Moss Kramer* law firm. He seemed satisfied with her stance on the situation. When he learned Hanna's son, Jonathan, was coming home to Pawleys Island that night, he insisted she get back to be with him.

Hanna was still an hour out from the coast when her cell phone buzzed on the seat beside her. She looked at the screen and didn't recognize the number but decided to accept the call.

"Hello, this is Hanna."

A woman's voice said, "Is this Hanna Walsh?"

"Yes, who's calling?"

"Hanna, this is Adrienne Frank."

Hanna's senses went on full alert when she realized it was Alex's ex. "Yes, what is it?"

Adrienne said, "I got your number from Alex's phone."

How did she get Alex's cell phone? Hanna didn't respond.

"Hanna, are you there?"

"Yes... I'm here."

"I'm sure Alex has spoken to you about us," Adrienne said.

Hanna felt her temper start to flare. Again, she didn't respond.

"I know you two were close and I just wanted to say how sorry I am that Scotty and I have complicated things for Alex."

"Complicated things?" Hanna repeated.

There was silence on the phone for a moment, then Adrienne said, "So, he hasn't spoken with you yet?"

Hanna put the phone on "speaker" and set it on the dash, gripping the steering wheel hard with both hands. "Adrienne, just tell me why you called."

"It really is best, for Scotty, I mean. He should be with his father and he should have a real family."

Hanna was stunned and couldn't think of what to say.

"Hanna, I'm sorry if I surprised you with all this. I just wanted you to know I appreciate how hard this must be for you."

Hanna reached for the phone and slammed the "end call" button, then threw it down on the passenger seat. Her hands were shaking, and she felt a sick hollowness in her gut. She drove for several miles, trying to calm her emotions, replaying the conversation with Adrienne in her mind. She was furious with Alex for not calling her to tell her he was getting back with his ex-wife.

By the time she reached the bridge across the marsh to the island, she had calmed herself some, but Adrienne Frank's smug voice still echoed in her mind. She had resigned herself days ago that things hadn't worked out as she had hoped with Alex Frank, but she hadn't been able to fully close the possibility of them reuniting. She still had strong feelings for Alex and secretly hoped there was some chance down the road they could reconnect. When she looked down at the phone beside her, she reconciled herself to the fact that wasn't even a slim hope anymore.

Hanna's spirits lifted some as they always did when she came out to the island. There was something about the place that was a safe harbor for her from the stress and challenges in her life. As she pulled up behind the beach house and opened her door, the smell of the salt off the ocean, the sound of gulls, the fresh breeze in her face, all helped to calm and renew her.

Her cell phone buzzed again. She reached over and saw "Alex Frank" on the screen. She didn't hesitate when she hit the "decline" button and threw the phone in her purse.

Chapter Forty-one

Alex saw his call to Hanna go immediately to voice mail and he knew she had declined to answer. He thought about it for a moment as he pocketed his phone. She had every reason to avoid talking to him with all the issues with her father's health and certainly, their latest discussions about his ex-wife.

He was walking back to his father's house after the confrontation he and Sheriff Stokes had with the widow, Meryl Bayes. The shade from tall trees along the river helped to cool the hot summer afternoon. A big sailboat under power caught his attention, making its way out toward the ocean. Alex turned and saw Connor Richards and his girlfriend, Lily, in the cockpit of the boat. Connor saw him onshore and waived. Alex nodded and continued on, suddenly thinking how odd they were heading out for a sail this late in the day. He looked up and saw there was barely a whisper of wind in the trees.

Alex's old family house was up ahead now, and he thought about Adrienne. He had no idea what to expect. With Adrienne, anything was possible.

When he opened the front screen door, the aroma of cooking came from the kitchen. He heard muted voices and walked back through the house. Entering the kitchen, Alex saw Adrienne working over the stove, stirring something. Their son, Scotty, was at the kitchen table, playing with a toy car. The boy looked up and saw him.

"Alex!" Scotty shouted and jumped out of his chair to rush over. "Mom says we can go for ice cream after dinner," he said, excitedly.

Adrienne turned and smiled at Alex. "Welcome home."

Alex took a deep breath. He sunk to one knee. "How are you, Scotty?"

"You've got a cool house," the boy said. "Mom says we can stay here.

Grandma's mad at us."

Alex looked up at Adrienne who turned from her work at the stove. She smiled at him and said, "Scotty, why don't you go out in the backyard and play with your car for a while 'til dinner. I'll call you."

The boy started to protest but she said, "Don't make me say it again."

"We can go for ice cream, right?" he asked.

His mother replied, "Yes, after dinner."

Scotty grabbed his toy from the table and pushed through the back door.

Adrienne said, "Thank you for taking us in."

Alex stood and walked to the refrigerator, reached in and grabbed a beer. "Would you like one?" he asked.

"Please."

Alex opened the beers and then sat at the table. His thoughts were spinning with his mixed emotions about this woman trying to make her way back into his life. He looked out the window and saw his son at the picnic table playing. He realized he was also feeling guilty for not taking more time to connect with his newfound son. *Why was he feeling so uncertain about all this?*

"My mother thinks you're a saint, by the way," Adrienne said.

He looked over at her and thought to himself about how much he would have welcomed the sight of her here in his kitchen years ago when they were starting out together, how much they had really cared for each other. *Was all that a myth from the beginning?*

Adrienne walked over to him and sat on his lap before he could protest. She put her arm around his neck and lifted her beer to his. "I know this all so strange for you," she said. "Can you please give it some time? We can make this work again." She leaned in and kissed him on the cheek.

After the dinner of spaghetti Adrienne had prepared, Alex did take them into town for ice cream and after, suggested they go for a boat ride up the river in his father's little skiff tied up at the docks in front of their house. Adrienne and Scotty sat in the front of the boat while Alex stood at the center console and navigated away from the docks and then east out toward the bay and ocean beyond. The sun was still high above the trees and with almost no breeze, the water was glassy calm. The heat and damp air pressed in on them. Scotty was fascinated by the gulls trailing the boat hoping for some morsel to be tossed overboard for them.

They passed slowly through the town and then out further through the lush canopy of Low Country foliage along the river in the wild country on the winding route out to the ocean. Alex looked down at Adrienne and Scotty and tried to come to grips with this new reality in his life. *Would they move to Charleston to be near him? When would they tell Scotty about his real father? Where would he go to school?*

Adrienne pointed to the riverbank where a long gator lay motionless in the mud. Scotty stood, excited to see the big animal. "How fast can they swim, Alex?" he asked.

"Pretty fast, but he won't mind us," Alex answered over the low rumble of the outboard motor.

Alex steered the boat around the next bend of the river and the wide bay opened before them. He could see the line of the horizon across the ocean between the south and north points of the bay. Several large cruising yachts and sailboats were anchored in the calm sanctuary of the bay for the night. He noticed Connor Richards with Lily on his boat, anchored furthest out toward the ocean. They were several hundred yards away from Alex's boat and didn't seem to notice them passing.

With the low wind, the ocean was also flat calm, and Alex continued out of the bay and turned north along the shoreline. There was protected National Seashore for two miles up the coast used as a park during the day. The sandy beaches pushed up into low dunes and broad green forests beyond. A few beach-goers were still settled in along the shore and some were swimming and playing out in the calm water of the Atlantic.

Alex had made this trip on many occasions, crewing on his father's shrimp boat. He remembered happy times pulling in large nets full of shrimp with his brother while his father barked out commands and kept the *Maggie Mae* on course. His heart suddenly felt heavy as he thought about the new evidence against his father.

Tomorrow, he would go to see Meryl Bayes again. Something wasn't sitting right with him about her account of the story the night of the murder. He was also having that "itchy" feeling, as he called it back at the police precinct, about the Richards. Another discussion with the girlfriend, Lily, was definitely needed.

Chapter Forty-two

Hanna was finishing a salad and sandwiches for dinner when she heard her son's car pulling into the drive behind the beach house. She washed and dried her hands and rushed to the door, opening it to see Jonathan and his new girlfriend, Elizabeth, climbing out of the low white Porsche that had been a gift from Jonathan's father when he graduated from high school. Hanna had pushed back on her husband, Ben, on the extravagance of the gift, but he had insisted. She noticed Jonathan had let his beard grow scrubby. The girlfriend was tall and lean with long blond hair and deeply tanned skin evident below short cut-off jeans and a light blue tank top.

Hanna hurried down the stairs and saw Jonathan wave before he reached in to grab bags for the weekend stay. He gave her a warm hug and kiss and then Hanna reached out her hand. "Elizabeth, it's so nice to meet you and welcome!"

"Hello, Mrs. Walsh. Thank you for having me out for the weekend."

"Call me Hanna, please."

Elizabeth smiled and nodded. Jonathan walked over and took the girl's hand to lead her inside. Hanna could tell they were deeply into each other and she was pleased that Jonathan looked so happy.

After the dinner, where Hanna updated Jonathan on the situation with his grandfather in Atlanta, they started a beach fire in the stone pit down in the dunes in front of the house. The sun was setting behind them and casting a soft orange glow out over the calm ocean. They sat in the sun-faded Adirondack chairs around the fire, each with a glass of red wine.

"So, Elizabeth," Hanna said, "I've been meaning to ask how the two of you met?"

Elizabeth smiled at Jonathan, then said, "He ran me off the road on my bicycle on the way to class and nearly killed me."

"What?" Hanna gasped.

Jonathan jumped in. "It wasn't like that. She rushed out from a side street without looking."

"So, you say!" Elizabeth responded and laughed before taking a sip from her wine. "He took me down to the Med Center to get my scraped knees attended to and then bought me a cup of coffee."

"And the rest is history," Jonathan said with a satisfied smile on his face.

Hanna lifted her wine glass to the others and said, "Well, welcome to Pawleys Island."

"Thank you, Hanna."

"What do the two of you have planned for the weekend?" Hanna asked.

"Just take it easy, Jonathan said. "Maybe take the kayaks back in the marshes."

"Sounds great," Hanna said. She suddenly remembered the last time she had been sitting here at the fire and the memory of the strange woman who had suddenly been beside her as she awoke from a nap or too many glasses of wine. She told Jonathan and Elizabeth about the unusual visit.

Jonathan said, "Sounds to me like one of Pawleys Island's ghosts, Mom."

Hanna chuckled. "Yeah, sure."

"You know all the old stories," Jonathan continued. "The Gray Man who appears on the beach every time there's a major storm coming."

Hanna was well aware of all the old ghost stories. They were a part of the lore of the island and much had been written and reported about the many ghosts on Pawleys Island. She hadn't honestly thought about it after that night on the beach and the weird appearance by the woman beside her at the fire. She had written it off to a strange dream after too much wine.

Elizabeth said, "So, there really are ghosts around here?"

"We have a book on them in the house," Jonathan answered. "I'll show it to you when we go up."

Hanna was trying to recall the few moments of memories she had of this ghost or spirit's visit that night at the fire. *What had she said? Listen to your heart.*

Chapter Forty-three

The alarm on Alex's phone began chiming at eight o'clock the next morning. He reached for it on the night stand and turned off the alert. He lay back in bed for a moment, gathering his thoughts. He had a meeting with the sheriff at nine to catch up on the latest with his father's murder case. He wanted to pay a visit to both Meryl Bayes and Connor Richards and his girlfriend, though he was still unsure what those discussions might reveal.

He showered and dressed quickly and left the house while Adrienne and Scotty were still sleeping. He had insisted again the night before on separate bedrooms for Adrienne. She had seemed to understand his continued reluctance to dive back in to something that had been lost so many years earlier. Scotty had slept in his parent's bedroom.

He got into his car to drive to the sheriff's office and thought again about trying to reach Hanna. He decided he had nothing to lose at this point and wanted her to understand what was really going on. He heard the phone ringing and was surprised when she answered on the third ring. He heard her say, "Good morning."

Alex responded, "Good morning. How is your father doing?"

"Better, thank you," her answer curt and guarded.

"I'm glad to hear that."

There was an awkward silence between them for a few moments, then Alex said, "Hanna, I've been trying to reach you. We need to talk."

Again, silence on the other end of the call.

"Hanna?"

Finally, she said, "Alex, I understand you need to be with your ex-wife and son. Adrienne called to..."

Alex jumped in, his heart beating faster, "Adrienne called you?"

"She let me know you were back together... as a family."

"Hanna..."

She cut him off. "Alex, you don't need to explain."

"I need to see you, Hanna."

He felt an emptiness grow inside as he heard her say, "I'm sorry this didn't work out," and then the line went dead.

It was all Alex could do to not run back into the house and throw Adrienne out on the street. What in the world was she thinking calling Hanna and then not telling him about it? But, then again, of course she would call her to make sure that threat was put aside for good. Hanna's final words replayed in his head, *"I'm sorry..."*

His phone rang, and he saw the sheriff's number on the screen. "Morning, Sheriff."

"Alex, good morning. Had a little excitement last night thought you should know about."

"What's that?"

Stokes said, "Can you meet me down at the Bayes' shrimp trawler?"

"I'm just down the road."

"Meet me on the dock."

Alex saw Sheriff Stokes standing on the dock next to the *LuLu Belle* with one of his deputies. He was surprised to also see two men and a woman with *DEA* for the Drug Enforcement Agency, stenciled prominently on the backs of their shirts. They were onboard the boat, apparently supervising a crime scene investigation crew.

"What's going on, Pepper?" Alex asked as he came up.

"Coast Guard came across your old pal Chaz Merton with his crew onboard the boat here last night. They were just outside the bay taking on a big load of pot."

"What?" Alex said in total surprise.

"The Bayes kid was with them, too."

"Horton's son?" Alex asked.

"Yessir."

"How much are we talking about?" Alex asked.

"The Feds tell me it's damn near a half million."

Alex was stunned. "And Chaz and young Horton were in the middle of all this?"

"Seems your friend Chaz has been very cooperative already with the Federal boys," the sheriff said. "Wants a plea deal for spilling all he knows about this drug ring that's apparently been operating around here for several years. We've been trying to chase down random reports of big drug shipments but had no idea."

Alex looked across the deck of the old shrimp boat and the Federal investigators scurrying about. "And you think Horton was tied up in all this before he died?" he asked.

"Don't know for sure," Stokes said. "Even one of my dispatchers was in on it, monitoring police and Coast Guard radio traffic to alert the boats out on the water. Guess he didn't do a very good job last night."

"Where's Meryl?" Alex asked.

"Up at the house with a couple more Feds," Stokes said. "She's sayin' she had no idea her old man and her son were mixed up in any of this."

"Of course she is," Alex responded. Random threads of circumstances were coming together in his head. "Sheriff, what do you think the odds are that Horton was getting skittish about the drug business and maybe thinking about getting out? Then suddenly, he turns up dead."

Alex was waiting for a call back from his father's lawyer when he walked up to his house. The news about the drug ring and Horton Bayes' involvement, suddenly created several new scenarios in his murder that needed to be quickly tracked down.

As he reached the front door, his thoughts returned to Adrienne and her call to Hanna. He tried to keep his anger in check as he heard her talking to Scotty in the kitchen. They were both at the small table eating breakfast when he walked in. She was wearing a short robe and her bare legs were crossed as she helped her son to more cereal. She looked up when he came into the room.

"Morning, Babe," she said, a big smile on her face.

"We need to talk," Alex said sternly. "Get some clothes on. We're going for a walk."

Alex led Adrienne out to the end of their dock on the river and then turned to face her. His face was flushed with anger and he tried to calm himself before saying, "What in hell were you thinking, calling Hanna?"

Adrienne didn't seem surprised at his accusation. "I just wanted her to know I was sorry about everything, about coming between the two of you."

"I'm sorry, but that's bullshit, Adrienne!"

Now she seemed alarmed at his anger. "Alex, please..."

"How did you even get her number?" he asked.

"I got it off your phone."

"And you didn't think you needed to tell me about this little conversation?"

"Alex, I'm sorry..."

"Not good enough," he interrupted. "I want you out of the house by the time I'm back at dinner tonight. I don't care where in hell you go, but it won't be here!"

Chapter Forty-four

Hanna watched her son and his girlfriend paddle their kayaks up ahead through another channel in the marshes behind Pawleys Island. She had let her own kayak drift back to give the two of them some time alone. She was genuinely pleased with Jonathan's new friend. Elizabeth was a smart and cordial young woman and she obviously had strong feelings for Jonathan.

Hanna had been struggling to put the memory of her call this morning from Alex in the back of her mind and not ruin this beautiful day with her son. The finality of it all was the most upsetting. She had been holding on to a distant possibility that things could work out with Alex Frank. The phone call from his ex-wife had dashed any of those hopes and she had made that clear with Alex this morning. Her track record with men continued the pattern of deep feelings, hopeful commitment, vulnerability, and in the end, crushing disappointment.

Jonathan and Elizabeth disappeared around a bend in the channel ahead. Hanna took in the early morning serenity of the water, the flowing grasses pushing in a light wind from the west, the smells of Low Country life all around her. A dock came into view ahead on the left leading back to shore. An expansive green lawn led to a shaded house up in the live oak and pines. Hanna watched as a woman walked out on the dock and stood facing away from her, looking out toward the mainland. She was dressed in a long flowing dress. Her hair was a deep reddish brown. She stood barefoot and seemed not to notice as Hanna approached on the far side of the channel.

When Hanna came abreast of the woman, she saw her turn and they made eye contact for the first time. Hanna felt a chill rush through her as the woman smiled back and waved. Her face was familiar, yet she couldn't remember where she'd seen her before.

"Good morning," Hanna called out.

The woman just continued to smile and didn't respond.

As Hanna paddled past, she looked back again and was stunned to see the woman was gone. There was no sign of her anywhere. The long dock was empty. There were no ripples or waves on the water where she might have fallen or jumped in, just the calm glassy surface of the channel.

Hanna sat across from Jonathan and Elizabeth on the outdoor deck of the restaurant that looked out over the marshes behind the island. The server had just left cold draft beers in front of them and taken their orders of fried grouper sandwiches for lunch.

Jonathan lifted his beer in a toast. "Thank you for having us out for the weekend, Mom." They all touched glasses.

"I wish you would come more often," Hanna said. "Elizabeth, what do you think of Pawleys Island?"

"It's wonderful! Do you mind if I never leave?" She laughed and sipped at her beer.

"Stay as long as you like, dear," Hanna said.

Jonathan said, "Mom, we wanted to share some news with you."

Hanna's first thought was an engagement, though she didn't see a ring on Elizabeth's finger. "And what news would that be," she said with both excitement and a little trepidation.

"Elizabeth and I are planning to take next term and study in Spain."

Hanna was relieved to hear the two of them weren't jumping too quickly into plans for marriage. She thought for a moment and then said, "I think that sounds wonderful."

"We're just starting to make plans," Elizabeth said. "Do you think you could come and visit while we're there?"

Jonathan continued, "Barcelona looks fabulous, Mom."

"Absolutely," Hanna said. "Just keep me posted on your plans and we'll make it work. I need a break from South Carolina." She tried not to think about her father and Alex Frank and Jenna Hall, and all the troubled cases she had waiting for her back in Charleston. Today was too grand to let herself get dragged down again in the realities of all that was churning in her life.

She suddenly remembered the lone woman on the dock back in the marshes and felt the goosebumps flush across her skin again, *how familiar the woman's face had been, her sudden disappearance.*

Hanna turned to Jonathan and asked, "Just before we got to the boat ramp, back around the bend, did you see the woman out on the dock? She was wearing a long dress."

Jonathan looked at Elizabeth and the two of them shook their heads. Jonathan said, "Didn't see anyone out on the marshes all morning."

Hanna said, "It was the strangest thing. She was there and then when I looked back she was just gone."

Jonathan laughed and said, "Sounds like your ghost is back!"

As Hanna prepared dinner that night back at the beach house, she started thinking again about the woman on the dock. She couldn't get her face out of her head. A thought came to her and she walked through the dining room and into the long room across the beach side of the house. On a wall next to the fireplace, she walked up to an old framed photo. It had been a gift from the woman who now owned *Tanglewood Plantation*, the property Hanna's family had owned back in the 1800's.

She looked at the faded photo now and saw the gathering of a large family in front of the old plantation house. The men were dressed in Confederate Army uniforms and the women in traditional dress of the day. In the middle of the grouping was a young woman who Hanna had learned was her distant great-grandmother, Amanda Paltierre Atwell. She had her arm linked with her husband, Captain Jeremy Atwell.

Hanna pushed closer and looked at the woman in the photo. She knew what she was going to see even before the face came into focus. *The woman on the dock.*

Chapter Forty-five

The drive from Dugganville to Charleston was slow with early traffic heading into the city. Alex watched the crawl of cars ahead of him on Highway 17. He had a meeting with his father's lawyer, Phillip Holloway, and then they were going to visit Skipper Frank at the County jail. His thoughts, though, were on his last conversation with Adrienne before he left the house.

He shook his head and thought about her treachery in calling Hanna and not bothering to tell him about it. When she showed up at his door after a fight with her mother, he should have walked her back home right then. His emotions had been swirling through a mostly sleepless night as his ex-wife slept in the bedroom beside his.

Alex knew in his heart he would do what was right by his son. He just couldn't imagine a path that would allow Adrienne back in. His feelings for her were so jumbled. They had been deeply in love in the early years and he knew some of that still lingered, despite her betrayal and behavior while he'd been away in the service. *And then, there was Hanna.*

He was so distracted in his thoughts, he had to slam on his brakes and swerve onto the shoulder of the road to avoid hitting a car making a left turn in front of him. He slapped his hands on the steering wheel and cursed silently.

Alex met Phillip Holloway in the lobby of the Charleston County Jail. They took two seats against the wall to talk.

Phillip started right in. "This knife evidence is going to take him down, Alex."

"I know."

"Have you found out anything else that can help?"

Alex felt his heart sink in his chest, knowing he'd found no other solid explanation for Horton Bayes' murder. He shared the news about the previous night's drug arrest aboard the Bayes' shrimp trawler.

Holloway stood, "Let's see what your father has to say about all this."

Alex and Phillip stood when Skipper Frank was led into the small interview room. The guard unlocked one of the hand-cuffs and secured it to a chain ring on the heavy metal table, then left them alone. Alex was not surprised by his father's desperate look. He appeared to have had little sleep and his face was gaunt and pale with several day's gray beard. His hair was combed straight back, shiny and unwashed. He looked up at his son and lawyer through bloodshot eyes.

Alex said, "You look like hell."

"Nice to see you, too."

Holloway pulled some papers from his bag and placed them on the table. "We have some bad news."

"It gets worse?" the elder Frank asked.

Alex said, "Pop, the divers found your knife under your boat."

"My knife?"

Alex showed him the picture of the knife on his cell phone.

Holloway said, "They will be able to identify it as your knife, we're quite certain."

"What the hell's it doing under the boat?" Skipper asked, his face showing sudden concern.

"We were hoping you could tell us," Alex said. "There's likely blood trace from Horton Bayes on the knife, Pop."

The old man's head slumped down. He pressed his hands together in a tight grip, but he didn't speak.

"Pop?"

He finally looked up and said, "I was up most of the night again trying to think through all that happened."

"And?" Alex asked.

Skipper looked up at his son. "I remember going to Bayes' boat after the fight."

Phillip and Alex looked at the man and waited for him to continue.

"We got into it again."

"What happened?" the lawyer asked.

Skipper took a deep breath, then said, "I remember a lot of pushing and yelling." He paused.

"What else?" Alex asked.

"Bayes' old lady came down and got between us."

"What!" Alex said. "Meryl Bayes was there?"

His father nodded. "Yeah, she must have come looking for Horton down at the boat after he didn't come home from the bar."

Holloway asked, "And you're sure she was there on the boat with you?"

"I don't know..."

"You need to be sure!" the lawyer pressed.

"The whole night's still a damn blur, but I can remember now, Meryl was yelling at me to go home and pushing me down the dock."

Alex looked over at his father's lawyer. "Why in hell hasn't she told us about this?"

Two hours later, Alex stood on the porch of the Bayes' house back in Dugganville with Sheriff Pepper Stokes. The sheriff knocked on the door for the second time when they heard footsteps coming. Meryl Bayes pulled open the door and looked through the screen. She was still in an old plaid robe and her hair was pulled up in a red scarf around her head.

"What?" she said, not opening the door.

"We need a few minutes, Meryl," the sheriff said.

She pushed open the screen door to let them in and led them over to a small living room with a couch and two chairs arranged around a television on a low wood table against the far wall. The house smelled damp and close, the furniture worn and cluttered with clothes and magazines. The two men sat across from her as she made room to sit on the couch.

The sheriff started, "Meryl, we need to ask you about the night of Horton's death."

Alex saw anger flare in her eyes, then she said, "What more do you want?" she hissed with a low smoky voice. "We've been through this how many times?"

Stokes said, "We're curious why you haven't told us about seeing Skipper Frank down at your boat the night of the murder."

She scrunched her eyes and pushed some loose hair away from her face. Her hands were starting to shake. and she held them in the lap of her robe. Finally, she said, "I told you everything."

"No, you didn't," Alex said. "You saw Skipper again down at the boat and broke up another fight between the two of them."

She looked back and didn't answer, a confused look coming across her face.

Alex continued, "You got between them and forced my father to leave. You pushed him down the dock to leave."

She didn't respond.

"Meryl?" the sheriff probed.

She took a deep raspy breath and started shaking her head. She reached for cigarettes and a lighter on the coffee table and lit one, blowing smoke to the side. "Yeah, he was there earlier. They were going it at it again."

"And why didn't you say anything about this?" Alex asked, the anger in his voice clear.

She looked away out the front window of the house, then said, "I don't know. It was a terrible night. I thought I'd told you everything. I did see Skipper earlier at the *LuLu Belle* after the fight at *Gilly's.* He was as drunk as Horton and they were pushing each other around again. I got Skipper out of there, but he must have come back later. I couldn't get Horton to come home with me. He wanted to sleep it off on the boat."

Stokes said, "Meryl, you didn't tell us this."

"I'm sorry," she said, tears starting to well up in her eyes. Then, a look of anger came across her face and she looked straight at Alex. "Your old man killed my husband! He came back and killed Horton!"

Chapter Forty-six

Hanna was beginning to doubt her sanity. Maybe it was stress or lack of sleep, but two encounters with the ghost of her great-grandmother was more than she could get her head around.

Jonathan and Elizabeth had gone for a walk on the beach. Hanna was making a salad with local shrimp for dinner. She was tempted to open a bottle of wine but poured a glass of iced tea instead. If it wasn't ghosts, she couldn't stop thinking about Alex Frank. She knew in her heart she had to move on and put all of that behind her, another lesson in commitments gone bad.

Hanna heard her house guests coming in from the beach. *Enough about ghosts and old boyfriends!*

During dinner around the big dining room table, Jonathan said, "Elizabeth and I need to head back first thing in the morning."

Hanna looked up, disappointed. "I thought you were able to go back Monday morning."

"I'm sorry, Hanna," Elizabeth said. "I got a call from work and they need me to take a shift tomorrow afternoon."

"Of course," Hanna said, trying to mask her feelings. The thought of being alone again in the big beach house was not appealing. She was thinking about heading back to Charleston early, too, to get back on her caseload when Jonathan stood to start clearing the dishes.

"Any more visits from the ghost of Amanda?" Jonathan asked.

Hanna frowned. "I think I need a good night's sleep. I truly think I'm starting to lose my mind with all that's going on with your grandfather and the cases we've been handling."

"And Alex Frank," Jonathan added. She had told him about the breakup. She nodded.

Jonathan said, "I like Alex a lot too, Mom, but sounds like there's just too much baggage there. You'll meet someone new... a catch like you!"

"Yeah, right."

After dinner, Hanna left the others back at the house to take a walk on the beach and watch the sunset. A cool wind from the east had kicked up and the waves had grown through the evening, now crashing loudly along the shoreline. She looked up when she noticed a sailboat making its way south in the rough water, sails down under power about a quarter mile out. The big boat rose and fell slowly in the long swells of the ocean.

The boat's slow progress up the face of one wave and then fast rush down the other side reminded her of the old adage about a *"following sea"*. In a gentler wind, a boat's progress downwind can be a calm and enjoyable ride, but as the wind builds and the waves grow, the same downwind tack can be the most dangerous course of all as large following waves can threaten to turn and sink even the most skilled sailor.

She watched the boat make its way precariously on through the growing seas, silently wishing them a safe return to port.

Chapter Forty-seven

Meryl Bayes was working on a flower box on the front of their house in Dugganville. Alex saw her back turned to him as he parked his car and got out. Meryl was a stout woman, nearing sixty. She was dressed in loose faded jeans and a torn Atlanta Falcons t-shirt. She had made no effort to hide the gray in her hair. When his car door closed, she turned and saw him coming up the walk.

Her face was flushed and sweaty from the work. She wiped at her forehead with the back of her arm. "Don't have nothin' more to say to the cops," she said with a gravelly voice.

"Just need a minute, Meryl." Alex said, standing now a few feet from the woman. "Sheriff Stokes says you're telling the DEA you knew nothing about Horton and your son running drugs."

"Get out of here," she hissed.

"Hard to believe your boat could be running drugs and you knew nothing about it."

She took her dirty work gloves off and threw them in a garden cart next to the house. "Like I told them cops earlier, my boys had nothing to do with those damn drugs. It's your friend, Chaz Merton, got my son mixed up in this last night. They were supposed to be runnin' shrimp."

Alex said, "Meryl, I hear Horton wasn't making a go of it shrimping and needed to find a way to make some extra money."

"Who told you that damned lie? Your old man?"

She started to walk away, muttering under her breath.

"Meryl, wait," he said, following after her. "There's something else that

I've been having a problem with."

She climbed the first step to the front door, then turned to face him.

Alex continued, "The night of Horton's murder, you say you went down to the boat and found my father and Horton getting into a fight again."

"That's right, they were really goin' at it."

"So, how'd you get between two big men like that and get them apart, get my dad to leave?"

Meryl hesitated and looked away.

Alex said, "Two men trying to kill each other, and you break it up?"

She looked back at Alex. "Those two were so drunk, I could have knocked 'em both over. I just kept yellin' and pushin' til they backed off."

"Do you remember seeing my dad's knife in the scabbard on his belt when he left?"

She seemed confused and just stared back at him.

"Meryl, the knife?" Alex insisted.

"It was dark, I don't remember," she said.

When Alex pulled down the long drive to Connor Richards' house, he saw the man getting into his car to leave. Alex pulled in behind the car, so he couldn't back up. Richards got out with an angry scowl across his face.

"What the hell you doin?" he said, slamming the door to the red Porsche and coming at Alex as he got out of his car.

"Just need a minute, Connor."

"Later, man," he said. "I'm late."

"Well, you're gonna be a little more late," Alex said. He turned when he saw Lily Johannsen coming out the front door of the house. She seemed surprised and a bit concerned to see Alex.

"Lily," Alex acknowledged.

She nodded back and came up beside Connor and took his arm.

Alex said, "You two hear about the drug arrests outside the bay last night?"

"Whole town's talking about it," Connor said.

Lily wouldn't make eye contact and stood silent.

Alex asked, "Thought you might have seen something while you were out on your boat last night."

Connor didn't hesitate. "We were just out for a sunset cruise and a few cocktails."

"Right," Alex answered and stared back at the man.

An awkward silence dragged on before Connor said, "Didn't see a thing. Must have been back before the bust went down."

Alex said, "Heard some Mexican Cartel might be running this operation. That's a dangerous bunch. You heard anything about that?"

Lily seemed to go pale and her feet shifted nervously. She looked away as Connor answered, "Lots of rumors going around."

"You ever hear about Horton Bayes tied up with these guys?" Alex asked.

Connor shook his head and pursed his lips, seeming to think about the question.

Alex said, "You let me know if you hear anything."

Connor nodded but didn't answer.

Alex looked over at Connor's girlfriend. "Nice to see you again, Lily. You hear of anything, call me, okay?"

She nodded back but didn't answer.

Alex was in the sheriff's office and watched as the man hung up the phone on his desk. Stokes said, "Feds won't let us near Merton or the Bayes boy yet. Say they haven't finished their interrogation."

"Who are they holding from the delivery boat?" Alex asked.

"Three Cubans, boat registered out of the Yucatan."

Alex said, "I'm gonna have my old man's lawyer file a motion to get us in to talk to these guys."

"Pretty thin narrative," the old sheriff said, "trying to link this drug deal to Bayes' murder."

"We need to track this down, Pepper."

He knew he should have gone back to his father's house, but he had no interest in running into Adrienne again. He wanted to give her as much time as possible to leave. Instead, Alex had gone down to *Gilly's* to order some dinner and have a beer. One had turned to three as he sat at the bar and talked to a couple of locals about drug runners along the Atlantic coast. He didn't learn much more but confirmed there had been stories of a new drug ring running marijuana all along the coast.

He was talking now to an old fishing guide, Billy James, who was a friend of the family. The man had nothing more on the drug ring that Alex hadn't heard. Alex asked, "You ever hear about Horton runnin' with these guys?"

"Runnin' weed?" the old man asked.

Alex nodded and took a drink from the last of his beer.

Billy shook his head. "No, can't ever remember Horton doing much more than chasin' shrimp and women."

"Women?" Alex asked, surprised.

Billy laughed. "That old bastard was gettin' more on the side than anybody I ever seen."

"Horton Bayes?" Alex asked, incredulous.

"Must be a lot of lonely women round these parts," the old guide said, and then finished his beer and got up to leave. "Sorry 'bout your old man, Alex."

Gilly walked up and grabbed his empty beer bottle. "Another?" he asked.

Alex said, "No, I need to get going." Gilly brought over his bill and Alex left some cash on the bar.

He walked down the steps into the cooling evening, palm fronds along the front of the place rustling in a heavy wind from the east. A sliver of moon was just over the treetops. His car was parked at the back of the lot by the river. His thoughts were spinning between Mexican drug runners, Connor Richards and Horton Bayes and how they may be part of it all.

He looked over when he heard a vehicle with a low throaty engine pull into the parking area. It was a late model pick-up truck that obviously needed a new muffler. The passenger side window was rolled down. Alex saw the gun and it took just a moment too long to register it was aimed at him. The first shot struck him in the left shoulder and he felt a searing heat that knocked him back and to one knee. He managed to keep moving in a roll away from the truck when the second shot spit into the gravel a few inches from his head. He kept rolling under a parked truck, trying to put the intense pain in

202

his arm aside. He heard two more shots explode and hit the dirt next to the truck as he rolled out the other side and forced himself to stand.

He reached for his 9mm Ruger service pistol on the clip on his belt. His head was swimming with the pain in his arm and the adrenaline racing through him. The loud roar of the other truck's engine cut through the night as it accelerated to speed away. Alex forced himself around the truck he was using for cover but couldn't see the license plate as it sped out of the parking lot and fishtailed away down the street.

Alex felt lightheaded and sank to the ground, leaning back against the wheel of the truck. He heard voices and then saw Gilly kneeling in front of him. He heard the man say, "Alex, you okay? We heard the gunshots!"

He couldn't answer and winced as Gilly pushed back the bloody sleeve of his shirt.

Gilly yelled out, "Somebody call 911!"

Chapter Forty-eight

Hanna woke on Sunday morning to the sound of gulls hovering over the beach in front of the house. She pushed the covers back and rubbed her eyes in the bright sunlight coming in the windows. She sat up and looked for her slippers on the wood floor. Her phone buzzed on the nightstand. She saw it was just past 8:30. She also saw it was Phillip Holloway calling. Reluctantly, she accepted the call.

"Good morning, Phillip."

Oh, Hanna," the lawyer said. "Glad I caught you."

"What is it?

Phillip said, "Just talked to Alex. He's okay but...

Hanna cut in, "What are you talking about?"

"He's going to be okay, Hanna, but Alex was shot last night up in Dugganville."

She felt a sick wave in her stomach. "He was shot?"

"He's in the hospital up there. Took one shot in his shoulder. Apparently, someone fired several more rounds that missed."

"Who was it?" she asked, the panic in her voice rising.

"Driver and a shooter in an old truck," Phillip answered. "They got away and Alex didn't get a plate number."

"Oh my god!" Hanna said, stunned.

"Alex says he's feeling okay and will probably be released later this morning, so there's no danger."

"Okay," Hanna said tentatively. "What's going on, Phillip?"

"Alex told me he's been asking a lot of questions about a drug ring that's been running in the waters up there."

"And they tried to kill him?"

"Someone did."

"Did Alex ask you to call me?" she asked.

"No, just thought you should know."

Hanna ended the call with Holloway, thanking him for filling her in. Of course, he offered to come up to the island to be with her if she was too upset. She managed to graciously decline the offer.

She went down to the kitchen to put some coffee on. While she waited, she fought the urge to call Alex to check on his condition. She wasn't sure she wanted to open the whole situation with him again. She was terrified at the thought someone had tried to kill him, but it sounded like his wounds weren't serious.

Her thoughts were interrupted when Jonathan walked in, his hair mussed and his face puffy from sleep. He pulled the coffee pot out and poured a cup even though it had barely started to brew. He sat down at a stool across the counter from his mother.

Hanna told him about the attempt on Alex's life.

Jonathan was as stunned as Hanna. He said, "What's he got himself into down there?"

Hanna just shook her head.

"You're sure he's going to be okay?" Jonathan asked.

"Apparently. I'm just not sure I should call. We've managed to put this behind us and I don't feel like opening it all up again."

Jonathan sipped at the hot coffee and nodded. "You know what's best. I'm sure Phillip will keep you informed."

Hanna scoffed, "Oh, I'm sure of that!"

Jonathan and Elizabeth left to return to Chapel Hill just after ten. Hanna gave them both a warm hug before they loaded up and pulled down the drive to leave. She decided to get back to Charleston to get some work done at the clinic before the craziness of a new week began tomorrow.

As she was packing, she called her father in Atlanta. He was still in recovery but feeling stronger.

"My partner came by to see me last night," Allen Moss said.

"Really?" Hanna said, surprised. "How nice of him."

"Wasn't just a social call," her father continued. "He's more than concerned about you coming in to the firm."

"What did you tell him?"

"I told him the Moss family was going to stay closely involved with the leadership of Moss Kramer, one way or the other."

Hanna said, "Let's just leave that as an option to keep him thinking. You sure you're feeling better?"

"The doctor thinks I can go home in a day or two. I'll need a full-time nurse at the house. Maybe a couple weeks 'til I'm up and about again."

"You take it easy, Allen," she scolded.

"I'm going crazy sitting in this room with doctors and nurses constantly buzzing around."

"They need to be buzzing around, Allen. You're sick!"

"I'm feeling much better," he said. "No need for all this fuss."

"Just do what the doctor says."

He didn't respond for a moment, then spoke with a weakness returning to his voice. "This transplant is scaring the crap out of me, daughter."

Hanna was surprised to hear her father admit to any sign of fear. It was so unlike him. "They know what's best, Allen."

"I feel fine. This old ticker's gotten me this far. Don't see any reason to trade it in at this point."

Hanna sighed. "One step at a time here, Allen, okay?"

On the way back to Charleston, Hanna called Alex's partner, Lonnie Smith. The detective had already spoken to Alex and confirmed he was out of danger and would be checking out of the hospital before noon. She had asked if Lonnie could meet later in the day to discuss the Moe Hall investigation. She wanted an update before going to see Greta at the clinic and check on the son, William.

Lonnie told her he was hosting a barbecue for friends at their house but insisted she come by to join them for burgers and a beer. He could fill her in on the latest on Moe Hall. She let her phone GPS guide her to the Smith house on the north side of Charleston. It was a beautiful old neighborhood sheltered with tall trees. Most of the homes had been updated and nicely landscaped with colorful shrubs and flowers.

Hanna found an open parking space on the street and walked up the drive, the sounds of laughter and music coming from behind the house. She came around and saw several children playing on a swing-set at the back of the fenced yard. Three couples were up on the deck, standing and sitting, drinks in their hands. Lonnie saw her and reached for his wife's arm to bring her over to meet Hanna.

"I'm sorry to interrupt your Sunday," Hanna said, genuinely upset for bringing work to his Sunday and his family and friends.

"It's not a problem, Hanna," Lonnie said in his deep voice. "Meet my wife, Ginny."

The two women shook hands. Ginny said, "We're glad you could join us. We were really concerned about Alex, but it sounds like he's going to be alright.

Hanna nodded and turned when Lonnie said, "Not sure what he's got himself in the middle of up there."

Hanna said, "Sounds like some very rough characters with this drug business." She felt a cold dread again as she thought about the men trying to kill Alex last night.

"Alex knows how to take care of himself," Lonnie said. "I may have to go up there for a little back-up. We'll see."

The Smiths took Hanna over to introduce her to the other guests, neighbors and friends from next door and across the street. Lonnie got Hanna a cold beer from a cooler on the deck and then said, "Let's get business out of the way." He led her away to a quiet shady spot on the back lawn.

Lonnie started, "I didn't want to say anything on the phone because I was waiting on a callback to confirm, but Moe Hall was spotted in Charleston last night. We have an informant who knows him and called it in."

Hanna felt her spirits lift. "Where is he?"

"We're following up on a couple of possibilities."

"Has anyone warned Greta down at the clinic?" Hanna asked. "I wouldn't want that man trying to go back for his son."

"I called her personally," Lonnie said. "She's got my number and the precinct number she can call if he shows up."

"Thank you," Hanna said, somewhat relieved.

Lonnie took a drink from his beer, then got a concerned look on his face. "Really sorry to hear about you and Alex. Thought you two were great together."

"You know about Adrienne and the boy?" she asked.

He nodded.

"Not much room for me in that little scenario," she said.

"Alex will do what's right."

"I know, that's why I don't want to be a distraction."

"You're not a distraction, Hanna," he said. "Alex is crazy about you. I haven't seen him like this before."

Hanna just shook her head. "Bad timing, Lonnie."

"Give it some time, Hanna. Alex will work this out."

Chapter Forty-nine

As Alex signed the release papers to leave the hospital on Sunday afternoon, he thought back to the first time he had been shot on duty. The bullet hole scar on the left side of his stomach was a continuing reminder of the dangers of police work. He had been investigating a homicide in Charleston five years earlier. He and his partner, Lonnie Smith, had tracked down a suspect to a boxing gym on the west side of town. They both saw the suspect run out the back of the building when they came in. Alex went after the man and Lonnie went out the front to try to head him off from the other direction.

When Alex opened the back door leading into an alley, he looked both ways and didn't see or hear the man running. He cautiously moved along the side of old brick building, his senses on high alert and his service pistol out and ready. He saw the man suddenly lurch out from behind a dumpster just ten feet away. He also saw the gun in his hand and started to yell to drop the weapon when the gun fired, hitting Alex in the lower abdomen. He went down immediately, intense pain and shock overcoming him. The rest of the incident was a blur of shouting and more gunshots as his partner came into the alley, fired back at the assailant and then found Alex as the shooter ran away in the other direction.

The wound had not been life-threatening, but it had been a long and arduous journey for Alex in recovery. He continued to condemn himself for allowing it to happen and for the suspect to escape. The man was arrested later in the day and eventually convicted for homicide and for the assault on a police officer. It hadn't helped Alex cope with the incident and he continued to have doubts and occasional nightmares about the day in the alley.

The shooting the previous night in *Gilly's* parking lot brought back all the old doubts and fears. Alex's shoulder would be fine, the bullet not damaging bones or the joint, but emotionally, he was reliving all the haunting memories of the first incident.

He was also struggling to work through who was behind the attack. *Who had he pissed-off enough to want him dead?*

Sheriff Pepper Stokes was waiting for him in his car at the curb outside the hospital. The old sheriff had been by to see him earlier and get his statement about the attack. Alex was pushed to the curb in a wheelchair by one of the nurses who had been attending to him. He stood and thanked her and then climbed slowly into Stokes' patrol car. His left arm was held securely in a tight sling, but the pain wasn't entirely masked by the drugs the doctor had prescribed.

"You need to learn to duck, Alex," the sheriff said beside him.

"Not funny, Pepper. You got anything on the truck and who was trying to take me out?"

The sheriff handed him a booking photo of a forty-something male with close-cropped gray hair, a scruffy beard and a snake tattoo showing on his neck above the shirt-line. "This guy look familiar?"

Alex studied the face for a moment. "No, don't think I've seen him before. Who is it?"

"Local "bad guy" named Hank Jameson, usually mixed up in the worst that goes on around here. Surprised he's out of jail right now. He has a truck that matches the description you gave us... late model, loud pipes."

"Where is he?"

"Got the boys out looking for him," the sheriff said.

Alex handed the photo back. "Who does he normally work for?"

"Anybody who needs nasty work done. He's already done time for armed robbery and manslaughter and avoided conviction on another murder charge. Seriously bad dude."

Alex asked, "You ever connect him with the Richards?"

"Beau and Connor?" the sheriff replied, seemingly surprised.

"Seems just a little too coincidental, I confront Connor about the drug deal out on the bay and a couple hours later someone's trying to put my lights out."

"That's a pretty serious charge, Alex."

"There were two of them in the truck, Pepper, as I told you. The shooter was on the passenger side."

"We know. Jameson has several other "friends" we're also looking for."

Alex said, "You and I need to go talk to Connor Richards again."

The sheriff hesitated, then said, "Alex, we can't go off accusing one of the county's most prominent families with attempted murder and drug trafficking without some real evidence."

"Pepper, I'm telling you, Connor Richards is dirty in this. I'm sure of it."

"Alex..."

"And I wouldn't be at all surprised if Beau is running the whole operation."

The sheriff started the car to drive away, then said, "Alex, you do what you think you need to do, but I'm not getting the Department out there harassing a family that's responsible for ninety percent of the economy around here without any real proof."

Alex stared back, concerned the Sheriff's Department wasn't going to take a more proactive approach to tracking this down. "Just take me back to my car, Pepper. I assume it's still down at *Gilly's*."

Alex pulled up to the gate at Beau Richards ranch and pushed the button for the intercom speaker. A few moments later, a voice he didn't recognize said, "Who's there, please?"

"It's Detective Alex Frank. I'm here to see Beau."

"A moment please," the voice said.

A minute later, Alex heard the motor engage and the gate start to swing open. The voice on the intercom said, "Please come up to the house."

Alex drove half way up the long drive-way and then stopped for a moment to check on his gun. He ejected the magazine and confirmed it was fully loaded with 9mm shells. He slammed it back into the pistol and placed it in the clip on his belt.

No one was waiting to greet him when he pulled up the circle around the front of the big house. He went up the stairs and rang the doorbell. An older man he didn't recognize, who must have been one of the servants, opened the door and said, "Good afternoon. Mr. Richards is out by the pool. I'll take you back."

Alex followed the man through the opulent rooms that led to the back of the house. He saw the large pool and outbuildings through several windows. The servant opened a set of French doors and held it for Alex to go out onto the back veranda and down the steps to the pool. He saw Beau Richards reclined on a deeply stuffed chair and ottoman and his wife, Amelia, on the chair beside him, deeply tanned and sunbathing in a revealing orange bikini. She didn't make any effort to cover herself as Alex walked up.

Beau Richards stood with a concerned look on his face and came up to meet Alex. "How you doing, Alex? Heard about the attack last night."

Alex ignored the man's offered hand to shake. "We need to talk, Beau."

Richards didn't appear to be miffed by the slight and just smiled back. "What can I do for you?"

Alex looked over at Amelia Richards and said, "Could we have a few minutes, ma'am?"

She stood slowly and reached for a short robe on the chair behind her. She said, "Sunday's no time for business, Detective."

"Won't be long," Alex said. He watched as she pulled on the robe and stepped into a pair of sandals before she walked away into the house.

"Get you something to drink, Alex?" Beau offered.

"No, I'm fine."

"You don't look fine, son," Beau said, looking at the sling around Alex's arm and shoulder. "What the hell happened?"

"Can we sit, please?" Alex asked, still a bit groggy and weak from the wound and drugs he'd been given.

Richards led them over to stools at a long covered bar area. Alex took one of the seats and watched as Beau walked around the back of the bar and poured some whiskey over a glass of ice." He said, "What's so important we need to interrupt this beautiful Sunday afternoon?"

"You tell me, Beau," Alex threatened. "I start sniffing around a drug deal out on the salt and talk to your son about why he was out there in the same area that night. Next thing I know, someone's trying to take my head off."

Richards put the drink down. "That's a pretty serious accusation, Alex."

Alex just stared back at the man and didn't respond.

"Why do you think Connor had anything to do with this?" Beau asked in a low challenging voice, all the hospitality in his demeanor clearly gone.

"Sounds like some serious drug traffic coming in around here, maybe the Mexican cartels involved. A lot of money. You follow the money, Beau," Alex said, looking out across the vast estate.

"You accusing me?" the man hissed.

Again, Alex didn't answer. He watched as Beau sipped at his drink and obviously tried to gather himself. He finally smiled back and said, "Alex, I'd be asking a lot of questions, too, if someone started taking shots at me, but you're way off base here. We run legitimate businesses, real estate, wholesale and retail seafood, investments, insurance. We're an open book, Alex."

Alex stood and said, "Looks like Horton Bayes was in on the drugs, too, Beau. You do much business with Horton before he was killed?"

"Is that what this is all about?" Beau asked.

"You didn't answer my question."

"We've been buying shrimp from Bayes for years, that's it."

"Right," Alex said. "My next stop is Connor's house. I'm sure you'll call to let him know I'm on the way."

Chapter Fifty

Hanna unlocked the door to her legal clinic offices in downtown Charleston and went up the back steps to her apartment on the second floor. She put her bags in the bedroom and went to the kitchen to get something to drink. She saw a half-full pitcher of iced tea and poured a glass over ice. She sat at the counter and looked through the mail that had been collected for her on the receptionist's desk, sorting bills, flyers and junk mail.

She pushed it all aside and looked at her phone on the counter in front of her. She resisted the urge to call Alex and check on his condition. She was certain once she re-opened that line of communication, she'd have to deal all over again with the situation with the ex-wife and son. *Not again!*

She did look at her messages and saw a text from her son. They had arrived safely back in Chapel Hill and he thanked her again for the weekend at the beach. The thought of her son and his great new girlfriend brightened her mood.

She went back down to her office and started in on the work that had been piling up. Soon, it was growing dark outside and she sighed when she realized she'd made barely a dent in what needed to be done by tomorrow.

A noise at the backdoor to the building sounded out of place and Hanna looked up with alarm. She listened and again heard something out in the back of the house. She reached for her purse and found her keys. A small key unlocked a bottom drawer of her desk. She pulled out a locked metal box and with hands shaking, found the key to open that as well. A small black handgun rested on the foam bottom of the box. Her late husband, Ben, had insisted she keep the weapon at the clinic. She was trained in handgun use and occasionally took the gun to a local shooting range to stay familiar with how to use it.

The silence was broken by the sound of glass breaking and Hanna gasped, standing quickly and reaching for the gun. She also grabbed her cellphone and managed to punch in 911 before she heard the back-door lock click and the door squeak open. She quickly whispered her name and location to the 911 operator and reported the unknown entry at the back of her house and offices.

Hanna knelt behind her desk as she heard footsteps coming down the hall toward her open office door. She held the gun in both hands as she'd been trained and took a deep breath to control her shaking hands.

She was not surprised to see the hooded face of Moe Hall as he came around and stood in the doorway.

He was startled and stepped back when he saw her and the gun. "Whoa!" he said, holding up both arms in the dirty gray sweatshirt, but he didn't back any further away.

"The police are on their way!" Hanna shouted.

"Calm down, lady," Hall said, regaining some confidence and starting to walk into the office. "I just want to talk."

"I *will* shoot you!" she yelled again.

This stopped him about ten feet from the other side of the desk.

"You need to turn yourself in," Hanna said. "The police will be here any minute."

Hanna could see his face turn grim and angry. "If you hadn't messed everything up, Jenna would still be here, and we'd be with our son."

"You killed her, Moe. You need to turn yourself in. It will go better for you if you turn yourself in."

The sound of a siren in the distance could be heard and Moe Hall looked back toward the open door for a moment. When he turned back to her, Hanna was stunned at the fury of his expression. "You stupid bitch!"

He started toward the desk.

"Moe, I *will* shoot you!" She stood now and held the gun out with both hands in firing position, aimed directly at his chest.

He kept coming and was now just a few feet from the chairs across her desk.

"Moe, stop now!" she screamed.

She watched as he reached into his back pocket and his hand came up with a long switchblade knife that he flicked open. "I should have carved you up a long time ago," he said in a low, angry voice.

He was only two feet from the side of the desk when he lunged. She pulled the trigger three times in rapid succession. The sound of the gunshots echoed through the room and she watched as the bullets all struck Moe Hall in the chest and threw him backward, stumbling to the floor.

Her heart was racing and her temples pounding. She suddenly thought she would vomit, but she kept the gun trained on the fallen man. The sounds of the siren grew closer and then she heard shouts out in the hallway.

"Police officers!" someone shouted. "Put all weapons on the ground and hands in the air.

Hanna saw a uniformed Charleston policeman peak around the corner of the office, his revolver held out in front of him. She placed her gun on the desk and raised her arms. "My name is Hanna Walsh!" she said, trying to calm her panic. "I'm an attorney. This man came at me with a knife."

The policeman came into the office, his gun aimed at Hanna. He saw Moe Hall lying on the floor, the blood from the gunshots evident on his sweatshirt and pooling on the floor beside him. Hanna noticed the man had a distant stare in his eyes and he wasn't moving.

Moe Hall was pronounced dead at the scene a short time after the first medical response unit arrived. Hanna had been taken to the lobby area of the office and was sitting in one of the chairs along the wall being questioned by a female police officer beside her. The officer had just told her of Hall's death. Hanna was shaking despite the blanket a paramedic had wrapped around her shoulders.

All of the police present seemed to be sympathetic to her story, particularly after they found the knife next to Moe Hall's body.

Hanna looked up when Lonnie Smith came into the room through the front door. He came right over and sat beside her, putting a gentle hand on her shoulder.

"Hanna, I got the call right after they learned it was you involved in the shooting," Lonnie said.

Hanna turned and fell into the man, wrapping her arms around him, the blanket falling from her shoulders. She had tried to keep her composure since the police had arrived, but the news of her attacker's death had sent her over the edge. She whispered to Lonnie, "I didn't have any choice. I warned him, and he kept coming. He had a knife!"

"We know, Hanna. You did the right thing."

Chapter Fifty-one

Alex stopped his car in the drive of Connor Richards' house. All the lights were out and there was no sign of a car. On a hunch, he looked for the number of the private air terminal at the county airport. He knew the Richards had a private jet they kept there.

The woman who took the call would not answer Alex's question about whether Connor Richards had left on the plane, but it was clear from her response the plane had recently departed. He pressed her, giving her his Charleston PD badge number. Reluctantly, she told him Connor and Lily Johannsen had left about an hour ago with two pilots. Their reported destination was Nassau in the Bahamas.

Alex was driving back into town to his father's house. He pushed the contact number for Sheriff Stokes and filled him in on his encounter with Beau Richards and the sudden departure of the man's son with his girlfriend.

"Maybe they're off on a damn vacation!" the sheriff said, seeming miffed at the call on a Sunday night.

"This wasn't a planned trip, Pepper," Alex said. "The pilots were brought in last minute for the flight, according to the woman at the hangar." There was no response. "You need to get a warrant in the morning for us to search Connor's house and office," Alex insisted.

"Be in my office at eight," Stokes said.

"I'd also suggest you have someone keep an eye on Beau Richards before he tries to get out of the country."

Alex was just walking into the house when his phone rang. It was his partner, Lonnie, calling. He pressed the button to accept the call.

"What's up, Lonnie?"

"She's okay, Alex, but Hanna was involved in a shooting tonight."

Before he could continue, Alex jumped in urgently, "A shooting? What the hell happened?"

Alex listened as Lonnie Smith filled him in on the details of Moe Hall's assault on Hanna. He couldn't believe what he was hearing and was both stunned and thankful that Hanna had the presence to confront the man and defend herself. "You're sure she's okay?"

"We're on the way down to the precinct to file the formal report," Lonnie said. "She's real shook up, as you can imagine."

"Can I talk to her?" Alex asked.

"She's in another patrol car. I'll tell her we talked when I get downtown."

Alex was reeling as his partner continued to share details of the attack and the fatal gunshots from Hanna Walsh that killed the man.

He ended the call and sat on one of the porch chairs, collecting himself and thinking through all that was happening, not only with the Richards and his father's murder investigation, but now with Hanna.

He pushed the contact for Hanna's cell phone. It rang five times and then went to voicemail. At the tone, he said, "Hanna, Lonnie called. I just want to check on how you're doing and if I can help with anything. Call me!"

Alex woke the next morning when he heard a loud commercial truck going by in front of the house. He looked at his phone and saw it was just past seven. He checked for messages and saw a voicemail from Sheriff Stokes but nothing from Hanna. He pressed the link to the sheriff's message.

"Alex, it's Pepper. Got a call from the DEA office first thing this morning. They're gonna let us talk to Chaz and little Horton. You want to drive down to Charleston with me this morning? Give me a call."

On their drive into Charleston, Alex learned from the sheriff that he had a deputy monitoring the movements of Beau Richards. He had also confirmed the flight plan of Connor to the Bahamas and that it was a hastily organized flight. He was waiting to hear back from a judge on a warrant to start searching Connor Richards's home and office.

Chaz Merton was brought in to the interrogation room at the DEA offices in Charleston. He was dressed in an orange jumpsuit with a number stenciled on the left chest. His hair was matted and in disarray and he clearly hadn't shaved in days. Merton seemed surprised when he saw Alex and Sheriff Stokes. He was accompanied by a woman who was introduced as his attorney.

"Morning Chaz," Alex said as the prisoner sat down across from them. The agent who brought Merton in left and closed the door. A mirror on the wall was actually a one-way window from the adjoining room where two DEA agents on the drug bust case were monitoring the discussion.

Merton just nodded and looked back at both men.

The sheriff said, "The Feds here tell us you've agreed to cooperate in the investigation of this drug ring."

"That's right," Merton said in a low, weak voice. He looked like he hadn't slept.

Alex said, "Chaz, how long you been involved in all this?"

Merton looked at his lawyer and she nodded. "Couple years," he answered.

"What about the Bayes family?"

The man hesitated a moment, then said, "Had little Horton out with me. He's made a few runs with us over the years, but he's been away at school mostly."

"What about his old man?" the sheriff asked.

Merton shook his head in the affirmative. "Horton's been doing runs as long as I've been out there."

Alex continued, "What role do the Richards have in all this?"

The prisoner looked over again at his attorney and then whispered something in her ear. She quietly conferred with him for a moment. Finally, Merton said, "Beau and Connor been runnin' this deal from the beginning. Connor sometimes even takes deliveries on his own sailboat or the "go fast" boat.

CHAPTER FIFTY-ONE

Alex wasn't surprised. He asked, "And there's a Mexican cartel involved?"

"Don't know for sure who's on the other end, but definitely some Mexicans and Cubans been bringin' the loads in."

Alex asked, "Horton ever tell you he was thinking about getting out of the deal?"

Merton hesitated a moment in thought, then said, "Last week, I know Horton and Connor were having a beef about something the morning after we brought in one of the loads. I figured Horton was unhappy about his cut in the deal."

"You didn't hear anything else?" the sheriff asked.

Merton shook his head *"no"*.

Alex leaned in over the table. "How much was Meryl Bayes involved in all this?"

Merton pursed his lips, considering his answer. "She's never been out on the salt with us, but she damn sure knows about the money. I've heard Horton bitchin' about her hidin' it all away for the future when he needed some repairs done on the boat."

Alex said, "Chaz, you think anybody involved in running this weed operation had any reason to want Horton Bayes dead?"

Merton looked back with an empty stare. He scratched at his unruly beard and then looked at his lawyer. She said something in private to him, then he said, "Horton's a damn unlikeable old cuss. Pissed a lot of people off, not just your old man."

Chapter Fifty-two

Hanna called her son, Jonathan, the previous night from the police station before she gave her formal statement. She wanted him to know what had happened and that she was okay, in case he heard something on the news. He had insisted on driving down to be with her and met her at the apartment early the next morning.

Jonathan was sleeping in the second bedroom when she woke and went into the kitchen to make coffee. She had slept little the previous night. The images persisted of Moe Hall coming at her with a knife and then the gun going off in her hands, the man lying on the floor of her office dying.

Hanna had also been thinking about Moe and Jenna Hall's young son, William. The boy was all alone now. She had called Greta at the clinic last night to let her know about the death of Moe Hall. Greta had assured her she would continue to take care of the boy.

She saw her phone on the counter next to her coffee cup and thought about the message from Alex Frank she received down at the police precinct. His call and concern had been comforting at the time, but she couldn't bring herself to call him back.

Jonathan came into the kitchen and walked over to give her a hug.

"How are you doing?" he asked, with obvious concern in his voice.

"Not great," she said, honestly.

He poured some coffee and sat beside her at the counter. "I just spoke with Elizabeth and she sends her best and hopes you're doing okay."

"That's sweet, thank you." Hanna was thankful her son had come down to be with her. She needed someone near.

Hanna walked down the back stairs to her offices on the first floor of the old house. Her own office was still closed off with yellow crime scene tape from the night before. She consulted with two police investigators and they agreed to let her get some files from her desk she needed to work on this morning. She wanted to be there when her staff came in to work to explain what had happened. In her office, she tried not to look at the blood stains on the carpet as she passed to her desk.

By mid-morning, she was deep into the flow of work again and thankfully, it helped her to put some of the past night's memories out of her mind. She was sitting at a desk in one of the extra offices when her assistant, Molly, stuck her head in the door.

"Detective Frank is here to see you," she said quietly, a confused and cautious look on her face.

Hanna was at once upset and then begrudgingly pleased to hear Alex had come to see her. She tried to push her anger and doubt about Alex's renewed entanglement with his ex-wife from her mind. "Tell him I'll be out in a moment." Molly disappeared from the door.

Her next thought was she must look a mess after a sleepless night and all that had happened. *Not much to be done about that now.*

When Hanna walked out into the reception area, she saw Alex waiting for her, standing by the front window. He smiled and started to walk toward her. She noticed Molly staring at her from behind her desk. As Alex came up, he opened his one arm that wasn't in a sling and took her in a tight embrace.

He said softly in her ear, "I'm so glad to see you're okay."

Hanna pushed back and returned a tentative smile. "Thanks for coming."

"Do you have a few minutes?" he asked.

"Let's take a walk." She turned to Molly, "We'll be back."

She led him down the steps and then waited for him to join her on the sidewalk under the shade of tall trees and the rush of traffic along the busy street. They walked for over a block without speaking.

Finally, Alex said, "Lonnie filled me in on what happened last night. It must have been terrible."

"I still have a sick feeling in my gut. I know I did the right thing, but..."

"You had to defend yourself."

"I know."

Alex said, "You need to find some comfort in knowing he won't be able to hurt anyone else again."

Hanna didn't respond, and they continued down the walk past other houses and then storefronts at the end of the block.

"Seven years ago," Alex said, "I had to use my weapon in an arrest and the man later died. It's going to take a long time to get beyond the guilt of taking someone's life, no matter how bad or evil the person is."

"That's reassuring," Hanna said sarcastically.

"Just know this will take time. I saw the department shrink for two years."

Hanna looked over at him, surprised.

Alex continued, "There's no shame in getting help for something like this, from friends and family and from professionals when you need it."

Hanna said, "I'm feeling worst about their little boy. He has no one now."

"He certainly didn't need the father in his life."

"Right." Hanna paused, then said, "My friend down at the clinic will help him find the right home, I'm sure. I'm going down to see her later today to see what I can do to help."

They stopped for a cup of coffee at a small shop on the corner with windows out to the busy intersection. Sitting at a small table at the front, Alex said, "I want to talk to you about what's going on up in Dugganville, if you're up to it."

"Okay," Hanna replied hesitantly, swirling the coffee in her cup.

"First, has Phillip told you about the developments in my father's case?" She shook her head *"no"*.

Alex went through all the details of the drug bust and the involvement of the Bayes family with a dangerous drug cartel, the flight of Connor Richards and Chaz Merton's cooperation with the investigators.

Hanna asked a couple of questions as he proceeded. He continued on about the revelation of Horton Bayes' infidelity and Hanna raised an eyebrow.

CHAPTER FIFTY-TWO

"What more have you learned about that?"

"I'm headed back this afternoon to talk with Meryl Bayes again."

Hanna asked, "What does Phillip think about all this?"

"We're following up on every possibility."

"Your father has to be feeling a little better with these new developments," she said.

"He's still not remembering all the events of that night and we've got a lot of work to do to prove he didn't kill Horton."

They both sipped at their coffee, then Alex continued, "I want you to know what's really going on with Adrienne... and my son, if you'll give me a minute."

"Alex..." Hanna started to protest, pushing back her chair.

"Please, just a minute," he pleaded.

She nodded reluctantly.

"Adrienne has tried to get us back together, for our child, she says. In a way, I can't blame her."

Hanna cut in, "Alex, you need to do what's best and I understand."

"No, you need to know I've ended any possibility of us reuniting. She stayed at my father's house a couple of nights with Scotty when her mother threw her out and she had nowhere else to go." He paused a moment to see how Hanna was reacting. She just stared back at him and didn't respond. "Nothing happened between us... physically, I mean, and I've asked her to leave."

Hanna was skeptical. "You can't tell me she didn't try."

Alex looked down at his coffee and sighed. He said, "Yes, but you need to trust me that nothing happened."

"Alex, that's all fine and thank you for being so honest with me, but you've still got a lot to work out with her and your son."

"I know, but I'm asking if you'll give me some more time."

"Take all the time you need," Hanna replied.

"No, I'm asking that you'll give us another chance," he said.

Hanna stared back at him and then looked away out the window. She tried to sort through all the conflicting emotions racing through her brain.

Alex reached across the table and took her hand. "Please, just give me a little more time."

She hesitated for a moment and then pulled her hand away. "I really need to get back."

She left him on the street in front of her office with no promises and no indication of where this all might lead, even when he pressed her again.

As she turned to go back up the steps, she said, "You need to focus on your father... and your son."

Chapter Fifty-three

Alex drove into Dugganville just before noon. The little town seemed to be moving on as if none of the drama of murder, attempted assassinations and drug deals was of any consequence. He pulled up and parked in front of his parent's house. As he walked up to the porch, he was thinking about Hanna and her admonition to deal with his personal matters before they could have any further discussion about their own future. On the drive back, he was considering asking Adrienne to move to Charleston with Scotty, find a job and a place to live. He could have joint custody of Scotty and help with his support. He wasn't sure how wild Hanna would be about his ex being in the same town, but there had to be some way to make this work.

He walked into the house and back to the kitchen. He saw the back door open and his senses went on immediate alert. He pulled his 9mm from the holster and flattened himself against the wall just outside the opening into the kitchen.

The familiar voice came from behind him. Beau Richards said, "Put the gun on the table, Alex."

Alex turned slowly and saw the man holding a long-barreled revolver with both hands out in front of him.

"On the table, now!" Richards demanded.

Alex slowly lowered his gun and then reached over and placed it carefully on the dining room table.

"Back away, now!"

He did as he was told and said, "Beau, you've got a lot of explaining to do. Assaulting a police officer is not going to help your cause."

Richards came around the other side of the table and took Alex's gun with a gloved hand, placing it in the waist of his pants," not taking his eyes off Alex. He said, "I was afraid you'd keep pressin' on all this. You just kept stickin' your nose where it didn't belong."

"Did you hire the hit on me, Beau?"

He didn't answer, but just smiled back. Then, his face got very serious again. "I assume you tipped the Feds off to the drug deal the other night. How'd you find out?"

"Didn't have a thing to do with it, Beau," Alex said. "Just blind luck they happened to be out there on patrol. Your spotters didn't do a very good job now, did they?"

Richards seemed to be thinking about Alex's response.

Alex said, "Chaz is being very cooperative with the DEA, Beau. He's spilled everything about you and Connor. They're out looking for you right now."

Richards nodded back slowly, his gun still fixed on Alex.

"Your best bet is to get the hell out of the country and hope they don't find you and get extradition papers to bring you back."

Richards said, "I have some loose ends to deal with first."

"And I'm one of your loose ends?" Alex asked.

"This is the same gun the idiot tried to kill you with the other night," Richards said. "He won't be needing it anymore. The cops are gonna think he came back and finished the hit on you and then had guilty feelings and used it on himself. This thing leaves a big hole, Alex. Really a mess over there. I'll drop the gun back before I leave town."

Alex was feeling more than helpless but was trying to keep an air of calm. He said, "People will hear the shot, Beau."

"I'll be long gone before anyone gets here. The timeline will look just fine when they find Jameson with a hole in the side of his head."

There was a knock on the door.

Beau Richards was distracted for just a moment and Alex reached quickly for the edge of the table and began pushing it as hard as he could. The pain in his shoulder was excruciating. Richards started to fall back, and he reached for a chair with one hand, the other trying to point the gun back at Alex.

228

Alex kept pushing as hard as he could and then dove for the floor as a deafening gunshot went off, barely missing him and slamming into the wall behind him. Under the table, Alex saw Beau losing his balance and starting to fall back. He crawled quickly across the floor under the table and grabbed on to one of his legs, pulling it out from under him.

Richards fell over one of the chairs and Alex was up and on him in an instant. He held his gun hand to the side with his knee and threw a straight punch as hard as he could into Richards' nose. The sound of bone and cartilage breaking was followed by a loud bellow of pain. Alex saw that he was stunned and his grip on the gun loosened. He pulled the big pistol away and stood with it, pointing down at Beau Richards' face, both men breathing heavily. Alex felt faint from the pain shooting out from his injured shoulder. He watched as Richards rolled over on his side, holding his nose and trying to staunch the flow of blood dripping down on the floor.

Alex heard someone coming in from the front room and raised the gun in that direction. Sheriff Stokes came in with his gun drawn and a look of astonishment washed over his face. "What the hell!"

Beau Richards had been led away in handcuffs by two of Stokes' deputies. He had a few choice words for Alex about being a *"dead man"* before he was escorted out.

Alex had asked the sheriff if he was sure his men could be trusted after discovering one of the department's dispatchers was on the Richards payroll. Stokes assured him these two men were solid.

After an hour of providing a full report to the sheriff and one other deputy on the attack by Beau Richards, Stokes had excused himself to take a call. He came back into the house a few minutes later.

"Just heard back from the crew I sent over to Hank Jameson's house," the sheriff said to Alex. "Beau was right. The man's brains are painted all over the wall."

Alex was sitting at the small table in the kitchen. His heart was still racing from the earlier attempt on his life. He looked up at Pepper Stokes. "We need to squeeze Beau on the Bayes murder. If Horton was threatening to pull out of the drug scheme, the Richards would sure have cause to make certain he wasn't another "loose end" as Beau called it. My father's fight with Horton that night would have been a convenient cover for the Richards to have Horton taken out."

Stokes said, "Pretty thin, Alex. I know you're looking for any way to get your old man off here, but we got nothing to back up that line of thinking."

"Chaz told us Connor and Horton were having an argument about something after the last drug deal," Alex reminded the sheriff. "We need to get Connor back in the states. Any word from the DEA?"

Stokes shook his head. "Connor and the girl are probably long gone from the Bahamas by now. Have to believe Beau and Connor had a pretty elaborate back-up plan if things went south."

Alex thought for a moment, then said, "Well, Meryl and young Horton are still around. We need to get back with the Feds and see what they've learned from the kid. I need to have another word with Meryl. Care to join me?"

Alex and the sheriff found no one at home when they went to Meryl Bayes' house. It was just past six. Sheriff Stokes left to go back to his office. Alex had a hunch on finding Meryl.

When Alex walked into *Gilly's Bar*, he saw several familiar faces along the bar and at a few of the tables. Gilly spotted him and nodded back. Alex walked through the crowd and then saw Meryl at a booth in the back, sitting alone with a shot of whiskey and half full glass of beer in front of her. When he sat down across from her, she looked up with an angry scowl.

"Get the hell out of here!" she snapped with a slurred voice, her eyes blurry and swollen.

"Pretty early, Meryl."

She didn't answer and reached for the shot and threw it back.

"Just took Beau Richards into custody, Meryl," Alex said.

She just continued to stare back, her head weaving some as she tried to focus on Alex.

"It's all coming out now, Meryl. Chaz Merton is telling the Feds everything about your husband and son's involvement with the Richards. Sounds like you were well aware of all this."

"You need to leave me alone!" she spat.

Alex pressed on. "We're hearing Horton was having a beef with the Richards about something. You know anything about that?"

"Why would I tell you anything?"

"Was Horton thinking about pulling out of the drug business?" Alex continued. "Maybe the Richards were getting worried about his intentions?"

Meryl took a sip from her beer and swallowed hard, then looked up at Alex with a flush of anger on her face. "Horton was too busy screwin' half the town to have time for running weed."

Alex didn't let up. "So, he was trying to pull out?"

The woman shook her head and looked away for a moment. "I don't know what that SOB was thinkin'!"

"Meryl, you need to help me here. Horton was running with a dangerous bunch. The Richards wouldn't think twice about taking him out if there was any indication he was pulling out on them... and these guys from Mexico don't play around either."

"Damn Mexicans!" she hissed. "I told Horton..."

"You told him what?"

"Just get outta here!" she snapped back at him.

Alex took another tack. "Meryl, who was Horton having an affair with?"

This really irritated her, and she started to slide out of the booth to leave. Alex reached out and grabbed her arm. "Meryl, sit down." She settled back and finished off the rest of the beer in the glass, looking across the bar for a server.

"Meryl, tell me who Horton was fooling around with."

She focused her gaze back on him and said, "Who wasn't he foolin' around with?"

"You tell me."

She took a deep breath, then said, "That bitch, Ella Moore is just the latest."

Alex wasn't surprised. Adrienne and her mother were cut from the same cloth. "How long had that been going on?"

"Like I said, just the latest."

Chapter Fifty-four

The bleak facade of the old women's shelter in downtown Charleston loomed ahead as Hanna and her son, Jonathan, crossed the street. Hanna had called Greta Muskovicz to make sure she was available to see them to discuss the situation of now orphaned, William Moe.

Greta met them in the lobby and took them up one flight of stairs to a large room where several young children were playing with toys spread on the floor, their mothers sitting along the periphery watching. Hanna saw William off by himself reading a book.

Greta said, "He hasn't spoken a word since we talked to him about his father's death. It was just too much after losing his mother such a short time ago.

Hanna felt her heart sink even deeper as she saw the overwhelming sadness in the boy's face. "How will he ever get beyond this?"

"We have one of our best counselors working with him," Greta said. "It will be a long process."

Jonathan asked, "Where will he go now?"

"We're working with the court to get assigned custody for now. We also have people trying to track down any other family members related to either the mother or father."

"Can I speak with him?" Hanna asked.

"It's probably better you didn't. He has so much going on right now, he doesn't need any more confusion."

Hanna said, "Please let me know what we can do to help. I have resources at the office to help with the search for his family... anything."

"Thank you," Greta said.

Hanna looked at her son sitting across the table from her at the small coffee shop down the street from her office. After the sad encounter at the shelter, she felt so blessed to have Jonathan with her, safe and healthy.

Jonathan broke the silence between them. "Mom, you can't take this all on yourself."

She offered a weak smile. "I just can't help think there was more I could have done when Jenna first came to see me."

"It was a bad situation from the start."

"I know," Hanna said, thinking back to the first meetings with the Moe family."

Jonathan said, "The man could have killed you. You did what you had to do."

She sighed and took a sip from her coffee. "I know he never would have been a good father for William, but..."

"You did the right thing."

Hanna said goodbye to Jonathan after they got back to the legal clinic. He needed to get back up to Chapel Hill. Their embrace was long and tearful before he got in his car and drove away. She was consumed with an emptiness and sadness for William and Jenna Moe, and when she was honest with herself, for her own life, mostly alone now.

As she started back into her office, she saw Lonnie Smith pull up and park. The big police officer got out of his car, ending a call on his cell.

"Hanna, I'm glad I caught you. Got a minute?"

"Of course."

"Has Alex called you about Beau Richards?"

"No, what's happened?"

Lonnie said, "Richards surprised Alex in his father's house and was there to kill him."

Hanna was stunned and couldn't respond.

"Alex is okay and Richards is under arrest, but it could have been... well, fortunately Alex was able to deal with the situation."

Hanna's thoughts were spinning, and she said, "Does this have anything to do with the case against Alex's father?"

"We're not sure yet. There's a lot going on up there."

"You're sure he's okay, with his arm and all?" she asked.

"I just spoke with him again a few minutes ago. I can tell he's a little shaken up. It looks like Richards hired the man who tried to kill Alex the other night."

Hanna shook her head in disbelief.

"They found the guy shot dead in his house. Richards admitted to Alex that he did it and was going to make it look like the hitman came back to finish the job."

"Does Phillip Holloway know about all this?" she asked.

Smith nodded and said, "Alex told me they've spoken, and Holloway is up to date."

"Okay, good," Hanna said, thinking about the fate of Alex's father, still sitting in the County Jail.

Smith said, "Alex asked me to check on you. See how you're doing."

She had to admit to herself she was pleased Alex was concerned and thinking of her, even with all that was happening. "To be honest, I've been better. We just got back from the shelter to check in on the son. He's not doing very well."

"They have the department helping in the search for other family members," Lonnie said. "We're trying to track down parents, brothers or sisters."

"I'm glad to hear that, but I'm not holding out much hope. Jenna seemed to have nowhere to turn."

"I'll keep you posted."

Chapter Fifty-five

As Alex pulled up to Ella Moore's house, he looked around to see any sign of Adrienne or Scotty. He wasn't in the mood for another encounter with his ex-wife, but he needed to speak to her mother. He got out of the car and walked up to the small house, looking around at the disrepair and neglect of the place. As he came up the drive, he was surprised to see a Sheriff's patrol car pulled up close to the garage in the back. His senses went on alert and he approached the front door cautiously.

He rang the bell and then rang it again when no one came to answer. He was about to walk around to the back when he heard someone moving inside. Both the screen and main door were closed, so he couldn't see in. Then, a small crack opened, and he saw the disheveled face of Ella Moore looking out.

"Ella, sorry to bother you."

"What?" she asked, pushing hair away from her face.

"I need to talk to you."

She hesitated and looked back into the house. "It's not a good time."

Alex heard a car door close and an engine start up. He looked over and saw the patrol car backing out of the drive. Sheriff Pepper Stokes was at the wheel. Alex watched as the car backed into the street and sped away.

Alex sat across the kitchen table from Ella Moore. She pulled an old robe up tightly around her neck. It appeared she didn't have anything on beneath. "You want a beer?" she asked.

"No. So, what's with you and the sheriff," Alex asked.

235

Ella flushed and didn't answer at first, then said, "Me and Pepper go way back."

"Surprised I never heard about that," Alex said.

She didn't respond.

"Just came from talking with Meryl Bayes." He watched as the woman blanched and squirmed a bit in her chair.

"Seems you and Horton were a pair, too."

"That's none of your business!" she said quickly.

"Oh, I think it is my business, Ella. How long you been seeing Horton?"

Again, she didn't respond.

"Meryl was pretty upset about the two of you, as you can imagine."

This set the woman off. "That old bitch..." and then she stopped herself.

"What, Ella?"

"Horton should have dumped her years ago. Can't see how he's lived with the woman all these years."

Alex considered her comments for a moment, then said, "So, was Horton gonna leave Meryl?"

Ella took a deep breath but didn't answer.

Alex pressed, "Was Horton going to leave Meryl for you?"

Finally, she said, "That bastard didn't know what the hell he wanted."

"When was the last time you saw Horton, Ella?"

She stood and backed away from the table, the anger rising in her face. "I don't need to tell you anything!"

"Why don't you want to talk about this, Ella?" he persisted.

"You need to leave!"

Alex pushed his chair back. He heard the front door opening. When he turned, he saw Adrienne and Scotty come into the house and then join them in the kitchen.

Adrienne said, "Alex, what's going on?"

"Just having a little chat with your mother."

"What in the hell for?" Adrienne demanded.

Alex turned back to Ella Moore and said, "She can fill you in." He knelt down. "Hey Scotty. How are you?"

"Good, Alex," the boy said. "Mom just took me to the movies."

"What did you see?"

"The super hero guys!" Scotty said.

"That's great, " Alex said, standing. He looked over at Ella Moore. "We're not done here, Ella."

As he walked back to his car, he couldn't put aside the guilt he was feeling in not taking more proactive steps to bring his son into his life. *A few complications at the moment*, he thought, trying to reconcile with himself.

Alex saw Sheriff Stokes' car parked in his assigned spot at the department offices. He went in and was cleared back through to see the sheriff. When the man saw Alex coming up to his door, he ended a call and stood, then said, "Alex, it's not what you think."

"What's that, Pepper?" Alex said, slamming the door behind him, "That you've been screwing a woman apparently close to this case with my father and you didn't tell me about it?"

"She doesn't have anything to do with your father's case," Stokes said.

"Oh, you don't think so?" Alex said, coming up and standing directly across the desk. "Meryl and Ella have been having a dispute over the woman's husband who is now dead, and you don't think that has anything to do with it?"

"Just settle down, Alex," Stokes said, taking his seat again. Alex remained standing. "No secret Ella and Meryl have a feud going." Half the town's seen them after each other."

"So, why am I just hearing about it now?"

"Alex, let's talk about something important…"

"This is important, dammit!" Alex snapped back.

"The Feds stopped Connor Richards and the girl trying to charter a boat out of Nassau," Stokes continued. "They'll be back in the country by tomorrow morning."

Alex paused for a moment, then said, "We need to get access to talk with them as soon as possible."

"I've already informed the DEA."

Okay, fine," Alex said. "Now, what has Ella told you about her relationship with Horton?"

"We haven't talked about it."

"Don't you think you should?"

"Alex, look, I'm a married man. Ella and me, is just an occasional thing. I don't know what she does with the rest of her time and I don't ask."

Alex tried to control his anger and frustration. He walked to the window and looked over the parking lot and people coming and going from the Sheriff's Department. A thought occurred to him and he turned back to Stokes. "We need to bring Ella Moore in, Pepper."

"What?"

"We need a complete statement from her on her relationship with Horton and particularly where she was the night of his death."

The sheriff stood and paced behind his desk, then picked up his phone and pressed two numbers. "This is Stokes. Have someone bring Ella Moore down here." There was a moment while he listened to the response. "No, do it now!"

Ella Moore sat across a small table from Alex and Sheriff Stokes. Her anger was clear at being asked to come down to the Department. She had thrown every conceivable expletive at the two men as she was led in.

She continued, "You have no damn right to treat me like this!"

Stokes said, "Ella, you need to settle down. You're not under arrest. We just need a few questions answered."

Ella fumed, "Pepper Stokes, I swear...!"

Alex cut in. "Ella, that's enough! We're going to ask you some questions and you're going to tell us everything we need to know. If you want a lawyer here with you, you have every right."

"I don't need a damn lawyer!" she spat, standing to leave.

"Ella, sit down," the sheriff demanded.

Reluctantly, she took her seat again.

Stokes began, "How long you been seeing Horton Bayes?"

"It's none of your damn business!"

Alex said, "Ella, we can be here all night, or you can make this a lot quicker by answering our questions. How long have you and Horton been having an affair?"

The woman sat, just staring back defiantly.

"Ella?" the sheriff asked.

In a low voice, she finally began, "Me and Horton have been off and on for a couple of years."

"Off and on?" Alex asked.

"It wasn't a regular thing," she said, "until more recently."

Alex perked up at the last comment. "Until recently?"

Ella hesitated, then said, "We were pretty tight these past few months."

"How tight?" Alex pressed.

Ella looked over at the sheriff as if she was feeling guilty about talking about this in front of him. "Pepper, I'm sorry, but you know what we have is just for fun, right?"

Stokes jumped in, "Let's not worry about that. Answer Alex's question."

She looked back to Alex and hesitantly said, "We were talking about moving in together. He was going to leave Meryl."

Alex was stunned, and his mind raced with the implications and contradicting facts and evidence surfacing in the case against his father.

Alex focused on Ella's face and asked, "Had Horton told Meryl about your plans."

Ella seemed flustered, searching for a response. "He never told me," she finally said. "He died before he told me."

Chapter Fifty-six

When Hanna returned to her office, one of the phone messages was from her partner at the firm she now worked part-time for on Pawley's Island. She called Trevor Hampton back and waited for him to take the call from their receptionist.

"Hanna, thanks for getting back," Hampton said. " Sorry about the late notice, but the Petersons want to meet with us in the morning and I need you here."

"What time?" Hanna asked, looking at the calendar on her cell phone.

"First thing. Can you be here by eight?"

"Sure, I'll drive up to the house tonight," Hanna said. "What's on their minds?"

Hampton chuckled and said, "Seems the reality of splitting half their stuff in this divorce has finally dawned on them. They want to discuss a reconciliation and new agreement on the property going forward. Alice is bringing her lawyer."

Hanna was not excited about the meeting. The Peterson divorce case had been particularly ugly. It was the kind of work she truly loathed, but with her husband, Ben, gone, she needed the money to help keep her free clinic open. "I'll see you in the morning," she said.

It was close to seven o'clock when Hanna assured herself the day's work was done and she had everything covered for the coming day. She found the paperwork she needed to take with her to Pawleys Island and stuffed them in her case. After packing a small travel bag in her apartment for the trip, she drove out of the parking space behind the house and began working her way through the city traffic, thinking about a quiet night at the beach house to clear her head.

Something triggered a thought about Alex and all that he was dealing with up in Dugganville. His father was still in jail on a murder charge that would likely carry the death penalty. There had been two attempts on Alex's life in the past week, and fortunately, all he had was a bullet wound in his shoulder. She shuddered when she thought about what could have happened. And then there was his ex-wife and new son to deal with.

Forty-five minutes later, she saw the turn-off to Dugganville and without allowing herself to second-guess the decision, she took the turn.

Hanna drove down the quiet main street of Dugganville, closing down now as the day faded. She saw Alex's car parked in front of the old diner and pulled in next to it. She took a deep breath and again, tried not to question her judgement in being here.

Alex was in a booth near the front of restaurant. He didn't look up when Hanna opened the door and a bell hanging from the knob clattered. She saw his left arm still in a sling and cringed as images of the attacks crept back into her mind. She walked up to the table and stopped. Alex finally looked up with a look of total astonishment.

"Hanna!"

He struggled to climb out of the booth and as he stood, she fell into his one-armed hug. As they held each other, she said, "I wanted to see how you're doing."

Alex drew back and smiled, then looked down at his shoulder. "I've been better."

"That's what I figured."

"Sit down," he said, gesturing for her to join him. "Have you eaten?

Hanna said, "Actually, no, and I'm starving."

Alex got the attention of the owner, Lucy. To Hanna, he said, "Get the meatloaf. The gravy is amazing."

Lucy took Hanna's order and then rushed off to the kitchen, sending the busboy over to bring her a cup of coffee and refill Alex's cup.

Alex said, "Thank you for coming."

"I have to be on the island for a client meeting first thing in the morning, so I'm headed up to the beach house."

Alex continued, "I'm the one who should be asking about how you're doing."

"It was pretty awful," Hanna said. "Not sure I'll ever have a good night's sleep. I can still see the man's face, lying on the floor dying in my office."

Alex reached over and placed a hand on her arm. "It will take some time. You need to keep reminding yourself it was self-defense. The man was a killer. He killed his own wife."

"I know," Hanna said, the sadness evident in her tone. "And I've left a little boy with no family and nowhere to go."

"Lonnie tells me the Department is helping to track down family members."

Hanna nodded and took a sip from her coffee. "How is *your* son doing," she asked and saw a look of concern. He scrunched his face and looked away for a moment. "What's happening?" she asked.

Alex looked back. "Adrienne and I don't have it all sorted out yet. Her mother has taken them back for now."

Hanna searched for any sign of his intentions for the woman and their son but decided not to pursue it further for the moment. "How's the shoulder?" she asked.

Alex gently touched the area of the wound on his left shoulder and said, "Good thing I'm right-handed."

Hanna smiled. "So, the guy who tried to kill you is dead?"

Alex recounted the story of Beau Richards hiring the man and then killing him before coming to Alex's house to finish the job on him.

"This is one crazy town." Hanna said.

Alex shook his head and said, "You're telling me." He went on to tell her of the arrest of both Beau and Connor Richards and then the new information about the feud with Ella Moore with Horton Bayes' widow, Meryl.

When he was finished, Lucy had placed Hanna's meal down and she was starting in on it. "Sounds like you have some new suspects," she said.

"A few too many loose ends," he admitted. "Connor Richards will be back in the States tomorrow. The sheriff and I will get to talk with him as soon as possible."

"How's your dad holding up?" Hanna asked.

"I spoke to him on the phone just a while ago. He doesn't seem too encouraged about all the new evidence in Bayes' death. He still can't remember anything after leaving the shrimp boat with Meryl Bayes there and Horton still alive. Meryl's continuing to claim Pop came back later and killed him."

Hanna thought for a moment about the murder investigation into Skipper Frank. She asked, "I was thinking about the blood evidence on your father. All they found was bruising and traces of Bayes' blood on his hands and a little on his clothes, probably from the fight at the bar. Seems he would have blood all over him and his clothes and shoes after stabbing a man to death like that."

"Yes, you'd think," Alex said. "Another one of those loose ends. Holloway thinks it's the key in Pop's defense."

As Hanna finished her meal, she looked out the window of the diner and saw that darkness had overtaken the town. She looked at her watch. "I'd better get going."

Alex hesitated, then said, "It's late, I've got a spare bedroom."

Hanna was tempted but said, "No, I need to get up to the island. Early start in the morning."

"Okay," Alex responded. "Thank you for stopping off on the way."

Hanna smiled and said, "Promise me you'll keep your head down."

They hugged again, tentatively, as she stood to leave.

As Hanna walked out of the door of the diner, she fought the urge to go back in and take Alex up on his offer to stay the night. She was exhausted and the thought of getting back on the road was the last thing she wanted to do. She reminded herself that sleeping in the same house with Alex Frank would create a few too many complications at this point. *Too soon!*

Chapter Fifty-seven

Alex saw the glow of a cigarette from someone sitting on the front screened porch as he pulled into the drive of his father's house. His senses went on high alert. He got out quickly, keeping the cover of the car between him and the person on the porch. He released the strap on his gun and pulled it out.

"Come out here now!" he yelled out.

"Alex, it's me," he heard the familiar voice of Adrienne reply.

He put his gun back and walked around the car. "Adrienne, what the hell?" He watched as she came out the door and down the steps. She threw her smoke down on the sidewalk and crushed it out with sole of her sandals. In the darkness, he could see she was wearing jeans and a white blouse. Her hair was piled loosely up on top of her head.

As she came up to him, she said, "Can we take a walk?"

"Just tell me what you're here for."

"Please," she insisted. "I need to talk to you about something."

They had walked in silence all the way out to the end of his family's dock on the river. His father's shrimp boat, the *Maggie Mae*, was tied up on one side, their small fishing boat on the other. Both rested calmly on the smooth surface of the river. The sounds of crickets broke the stillness of the night. A small light at the end of the dock reflected down in the water and fished darted in to chase minnows attracted by the glow.

"You want to tell me what's going on?" Alex finally asked. He turned to face his ex-wife. Adrienne reached for his hand and he pulled it away. "Just tell me what you have to say."

Adrienne said, "I want you to understand something."

"And what is that?"

"Scotty and I really had nowhere to go."

"I know that."

"No, I mean when Derek left us in Florida. I didn't have any money and couldn't find a job and someone to watch Scotty. I had to come back home."

"Yes, I know," Alex said, the impatience clear in his voice.

Adrienne hesitated and walked over under the light, then turned and said, "I never wanted to lie to you, but I just didn't have any other options."

"What are you talking about?"

"I never thought we would see Derek again. We had been fighting constantly for weeks and I knew he'd had enough."

"Adrienne..."

"No, let me finish," she cut in. "I wanted Scotty to have a real family. Not like me. I hardly knew my father growing up."

Alex closed the distance between them and said, "What are you trying to say?"

"Derek came back for us today. He's over at my mother's house."

"Okay," Alex responded cautiously.

"I think we can make it work. He's got a new job down in Florida. He wants us to come back."

Alex's mind was racing, and he immediately thought about his son. "And what about Scotty?"

Adrienne came to him and put her arms around his waist. This time, he didn't pull away. She looked up at him and said, "Derek is Scotty's real father, Alex."

He let the words sink in for a few moments, his emotions racing between anger and relief. Anger won out. He pushed her away. "You've got to be kidding me! How could you lie to me about something like this? He looks just like me, Adrienne. You told me this Derek guy has red hair and there was no way he could be the father."

She didn't respond.

"Adrienne?"

245

"I told you I never wanted to lie to you, but I didn't have any other place to go," she said, her tears shining on her cheeks in the dim light. "Scotty looks a lot like his real father, Derek."

Alex stood there, stunned at all he was hearing, looking back at this woman who he had once loved with all his heart and now, found himself again, wishing he had never seen her face.

Alex sat in the captain's chair of his father's boat. Adrienne had gone back to her mother's over an hour ago. She was leaving for Florida in the morning with her husband and *their* son. His only hope regarding Adrienne was he would never see or hear from her again.

He was on his second beer, letting the alcohol numb his mind and the pain in his shoulder. He thought about calling Hanna and telling her about Adrienne's deception but decided it was too late. He found his emotions mixed about the news of Scotty's real father. He had been preparing himself for the reality of taking the boy into his life and raising a son together, somehow, with Adrienne. He had never doubted his ability to be a good father for Scotty, he just couldn't find a path that would allow Adrienne back again. Now, that was not an issue... *and how was Hanna going to react?*

Sheriff Stokes called him the next morning at 7:30 to tell him the DEA was going to let them talk to Connor Richards at noon. He was locked up with the Feds all morning down in Charleston.

"Any news on what Connor's telling these guys?" Alex asked.

"No, they're not sharing," the old sheriff said.

"You got time for a cup of coffee and some eggs," Alex asked.

"Sure."

"Meet you down at *Andrews* in thirty minutes?"

"I'll be there," Stokes said.

Chapter Fifty-eight

Hanna had fallen asleep moments after she had arrived at the island the night before. The past day's events and stress had been exhausting and she had a deep restful sleep before her alarm went off at 6:30 the next morning.

She put some coffee on in the kitchen, then went back upstairs to shower and dress for her meeting down at the law firm offices at eight. As she was coming out of her closest, she happened to notice several books stacked on the top of her dresser. In the middle of the pile was a well-worn black leather-covered book. She reached for it and pulled out her great-grandmother's journal, written during and after the Civil War. Hanna had found it in the attic of the beach house over a year ago in an old trunk when she was cleaning out the house, expecting to have to sell it after her late husband's murder.

The journal chronicled Amanda Paltierre Atwell's life and family during the war and the year's afterward when her husband, Captain Jeremy Atwell, never returned from a battle fought weeks after the war had ended in a remote battlefield in southern Texas called Palmetto Ranch. It also chronicled a new relationship with a mysterious stranger who returned to South Carolina to tell Amanda of her husband's death in the senseless battle. The stranger ultimately confessed to Amanda that he was the man who killed her husband during the fight. Through some difficult times, she found a way to forgive the man and they were married some years later and lived a mostly happy and fulfilling life together.

Hanna sat on the bed and turned the fragile pages of the journal carefully to a passage she recalled reading many times.

Colonel Morgan returned to the plantation last night. It's been months since I sent him away. I'd thought I would never be able to forgive him for killing Jeremy. As these months have passed, I've thought of little else. I've come to realize the war put many men in situations that can never be justified or fully understood.

Before I learned Colonel Morgan was actually a Union Officer, the man who killed Jeremy in Texas, I had been troubled with a growing affection for the man. Jeremy had been gone for so many years and I knew I had to move on with my life. We have so little time on this earth and if we're fortunate enough to find someone we can be happy in sharing those years together, how can we deny those feelings?

Hanna glanced up from the journal when she heard the chime on the coffeemaker in the kitchen. She looked again at the passage from her grandmother's journal, then placed the old book gently on her nightstand. She saw the alarm clock and realized she had time for a quick breakfast before having to get down to the law offices for her meeting. Her grandmother's words echoed in her mind as she went down the stairs. *How can we deny those feelings?*

The Peterson divorce meeting had been more dreadful than Hanna could possibly have imagined. She had watched incredulously through the morning as two people who clearly detested each other struggled to find some middle ground where the couple's substantial fortune and real estate holdings could be protected and shared going forward in some greedy alliance. She felt like she needed another shower when she came out of the meeting.

It was approaching noon when the couple finally left the offices, Mr. Peterson in his Maserati GranTurismo and Mrs. Peterson in her white Mercedes SUV. He would be taking their Gulfstream jet back to Manhattan and their elegant Park Avenue apartment and she would continue to reside alone in the palatial home on the coast here on Pawleys Island.

Hanna decided to take a break and drive home for a quick lunch before returning for an afternoon of work. She pulled into the drive at the beach house and parked in the shade of several palm trees. The afternoon winds were building and rattled through the palm fronds, offering some relief from the heat.

The cool rush of air conditioning greeted her as she went inside and into the kitchen. Opening the refrigerator, she sighed when she saw the sparse array of edible food. She found a *Lean Cuisine* in the freezer that looked like her best solution and placed it in the microwave for a three-minute instant meal. She pulled a chilled bottle of water from the refrigerator and sat at the bar to wait for the microwave and to catch up on her phone messages and email.

Something on the counter caught her attention and she looked up to see her grandmother's journal lying open across from her. At first, she didn't think much of it and looked back to her phone and then suddenly, she clearly remembered leaving the book on her nightstand upstairs in her bedroom before she left for work that morning.

A chill of alarm caused her to look around and listen to hear if anyone was in the house. She sat for several moments listening and trying to understand how the book could have been moved. She stood to walk through the house to see if anything else was askew. She happened to look down at the journal and noticed it was open to the passage about the return of her grandmother's soon-to-be second husband, she had read earlier in the morning.

Hanna again read the entry about the return of Colonel Morgan to the *Tanglewood Plantation* outside Georgetown after the end of the Civil War... *how can we deny those feelings?*

Chapter Fifty-nine

Lucy was clearing their dishes from breakfast at *Andrews Diner* when Alex finished the last of his coffee and said to Sheriff Pepper Stokes across from him, "We need to get formal statements from both Ella and Meryl."

"Alex, I know you think this whole thing with Horton and these women smells bad, but I can't believe either of them could have killed him. You've seen how badly he was attacked and stabbed. Could you see either of them able to physically manage that?"

Alex thought for a moment, then said, "Horton Bayes was really drunk that night. It wouldn't take much to overpower him. He might have even been passed out."

Stokes shook his head. "I don't see it."

"We need to get them in for a statement, Pepper."

The sheriff looked at his watch. "We have to get started down to Charleston. They'll have Connor Richards ready for us at eleven."

Alex said, "I've called Holloway to join us. My dad's lawyer needs to be there, too."

"Let's see what Connor has to say before we decide what to do about Ella and Meryl."

Phillip Holloway was waiting for them in Charleston when they came off the elevators. As always, he looked like he was dressed for a cover of *Gentleman's Quarterly*. He gave Alex a warm smile and firm handshake, then the same for the sheriff. "Good to see you both," he said. "They're ready for us any time. Richards has "lawyered up" as you can imagine, so I doubt we'll get much from him this morning, but let's take a try."

Alex asked, "Do you have some time later to see my father with me?"

"Sure, we'll make it work."

Stokes said, "Have you gotten anything more from the DEA on Richards?"

"No, they're still not sharing. We're on our own."

Connor Richards was dressed in a jail jumpsuit with a prisoner number stenciled on the chest. His hair was slightly askew, and his face looked drawn and tired. He didn't look up when Alex walked into the small interview room with the sheriff and Phillip Holloway. The three sat down across from the prisoner and his attorney, a woman with graying hair and an immaculate gray business suit. Introductions were made. Her name was Mary Bronson.

Stokes said to the attorney, "We need to speak to your client about recent events regarding the murder investigation of Horton Bayes and the attempted murder of my friend here, Mr. Frank, who is a Charleston Police Detective working with me on all this."

Richards' lawyer smirked and said, "And his father is sitting in jail, charged with the murder of Bayes. Hardly an unbiased member of the investigation team."

Stokes didn't respond.

Holloway jumped in. "Ms. Bronson, your client's father has already confessed to hiring the hitman that tried to kill Alex here, earlier this week."

"He did no such thing!" Bronson protested. "Mr. Frank is *claiming* he admitted to all of this, but Beau Richards completely denies the allegation and he hasn't been formally charged."

"There is no question that he personally tried to shoot and kill Alex," Holloway replied. To Connor he said, "Would you like to tell us your involvement with your family hiring this hitman, Hank Jameson, and why you needed Alex Frank to be killed?"

Mary Bronson exploded, her face turning a flushed red, "That is completely out of line! There is no evidence to suggest my client had any involvement in any of this."

Calmly, Holloway said, "Connor, would you care to speak for yourself today or are we wasting our time?"

The prisoner looked over at his lawyer and she whispered something in his ear. Bronson said, "I've advised Mr. Richards that he has no obligation at this point to address any of your questions."

Alex had heard enough, and the frustration was clear in his voice when he jumped in, "Connor, why in hell did you suddenly take off to the Bahamas in the middle of the night if you weren't running from all this?"

Connor responded quickly, "Lily and I left on vacation. It had nothing to do with any of this."

Alex couldn't hide his skepticism, "Amazing timing to have a Caribbean vacation planned right after there's an arrest warrant out for you on a drug bust."

Richards protested, "I didn't have anything to do with that!"

His lawyer whispered in his ear again, trying to silence him.

Sheriff Stokes said, "Connor, we have a witness under arrest who implicates you and your father in this drug ring and several other criminal enterprises."

Richards spat back, "If you're talking about Chaz Merton, he's a damn drunk who would turn his mother in if it would save his ass!" His lawyer put her hand on his arm to stop him, but Connor continued. "If you're looking for who killed Horton Bayes, you better give Merton a serious look. He bragged to me about getting Bayes out of the way, so he could take over as captain of their family's shrimp boat. The man's a damn mess and was on his last legs. Your old man had already fired him and no one else would give him any work except us, canning fish. He was up to his ass in gambling debts."

Alex was stunned at the man's revelations. *Chaz Merton!* He looked Connor Richards straight in the eye and said, "You're telling us Chaz Merton confessed to you he killed Horton?"

"Might as well have. He was drunk down at *Gilly's* the next night, telling me and my father he'd taken Horton off the board and his old lady was going to let him take on the *Lulu Belle* as captain."

Alex was furious and had to stifle the urge to reach across the table and grab Richards by the throat. "And you didn't think you should report this to the sheriff? My father's looking at a death sentence!"

Richards didn't answer, and his lawyer broke in, "That's really enough! My client has nothing further to say about any of this."

An hour later, Alex, the sheriff and Phillip Holloway were sitting in another interrogation room with Chaz Merton. When the man was brought in, he had a wide smile that quickly disappeared when Alex confronted him. "Chaz, we just came from an interesting conversation with Connor Richards. He tells us you confessed to him and Beau that you "took Horton off the board" to take over as captain of their boat."

Merton's smile quickly disappeared. He looked confused and didn't respond.

Stokes said, "Chaz, tell us what happened that night."

"I got nothin' to say," Merton suddenly said.

"Chaz, how'd you get my father's knife?" Alex asked.

Merton started shaking his head, "What are you talking about?"

"You had my father's knife and you went back to the *Lulu Belle* and killed Horton Bayes. You knew it would look like my father did it after their fight down at the bar."

"No, no!" Merton protested, squirming in his chair and looking back at the door for the guard. He stood up and said, "You got it all wrong..."

Alex interrupted, "How'd you get the knife, Chaz?"

Chapter Sixty

Hanna had returned to the beach house an hour earlier after a long afternoon and early evening of work. She was sitting at the counter in her kitchen, a bottle of red wine half empty beside her glass.

She had called her father and was pleased to hear the strength returning in his voice.

"The doc says I'll be out of here in a couple of days."

"Why don't you and Martha take some time and get away?" Hanna asked. "When's the last time you took a vacation?"

"Do you have any idea how far behind I am at the office?" he protested.

Hanna couldn't contain her frustration. "Allen, there is no way you're going back to the office any time soon! Get over it!"

"Hanna, settle down. I'm feeling much better."

"You need to have a heart transplant, for Pete's sake!"

"I'm not going to sit around and wait for them to find me a ticker."

"Alan, I swear I'll come back to Atlanta to work if that's what it will take to keep you out of the office."

"No need, daughter dear..."

"Allen!"

They had ended the call with a thinly veiled promise from her father he would follow his doctor's orders on when it would be safe to return to work. Her next call had been to her father's wife, Martha, to insist she sit on the man if he tried to leave the house or started having them bring work to him there.

She took another sip from her wine and considered putting the cork back in the bottle and trying to find something to eat for dinner, but instead, she poured another small splash in the glass. The silence of the house suddenly became very apparent to her. She started thinking back on happier, noisier times in this kitchen with family and friends... and Alex Frank. She had been trying to mask her loneliness for some time. Her work and the chaotic events of the past days had helped to keep her mind occupied, but the quiet house was now closing in on her.

She reached for her grandmother's journal, still open on the counter from lunch. She flipped through a few more pages, reading familiar passages she had read many times. She looked out the window to the beach and tried to imagine the days, over a century and a half ago, when Amanda had been here in this house, in this kitchen and walking out on that beach. She felt such a close bond with the woman and whenever she looked at the old Civil War-era photo of the family on the wall, she could easily imagine the face of Amanda Paltierre Atwell coming alive and speaking with her.

Pouring more wine into her glass, she had a sudden urge to get some air. She walked out onto the veranda looking over the beach and then walked down the steps and over to the firepit, nestled in the dunes. She sat in one of the chairs and watched as the day faded and the first stars began to show in a sky tinged orange and pink against the clouds. The wind was blowing offshore, and the ocean was a calm gray, broken only by a few gulls diving here and there searching for a late meal.

Hanna looked at the empty wooden chair beside her in the sand and thought back to the night the mysterious woman had suddenly been sitting there beside her. In her mind, she had chalked the experience up to the excess of wine that evening and probably, just a drunken dream. *Then what about the woman on the dock who had been there and then suddenly gone?* She shook her head and took another sip from the wine. *You're losing your mind, Hanna Walsh!*

She woke suddenly, feeling an arm on her shoulder. She heard a voice. "Hanna."

It was dark, and she was still sitting in the old Adirondack chair on the beach and as her head cleared, she turned to see Alex Frank sitting down beside her. He reached for her hand.

"Sorry to startle you," he said, softly.

"Ohmigod, you scared me half to death."

"I'm sorry."

The silence between them was broken only by the sounds of the gulls.

Hanna finally said, "What are you doing here?"

"I have a lot to tell you."

"About what?" she asked.

"How about a glass of that wine first."

Hanna stood. "Let's go up and get another glass."

Alex picked up the bottle and followed Hanna up the path to the house.

In the kitchen, he poured a glass of the wine. Hanna held her hand over the top of hers and said, "I need some coffee." She started getting a pot ready. Alex was sitting at the island counter. He saw the old journal and pulled it over. Hanna had shared it with him during past visits to the beach house and he had read some of it.

"Catching up again on your great-grandmother?" he asked.

Hanna turned and faced him, then came over and sat beside him. She took the book from him and caressed the old leather cover. "I swear at times she's still here with us."

Alex smiled back at her but didn't respond.

"So, you said you had a lot to tell me." she asked.

"My father has been released."

"What!"

He relayed his earlier meetings with Connor Richards and Chaz Merton. When he finished, Hanna asked, "And Merton confessed?"

Alex nodded. "The more we pressed, the more nervous and agitated he got. When we continued to confront him with all we'd learned from Connor Richards, he actually broke down and finally came out with all of it. When he left *Gilly's* that night, after the fight between my father and Horton Bayes, he went to Bayes' boat to plead with him again for more work on the man's shrimp boat. Apparently, Horton told him to get lost. They got into an argument and Chaz admitted he just snapped and hit the old man across the face with a piece of the boat's rigging there on the deck. When he realized what he had done, he really flipped out when he saw that Horton wasn't breathing. He panicked and pulled the knife he had from my father's boat the previous day when he'd been filleting some fish they'd caught on the last shrimp run before my father fired him."

"He thought he could make it look like your father did it?" Hanna asked, incredulous.

"And then he took the knife back to my father's boat and threw it in the water by the dock."

Hanna sighed and leaned over and gave him a hug. "Oh, Alex, I'm so happy for you and your father. He must be so relieved."

"I dropped him off down at *Gilly's* to celebrate before coming out here," Alex said and laughed.

The coffee pot alarm beeped, and Hanna walked over to pour a cup. She returned and lifted her cup in a toast. "To the release of Skipper Frank!"

"Thank you!" Alex said, then took a long drink from the wine. "There's something else I need to speak with you about."

Hanna just looked back without responding.

Alex cleared his throat, obviously trying to figure out how to begin.

"What is it?" Hanna asked.

"Adrienne is gone, Hanna."

"She's gone?"

"She's gone back to Florida with Scotty, back with her husband."

Hanna felt some sense of relief but was confused about Alex's tone and nervousness. "That's good... I suppose," she said, "but what about your son?"

Alex looked intently at her. "He's not mine, Hanna. Adrienne has been lying. She was desperate when the man abandoned her, but Scotty is his son. He's taking them back."

"She would lie to you about that?" Hanna couldn't believe what she was hearing.

"You've met Adrienne. There's not much I wouldn't put past her."

"And she's already gone?"

Alex nodded.

Hanna's thoughts were swirling and all she could think to say is, "I'm sorry about Scotty. I know you were embracing all that and ready to take him in."

He shook his head, taking another sip from the wine. "I really don't know what to think, but I'm damn glad Adrienne is a thousand miles away!" He smiled back at Hanna.

She lifted her mug to his glass again.

There was an awkward silence between them. Hanna went to get more coffee and then stood with her back to the counter, facing Alex.

He finally said, "I know this has all been hard for you. I'm sorry for what I've put you through."

"It wasn't you, Alex."

"I know, but I should have kept Adrienne and this whole mess away from you."

"Alex..."

"I just wanted to come and apologize."

"Thank you, but..."

Alex interrupted. "I don't expect you to just forget about all that's happened...," he paused to gather himself. "I'm hoping you and I can take another run at this."

"Another run?"

"I love you, Hanna."

She heard the words but couldn't respond. Her mind raced with sudden mixed feelings of relief and then her old concerns about committing to another man after past failures and the hurt it led to. Alex was obviously waiting for her to respond. She looked back and felt the familiar attraction and deep feelings.

"Hanna?"

Her face glazed over as she thought back to the loss and betrayal of her husband and then Sam Collins who she had been madly in love with, who abandoned her after college. She finally looked back at Alex. His face was full of concern and expectation. She walked across the space between them and he stood as she approached. She watched as he opened his arms and she fell into him and felt him pull her close.

Hanna heard him say again, "I love you, Hanna. Please, let's give this another try."

She pulled back and looked up at him, pushing all doubt aside, "I love you, too."

A complete sense of relief and joy came over her and she pulled him close again. "I do love you, Alex Frank."

The sunlight through the thin curtains on the windows from the beach side of the house caused Hanna to wake with a start. She lifted her head from the pillow and looked around to clear her head. Alex was turned away, his bare back to her, still sleeping soundly. She pulled the covers up to cover herself and lay back on the pillow. She suddenly remembered a dream, or was it a dream? She recalled making love with Alex as a soft breeze blew through the second-floor windows, blowing the curtains back in a lazy rhythm. Later, when he was sleeping, she had gone out on the veranda to see the moon and stars with a comforter wrapped around her against the cool of the night.

In her mind, she was sure Amanda Paltierre had suddenly been there beside her, smiling back and pushing her long red hair away from her face in the gentle wind. As Hanna thought back on it now, in the gauzy haze of shaking off the night's sleep, she was certain Amanda had been there. It was too real to be a dream. What had she whispered? *Follow your heart.*

THE END

A note from Michael Lindley

Thank you for reading **A FOLLOWING SEA**. I hope you enjoyed this next installment of Hanna Walsh and Alex Frank in the Low Country of South

Carolina.

The danger and intrigue continue in Book #3, **DEATH ON THE NEW MOON**.

Alex encounters a tragic loss and near-deadly run-in with a ruthless crime syndicate. As Hanna helps him search for a dangerous killer, the surprise return of a lover from her past sends all hope of her future with Alex into a tailspin.

The story plays out against the idyllic backdrop of Charleston, Pawleys Island and the fictional Dugganville, South Carolina.

Amazon #1 for Crime and Psychological Thrillers; a captivating and twisting tale of love, betrayal and murder in the Low Country of South Carolina and the tenuous love affair of Hanna Walsh and Alex Frank.

Amazon Five Star Reviews for *Death On The New Moon* ☆☆☆☆☆

"A page-turning thriller."
"This is a sit at the edge of your seat thriller."
"Loving this series!"
"Awesome book! I could hardly put it down."
"Fast-paced with lots of twists and turns."
"A 10 star thriller!"

If you love mystery and suspense with twisting plots, compelling characters and settings that will sweep you away, find out why readers are raving about *Death On The New Moon.*

To keep reading **DEATH ON THE NEW MOON**, go to Michael Lindley's online store to buy direct at store.michaellindleynovels.com.

About the Author

Michael Lindley is an international bestselling author of mystery and suspense novels. His *"Hanna and Alex"* Low Country series has been a frequent #1 bestseller on Amazon in that genre.

His previous books include the "Troubled Waters" novels of historical mystery and suspense begins with the Amazon #1 bestseller, THE EMMALEE AFFAIRS.

"I've always been drawn to stories that are built around an idyllic time and place as much as the characters who grace these locations. As the heroes and villains come to life in my favorite stories, facing life's challenges of love and betrayal and great danger, I also enjoy coming to deeply understand the setting for the story and how it shapes the characters and the conflicts they face.

I've also loved books that combine a mix of past and present, allowing me to know a place and the people who live there in both a compelling historical context, as well as in present-day. I try to capture all of this in the books I write and the stories I bring to life."

Copy the Bookfunnel link below to sign up for my "Behind The Scenes" newsletter to receive announcements and special offers on new releases and other special sales and we will also send you a FREE copy of the *"Hanna and Alex"* intro novella, *BEGIN AT THE END.*

You can connect with me on:

🌐 https://store.michaellindleynovels.com

Subscribe to my newsletter:

✉ https://dl.bookfunnel.com/syy533ngqn

Also by Michael Lindley

The *"Troubled Waters"* novels of historical mystery and suspense.

THE EMMALEE AFFAIRS
  THE SUMMER TOWN
  BEND TO THE TEMPEST

The *"Hanna and Alex"* Low Country Mystery and Suspense Serie

LIES WE NEVER SEE
  A FOLLOWING SEA
  DEATH ON THE NEW MOON
  THE SISTER TAKEN
  THE HARBOR STORMS
  THE FIRE TOWER
  THE MARQUESAS DRIFT
  LISTEN TO THE MARSH

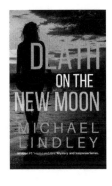

DEATH ON THE NEW MOON
To keep reading **DEATH ON THE NEW MOON**, go to Michael Lindley's online store to buy direct at *store.michaellindleynovels.com.*

Made in the USA
Middletown, DE
06 September 2024